The BRIDESMAIDS

The BRIDESMAIDS

CHERIE BENNETT

SCHOLASTIC INC.
New York Toronto London Auckland Sydney

No part of this publication may be reproduced in whole or in part, or stored in a retrieval system, or transmitted in any form or by any means, electronic, mechanical, photocopying, recording, or otherwise, without written permission of the publisher. For information regarding permission, write to Scholastic Inc., 555 Broadway, New York, NY 10012.

ISBN 0-590-54335-0

12 11 10 9 8 7 6 5 4 3 2   6 7 8 9/9 0 1/0

Printed in the U.S.A.   01

First Scholastic printing, July 1996

For J.G., the prince at the end
of a long line of frogs

The BRIDESMAIDS

Prologue

THE HONOR OF YOUR PRESENCE
IS REQUESTED
AT THE MARRIAGE
OF
FAWN ELIZABETH MUNDY
TO
AUSTIN BAYLOR STANFIELD

The engraved words from the wedding invitation kept echoing in sixteen-year-old Lexi Mundy's head as she stood nervously at the back of the chapel. Just in front of her was her best friend, Juliet Stanfield, and in front of Juliet was her other best friend, Paris Goldman, each of them waiting for her moment to walk down the aisle with a groomsman.

My sister, Fawn, is really marrying Juliet's brother, Austin, Lexi told herself. *Right now.*

Right this minute. And there's nothing I can do about it.

Married. Married forever.

The beautiful organ music began, and little five-year-old Betsy Stanfield, Austin's cousin, was the first one down the aisle, tossing rose petals to her left and to her right from a basket she held in her left hand. She looked absolutely darling, and everyone smiled.

Then, slowly, the first couple of the bridal party made their own way down the aisle toward Reverend Collie, who looked on with encouragement.

Now it was Paris's turn, then Juliet's, and then, finally, it was Lexi's turn. As her sister's maid of honor, she was last, before the bride. She caught Juliet's eye as she slowly walked toward the altar, on Greg's arm.

Is it my imagination, or does Juliet look as troubled as I do? Lexi thought. *No, it couldn't be. Juliet doesn't know Fawn's terrible secret. I only wish I could have told her. But it wouldn't be fair. She's Austin's sister.*

Lexi took a deep breath and forced her feet forward down the narrow aisle, toward the minister's welcoming face.

What else can I do? Lexi thought helplessly. *I can't possibly stop the wedding. I don't have the right. And Fawn would never forgive me in a million years.*

At that exact same moment, something similar was going on in Juliet's head. She watched as Lexi walked slowly down the aisle, and there was a terrible dread in the pit of her stomach.

I wish I could have confided in Lexi about Austin's secret, she thought. *But Lexi is Fawn's sister. And I wanted to give Austin a chance to tell Fawn himself. How can he marry her if he can't even tell her the truth about himself?*

But he never said a word. And now it's too late.

"Dearly beloved, we are gathered here today to witness the marriage vows of Fawn Elizabeth Mundy and Austin Baylor Stanfield," Reverend Collie intoned.

Fawn smiled tremulously, her hands shaking a bit. She looked over at Austin, who stood beside her, and he met her gaze, looking just as nervous as she did. She brought her eyes back to the reverend as he continued to speak about the holy state of matrimony.

And then, finally, he was at the vows.

"Do you, Fawn Elizabeth Mundy, take this man, Austin Baylor Stanfield, to be your wedded husband in sickness and in health, for richer or for poorer, in good times and in bad, till death you do part?"

Oh, Fawn, Lexi thought, her heart catching in her chest. *I love you. And I'm so sorry if I hurt you in any way, but how can you go through with this without telling Austin the truth, and —*

"I do," Fawn managed in a shaky voice.

"And do you, Austin Baylor Stanfield, take this woman, Fawn Elizabeth Mundy, to be your wedded wife in sickness and in health, for richer or for poorer, in good times and in bad, till death you do part?"

Juliet gulped hard. *I should have talked to you, Austin. I'm a terrible sister,* she thought, *to let you agonize about everything alone. I'm so sorry. But please don't go through with this without being honest with Fawn, because how can you even start a marriage that isn't based on honesty, and —*

"I do," Austin replied solemnly.

Reverend Collie smiled and raised his head to look out over all the faces in the chapel. "If there is anyone present who does not feel that these two should now be joined in holy matrimony, let him or her speak now, or forever hold your peace."

Silence. And more silence.

And then a voice, one voice, which seemed to boom and echo throughout the hushed, sacred chapel —

"I do! I object!"

Reverend Collie looked shocked.

Everyone at the altar turned, aghast, to the person in the wedding party who had spoken, their faces full of anger and disapproval.

"I object!" the voice repeated. "Stop this wedding!"

Chapter 1

"Hi, you guys, I thought you'd never get here!" Juliet Stanfield cried to her two best friends, Alexis Mundy and Paris Goldman, as the two walked across the redwood deck that led to the pool in Juliet's mammoth backyard. "Is today the best day of our entire lives or what?"

"Ask me after I fall into your pool," Paris said irritably, blowing her shaggy blond bangs out of her eyes. She set her canvas bag with her bathing suit in it down on the lounge chair. "It's too hot to think."

"But it's perfect!" Juliet insisted, throwing her arms wide. "We have the entire summer ahead of us, and then senior year!"

Paris plopped down on the chaise longue and wiped the sweat from her forehead. "What did you do, take extra rah-rah pills this morning?"

"Oh, stop," Lexi chided her good-naturedly.

"You're psyched to be out of school for the summer, and you know it."

"Marginally," Paris allowed.

"And senior year is going to be fantastic," Lexi continued. She sat on the end of Paris's chaise longue. "When I was a little kid, I used to dream about what it would be like to be a senior in high school."

"My idea of bliss would be to skip it entirely and move right on to college," Paris said. "Preferably, as far away from tiny Stanfield, New York, as is humanly possible."

"Oh, let's not talk about school," Juliet insisted. "We just got *out* today! And you know I hate everything about school!"

"No, you don't," Paris said, scratching at a bug bite on her leg. She got up and walked to the edge of the pool. "You hate studying. But planning your outfits? Flirting with guys? That you love." She slipped off a sandal and dipped her toe into the pool. "It's still kind of cold."

Juliet put her hands on her hips, and edged toward Paris. "You were just complaining about how hot it is."

"So?" Paris asked.

"So, this should cool you off!" Juliet said. Then she quickly pushed Paris, who was dressed in baggy shorts and an even baggier T-shirt, into the pool.

Paris came up sputtering, her long, dirty-blond hair plastered to her head. "Oh, very cute!"

Juliet laughed. "It was, wasn't it?"

"Come on, we can't let her look like a drowned rat alone!" Lexi said, pulling Juliet toward the edge of the pool.

"Let me go change into my bikini — " Juliet began.

"No fair!" Paris cried. "Push her in, Lexi!"

"Jump or get pushed," Lexi warned Juliet. "Fair is fair!"

Juliet rolled her eyes, stepped off her sandals, and dove into the pool. "Satisfied?" she asked when she resurfaced, treading water.

"Very," Paris said with a grin. "It's not often I get to see Miss Juliet I-can't-be-seen-without-a-perfect-French-manicure Stanfield looking like dogmeat! Your mascara is even running down your cheeks!"

Juliet held up her hand. "But my nails still look perfect!"

Paris and Juliet both laughed and began to splash each other playfully.

Lexi smiled, happy that her two best friends weren't really mad at each other. Not permanently, anyway. It was never permanent, but Lexi did spend a lot of her time smoothing out their fights.

The threesome had met at the Stanfield College preschool twelve years earlier, when they'd all been four years old. During the first week of preschool, Lexi and Paris had become inseparable. Or rather, Lexi had become Paris's shadow.

A chubby girl with long, dirty-blond hair that was always in her eyes, Paris lived with her dad, who was a professor of theology at Stanfield College. Her mom had split the year before for parts unknown. Paris was very independent, and even at age four she had always picked out her own clothes, which tended to be very baggy and wrinkled, and were often missing a button or two. Lexi's mom, who had been something called a "hippie" years ago, claimed to give Lexi complete clothing freedom. Actually, her mother made Lexi tuck in her shirt neatly every day and insisted on "helping" Lexi pick out her clothes — which really meant that her mother picked them out. So Lexi thought Paris was the luckiest thing walking.

Also, Paris knew everything about everything. Like you could make two worms out of one by cutting it in half. And where babies came from. And you could make your hair grow faster by tugging on it at night.

Lexi was hungry for Paris's undivided attention. At home, her parents were always busy running the Stanfield Inn, the nicest bed-and-breakfast in their small college town, or else they were working on one of their many political causes, like no nuclear power or rights for American Indians. And her eight-year-old sister, Fawn the Perfect, would not give Lexi the time of day.

Per Paris's instructions, Lexi had dutifully tugged on her short, wispy brown hair every night until her scalp pulsed with pain. And Paris swore it was getting longer. She said it with such conviction that Lexi began to really believe it, and she swung her hair around in preschool, imagining herself with perfectly glorious hair all the way down her back, like a fairy princess.

That is, until a real princess showed up at preschool.

Lexi could still remember how exotic and beautiful Juliet Stanfield had looked when she'd walked into the preschool one week after everyone else had started, her hand tucked into the hand of a lovely, blond-haired woman.

Lexi couldn't take her eyes off of Juliet. She had almond-shaped eyes, golden-colored skin, and long, shiny black hair that shimmered like a waterfall down to her waist, held back with the narrowest of pale pink ribbons. She wore a white smock dress with pink ribbons, white tights, and black patent leather Mary Janes. Lexi thought Juliet was the most beautiful thing she had ever seen.

Unfortunately for Juliet, Lexi was the only one who felt that way.

"She's dumb or something," a red-faced little boy named Pete said, hitching up his blue jeans.

"Her eyes are all funny," another girl said, holding her fingers at the corners of her own eyes to make them slant like Juliet's.

"Why's she wearing a party dress?" another little girl wanted to know.

" 'Cuz like I said, she's dumb," Pete explained.

"She's just adopted," Paris told him calmly.

"How do you know?" Lexi had asked her.

" 'Cuz she's Chinese and her mom is American," Paris told Lexi.

"What's Chinese?" Lexi asked.

Paris sighed with exasperation. "It's a foreign country. All the people there are slaves. Americans went over there and set the slaves free. It's in every history book."

All the little kids had stared at Paris.

"Uh-uh," Pete finally said. "She looks weird 'cuz she's dumb."

"*You're* the dumb one," Paris replied.

"Take that back, fatso!" Pete yelled.

"Don't call my friend fatso!" Lexi yelled, stomping her foot.

"Fatso! Fatso!" Pete had jeered at the top of his lungs.

Paris walked up to him, calmly drew her fist back, and socked him in the stomach. Then she turned to Lexi. "Come on. Let's go ask that girl if she's Chinese."

"We can't do that!" Lexi said in horror.

"Lexi, we can do anything that we want to do," Paris had replied.

We can do anything that we want to do. The concept was so foreign, so daring, that Lexi could hardly take it in.

"Come on." Paris dragged Lexi over to the new girl, who was calmly playing in the sandbox, careful not to get her beautiful dress dirty.

"Hey," Paris called to her. "So, are you Chinese?"

The new girl stood up, daintily brushing off her hands.

"No. I'm American."

"Can't be," Paris said, folding her arms.

"My parents adopted me from Viet Nam when I was a baby," the girl explained. "Mommy says that makes me American."

Lexi looked at the new girl with fascination. There were tiny little diamonds shining in her pierced ears. She remembered that the teacher had introduced her to them as Juliet.

"Juliet?" Lexi asked, her voice filled with awe. "Were you a slave in . . ." Lexi had forgotten the name of that other country.

"Oh, no," Juliet said. "I was a princess."

Lexi instantly believed her.

"No way," Paris insisted.

"Yes," Juliet had said calmly. "And I'm still a princess."

Paris looked skeptical.

"She might be," Lexi whispered to her friend.

"Do you want to build a sand castle with me?" Juliet asked them, her voice full of excitement. "Then all three of us could be princesses and live in it together. And we'll all marry handsome princes!"

"Yes!" Lexi had cried, at the same time Paris had yelled "No!"

"Come on," Lexi wheedled. "It'll be fun. If it's not fun I promise to do everything you tell me to do for an entire week."

That was the beginning.

The three of them had built such an incredible sand castle that the teacher left it up for two weeks, finally taking a photo of it to mount on the board before she let the other kids stomp it gleefully into oblivion.

After that they were inseparable.

For twelve years now it had been Juliet, Lexi, and Paris. Where you found one, you found all three. Their personalities hadn't changed much in all those years, either. Ethereal Juliet was still a princess, chubby Paris was still a rebel and still liked to make it up as she went along, and peacemaker Lexi was still the glue that held the three of them together.

They even still dressed the same way. At that moment Juliet was dressed in white Ralph Lauren shorts with a delicate lace–trimmed T-shirt. Paris, per usual, had on baggy shorts and an even baggier T-shirt, and Lexi wore fresh, faded jeans and a white cotton shirt.

And of course, at the moment they were all soaking wet.

"You know what would be fantastic?" Juliet asked, turning to float on her back. "To fall in love this summer."

"With someone incredible," Lexi added, reaching for an inflatable raft and climbing on it. Of course, in her case she knew exactly who that incredible someone actually *was*.

"That lets out every guy at Stanfield High,"

Paris said, pushing her long, wet hair off her face.

"Oh, forget high school boys," Juliet said. "They're only good for flirting practice. I'm talking about college guys!"

"Everything in life is not guys, you know," Paris griped.

"Not everything," Juliet agreed. "But the most fun thing! I have this feeling . . . that tomorrow night at the party something really incredible is going to happen for all three of us!"

"Here she goes again," Paris groaned. "I don't even *like* parties."

"Come on, it's going to be fantastic," Juliet insisted. "And my brother invited all his friends. College guys!"

"They probably went to Stanfield High two years ago and now they're at Stanfield College," Paris guessed. "Major bor-ing!"

"Austin isn't boring," Lexi said, letting her fingers dangle off the raft into the water.

"Love is *so* blind," Paris muttered.

"Austin will definitely be at the party?" Lexi asked with exaggerated casualness.

"Of course," Juliet said. "According to my parents, it's a party for me and for Austin. Didn't I tell you that?"

"No," Lexi said.

"I guess I just forgot," Juliet replied. "The plans keep getting bigger and bigger. Mom decided it should be this huge family thing. Between my friends and Austin's friends and my parents' friends, they're expecting over two hundred people — "

"Only their closest buds, no doubt. And here we thought we were going to some cute, little high school barbecue thing on the back forty . . ." Paris mused.

"You know Mom," Juliet said with a shrug. "It's turned into this major deal. Very *Great-Gatsby*-on-the-lawn kind of thing."

"Gag me," Paris muttered under her breath.

Juliet ignored her. "Hey, my parents are thrilled that I actually managed to finish junior year with a B average. And Austin just got elected president of his fraternity house. Hence, the big celebration."

"Of course he got elected president," Paris said. "Austin Stanfield. Stanfield College. What rings a bell here?"

"They didn't vote for him just because he's a Stanfield," Juliet insisted. She looked over at Lexi. "Austin asked me if you were going to be there."

"He did not!" Lexi exclaimed, practically sliding off the inflatable float.

She'd had a crush on Juliet's older brother, Austin, ever since the first day she had laid eyes on him. Juliet had invited her and Paris over for dinner. A guy in a uniform served it. And for dessert you could make your own sundae at an ice cream bar. But those things hadn't impressed four-year-old Lexi nearly as much as eight-year-old Austin, with his tousled blond hair that fell into his blue eyes and a smile that lit up his face. After dinner they had all gone swimming in the huge built-in pool, and Lexi had gotten a bee sting. Austin had pulled the stinger out, careful not to hurt her.

That was the day she had given him her heart.

There were only two minor problems.

One was that Austin still thought of her as Juliet's little friend. A mere child.

And the other one was that twenty-year-old Austin was dating Lexi's twenty-year-old sister, Fawn.

Fawn the Perfect.

Fawn was the kind of girl who had never had a bad hair day. She never got a pimple. In fact, Lexi was pretty sure Fawn didn't go to the bathroom.

Lexi sighed and let herself roll off the raft, plopping into the cold water.

"Why am I getting all excited?" Lexi asked

out loud. "I might as well be dreaming about Brad Pitt."

"That's not true," Juliet insisted, swimming over to Lexi. "Fawn and Austin have only been dating for a few months. And you know Fawn. She always has a million boyfriends."

That was true. Lexi's older sister, who in addition to being perfect-looking was sweet and kindhearted, had one little flaw. She was . . . well, she was kind of fickle when it came to guys. Basically, she'd never met a guy she couldn't dump.

"Maybe it's because it's so easy for her to get any guy she wants," Paris guessed. "It's like she just likes the flirting part. But once she gets the guy, she wants to find another one."

"Right," Juliet agreed. "And Austin only broke up with his last girlfriend, Penny, a week before he started going out with Fawn. So I don't think it's going to last."

"Is she coming to the party tomorrow night?" Paris asked.

"She must be," Lexi said with a sigh.

"Well, she lives at home," Paris said. "Didn't she tell you?"

"I never see her," Lexi explained. "She might live at home but she spends all her time at the college. She's supposed to help me serve breakfast at the inn in the mornings, but she's never there."

"Sure, she's too busy making every guy at Stanfield College fall at her feet," Paris said.

Including gorgeous, smart, rich Austin Stanfield.

Not just rich. Very, *very* rich. In fact, Austin and Juliet's great-grandfather was the founder of Stanfield College, the small, elite private college around which their small town in up-state New York had been built. The Stanfields lived in a huge, colonial-style mansion at the top of a hill, surrounded by acres of perfectly manicured lawns. There was an oval-shaped built-in pool, a tennis court, and even two guest cottages where the girls had played dress-up when they were little.

Ever since he had entered as a freshman, Austin Stanfield was the John F. Kennedy, Jr., of Stanfield, New York. Every girl — freshman, junior, senior, whatever — wanted him. And at the moment, it seemed Fawn Mundy had him.

"They'll break up, you'll see," Paris told Lexi loyally.

"How do you know?" Lexi asked. "My sister is crazy about him."

"Only for the moment," Paris predicted.

"Who am I kidding?" Lexi sighed. "Austin still thinks I'm a little kid."

Juliet's eyes lit up. "I have a fantastic idea."

"Oh, no," Paris said. "I know what happens when you get that look in your eyes, Juli."

"But this is an amazing idea!" Juliet insisted. "We'll do a makeover on you, Lexi! Tomorrow night when Austin sees you, it'll be like he's never seen you before!"

"A makeover like what?" Lexi asked nervously.

"A thong bikini and a sign around your neck that reads AUSTIN: TAKE ME is my suggestion," Paris put in.

"I'll do everything," Juliet went on, ignoring Paris's remark. She turned to Paris. "And I'll do you, too!"

"Oh, no, you won't!" Paris shot back.

"Yes, it'll be terrific!" Juliet insisted. "You guys can come over in the afternoon and we'll work on it. I've got tons of clothes — "

"Excuse me," Paris interrupted, dog-paddling over to Juliet, "but you are, like, a size three. Lexi is a size eight. And I am a size sixteen. I could use one of your designer T-shirts as a bib."

"There is no stopping a woman with a

makeover mission," Juliet said. "You guys, this is going to be so awesome! I have a feeling something truly incredible is going to happen for us this summer! And it's all going to begin tomorrow night!"

Chapter 2

"Juli, this is a really, really bad idea," Paris said, as Juliet draped a towel around her neck. "I'm dying with these stupid hot rollers all over my head. I'll just sweat off all your makeup, anyway. You know I never wear any."

It was late the next afternoon, and Paris and Lexi were with Juliet in her room, getting the full Juliet beauty treatment.

Juliet had done Lexi first. At the moment Lexi sat on one of Juliet's beds wearing more cosmetics on her face than she ever had in her life. Juliet had also changed Lexi's usual hair-style, a simple ear-length bob, by gelling the sides back and blow-drying the front so that it fell over one eye. Lexi couldn't decide if she looked terrific or really, really stupid.

"You'll look fantastic with makeup," Juliet insisted to Paris. "I've been telling you that for six years." She dotted some base on Paris's face.

"Just because you started wearing makeup at age ten doesn't mean the rest of the world had to follow suit," Paris pointed out.

"Call me Michelangelo," Juliet said dramatically, gently sponging the makeup base onto Paris's face.

"Sign my face when you're done and you're dead," Paris warned.

"Stop talking," Juliet admonished her. "I can't work on a moving canvas."

"Why did I let you talk me into this?" Paris exclaimed.

"Because deep down you want to look like a babe just as much as the next girl," Juliet explained. "Besides, I did a great job on Lexi, didn't I?"

Paris gazed at Lexi, who was sitting on Juliet's bed. "You look like you belong in an MTV video," she decided.

"Really?" Lexi asked, thrilled.

"It wasn't meant as a compliment," Paris added.

"Stop talking!" Juliet commanded, as she brushed some eye shadow on Paris's eyelids. "Honestly, Paris, you have such a beautiful face."

"A remark utterly unworthy of you," Paris replied. "That's what everyone says to fat girls."

"You could lose weight if you wanted to," Juliet said.

"Perhaps, O Self-Righteous One. So maybe I just don't want to."

"Everyone doesn't have to be thin," Lexi added. "Beauty comes in all sizes and shapes."

"Then how come all the top models are five foot ten and thin?" Juliet asked.

"There's a new study that scientifically proves that women who are twenty pounds overweight live longer than women who are twenty pounds underweight," Paris said.

Juliet picked up the mascara and stared at Paris. "Is that true or is that one of those stories you made up like you always did when we were kids?"

"I'll never tell," Paris said.

"Just a little blush . . ." Juliet said, dusting the brush over Paris's cheekbones. "I really should open Juliet's House of Beauty one of these days."

"Oh, right," Lexi laughed. "Your parents would *love* that!"

"Just because I'm rich doesn't mean I shouldn't do what I really want to do," Juliet said, reaching for a tube of lipstick.

"Imagine," Paris breathed, "a girl strong enough to stand up to the Stanfield millions! I could cry!"

"Cry and I'll kill you," Juliet said. "This mascara is not waterproof! And stop talking so I can finish your lips."

"Yuck!" Paris cried. "Lipstick is so goopy-feeling!"

"You have to suffer for beauty," Juliet insisted. She stepped back from Paris, eyeing her critically. "I am a genius, if I do say so myself."

"Does that mean I can look now?" Paris said. Juliet had covered her mirror with a hand towel before she began her work.

"Of course not," Juliet said. "I have to take out your rollers and do your hair first." She began to pull the rollers out of Paris's long hair.

"Can you imagine going through all this every day?" Paris asked. "What a waste of time!"

"Oh my gosh, incredible blond waves," Juliet murmured happily, as she took out the last hot roller. "Now turn your head upside down and shake it."

Paris complied, then swung her head back up. "Are we done now?"

"Spray," Juliet mumbled, picking up some

hair spray and carefully spraying Paris's hair at the roots.

"Voilà!" Juliet cried, pulling the towel off the mirror. "What do you think?"

Paris stared at her reflection. The makeup Juliet had applied was actually subtle and tasteful. Her hair, which she had never set before in her life, could have been in a shampoo advertisement. She looked . . . kind of great.

Much as she hated to admit it.

"It's . . . okay," Paris said carefully, turning her neck this way and that to get all views of her face.

"You look beautiful, really," Lexi said. "Your hair is fantastic!"

"Imagine what we could do if you let me highlight the front!" Juliet said eagerly. "A few lighter strands around your face. Your face is so pretty, and — "

"What if every fat girl who got told she had a pretty face lost weight and found out she really had been a dog all along?" Paris asked. "Major depression!"

"As far as I'm concerned you look gorgeous just the way you are," Lexi said loyally.

"Not if she wants to get cute guys," Juliet said with a shrug.

Lexi shot Juliet a warning look.

"I'm sorry! I don't make up the guy rules!" Juliet cried.

"Wow, is that a guy rule?" Paris asked, her face flushing with anger. "You mean it's, like, in a *handbook?* Guys aren't *allowed* to like girls who are overweight?"

"I didn't mean it like that — " Juliet began.

"You guys, let's not fight about it," Lexi said. "Some guys wouldn't like any one of us for one reason or another. What difference does it make?"

"Besides, who gives guys all the power, answer me that!" Paris said. "It's not like I'm pining away for some jerk to decide whether I'm thin enough for his undivided attention!"

"True," Juliet agreed. "But what if there was some special guy who you really, really liked, and he didn't like you because he thought you needed to lose weight?"

"Well," Paris said, "then that guy is a superficial loser who isn't good enough for me, anyway!"

"Good point," Juliet allowed.

"Absolutely," Lexi added. She walked over to Paris and stared at both of their reflections in the mirror. "We look quite babelike, don't you think?"

"Yeah," Paris admitted, a smile playing at

the corner of her mouth. "From the neck up, anyway."

Both girls were still wearing oversized T-shirts and cutoffs.

"Aha!" Juliet exclaimed. "I have surprises!"

She ran to her closet and pulled out a simple, sleeveless white minidress with a scoop neckline. "Size eight," she said triumphantly, handing it to Lexi.

"Where did you get this?" Lexi asked in shock.

"My cousin Beth Anne!" Juliet exclaimed happily. "She's exactly your size! And it's a Versace!"

"Who's that?" Paris asked.

"A famous designer," Juliet explained, rolling her eyes.

"Excuse me!" Paris exclaimed. "My idea of fashion is a clean T-shirt!"

"It's fantastic," Lexi admitted, "but I can't wear your cousin's dress! What if I spill something on it?"

"She was going to give it to the thrift shop anyway!" Juliet explained. "Try it on!"

Lexi slipped out of her clothes and dropped the minidress over her head. It fit her perfectly. "I can't believe it . . ."

"Believe it!" Juliet insisted. "Oh, I love this!"

"I don't suppose you have anything in that magic bag for me, O Great and Powerful Oz," Paris said in her best Dorothy voice.

"O ye of little faith," Juliet replied, running back over to her closet. She pulled out a black minidress with short sleeves and a low-cut back. "Size sixteen. Carole Little."

"Don't tell me, she's a famous designer," Paris muttered. "And you just happen to have a relative that wears a size sixteen."

"No," Juliet admitted. "I found it at Second Hand Rose near the college."

Paris's jaw dropped. "You went shopping for me?"

Juliet nodded. "It was fun. Go ahead, try it on."

Paris slipped out of her clothes and pulled the dress over her head. It was a little tight in the bust, but not too much, and it was short enough to show off her great legs.

"Hot momma!" Lexi teased.

Paris studied her reflection. "But I never dress like this . . ."

"Never say never!" Juliet sang out. "You two look fantastic!"

"So what are you wearing?" Lexi asked.

"I just happened to stop into The French Shoppe while I was downtown," Juliet said, walking over to her closet. She pulled out a short, floaty lavender skirt made from layers of chiffon, and a matching camisole. And tiny lavender ballet slippers.

"Wow," Lexi said, eyeing the outfit. "It's gorgeous."

"And I'll bet it cost enough to feed a small third world country for a week," Paris added.

"It's a Christian Lacroix," Juliet breathed, holding the outfit up to herself. She looked over at her friends. "Tonight three Cinderellas are going to the ball!"

"Are you sure I look okay?" Lexi asked Juliet nervously, when the three girls walked into the party a couple of hours later.

They had stayed upstairs in Juliet's room until the party was already under way so they wouldn't be the first to arrive. Juliet's mom had come by the room and told Juliet to come downstairs and greet the first guests, but after that her mother got too busy to realize that Juliet wasn't around.

"Whenever possible, make an entrance," Juliet had decreed regally to her friends.

"You look good, honest," Paris told Lexi, as she nervously pulled at the hem of the short black dress she was wearing. She put her hand up to her forehead. "Oh, God, I'm sweating this crap off my face already."

"Think chilly, serene thoughts," Juliet advised her.

Paris eyed her friend, who really did look like a princess in her pale lavender outfit, with a small diamond suspended from a slender lavender ribbon around her neck. "I just realized something. You don't sweat."

"I sweat."

"No, no, you don't," Paris insisted. "I've never seen you sweat."

"Well, I don't sweat when I'm wearing a designer original!" Juliet exclaimed, as if the idea were comparable to, say, the murder of small children.

"Medical science should study you," Paris murmured, pushing her mane of blond waves off her face.

Juliet looked around at her backyard, which had been transformed for the party. A huge green-and-white tent had been erected over part of the lawn, under which a buffet was being served by attractive young men and women in perfectly cut tuxedos. Other waiters and waitresses carried trays of peach juice and champagne, which they offered to people as they entered the party. Near the pool a band played an old Stevie Wonder tune, fronted by a girl singer in a black, sequined minidress. A few older couples were dancing to the music on the patio. Everywhere Juliet looked well-dressed people were laughing, talking, drinking champagne. She noted that none of her other friends had arrived yet.

"I have to get the band to improve the music before our friends get here," Juliet worried. "They won't even want to stay!"

"Ha," Paris barked. "There's free food. They'll stay."

"Oh, no, there he is!" Lexi hissed, grabbing Juliet's hand.

Austin had just ambled into the backyard. He was wearing jeans, a white linen shirt, and a navy sports jacket, and his blond hair fell into his eyes in that way that made Lexi long to brush her hands over it. He was standing with two other guys, laughing about something. One of the guys was tall and thin, with longish brown hair and a handsome, friendly face. He was wearing jeans and a denim shirt, with a colorful tie. The other guy had black hair cut short and a face so perfect it deserved to be on a movie screen. He had on a double-breasted, cream-colored linen suit.

"Who's *that?*" Paris asked, her eyes on the black-haired guy.

"Greg Cambridge," Juliet reported. "Austin's best friend. He was away at prep school for years, and he went to some college on the West Coast last year. I heard he got kicked out."

"For what?" Paris asked.

Juliet shrugged. "Austin won't tell me. Next year he'll be at Stanfield. Want to go meet him?"

"No," Paris said quickly.

"You lie like a rug!" Juliet said with a laugh. "Your IQ slumped just looking at him!"

"It did not," Paris insisted. "Guys that look like that are always obnoxious."

"That's not fair," Juliet said.

"What, you're gonna tell me he does volunteer work for the homeless and he's engaged to a horse-faced girl with an overbite the size of New Jersey, but he loves her for her inner beauty?"

Juliet gave Paris one of her patented looks. "Very funny."

"What should I say to Austin?" Lexi asked, biting her lower lip nervously.

"Lexi, you've known Austin for twelve years," Paris reminded her friend.

"But tonight's different," Lexi whispered. She craned her neck around. "I don't see my sister."

"Good!" Juliet said. "Then this is the time to make our move."

"To do what?" Lexi asked.

"To assist with destiny, of course," Juliet replied. Then she led her two friends across the yard toward her brother.

Chapter 3

"Hi," Juliet said casually when the girls reached the three guys. "Having fun?"

"Oh, hi," Austin said. "We were just laughing about Mom. She won't let us drink any champagne because we're not twenty-one yet."

"I've had a fake ID since I was fifteen," Greg said, still chuckling.

"Hello, Austin," Lexi said, trying for her most sultry voice.

"Hi, Lex," Austin replied easily. Then he really seemed to look at her for the first time. "Wow, you look great!"

"I do?" Lexi asked in shock, then she caught herself. "I mean, thanks, Austin." Little thrills ran up Lexi's spine.

"You're welcome," Austin said, smiling at her. He looked over at Paris. "You're looking pretty fine, too, Paris. Have I ever seen you in a dress before?"

"Probably not in this lifetime," Paris allowed.

Greg grinned at her. "I'm glad I caught you tonight, then."

Paris gulped hard. Was he actually *flirting* with her?

Nah. Couldn't be.

"This is Greg Cambridge," Austin said, "and this tall guy is Tyler Finn. He transferred to Stanfield from the University of Tennessee. He moved into the frat house when summer-semester started. He's gonna be a sophomore in the fall. This is my sister, Juliet, and her two best friends, Lexi Mundy and Paris Goldman."

"Pleased to meet y'all," Tyler drawled with a thick southern accent. "Call me Ty."

"I love your accent!" Juliet cried. "It's so cute!"

Tyler shook his head ruefully. "Don't remind me. I'm tryin' my darndest to get rid of it!"

"But why?" Juliet asked.

"Because I'm a drama major," Tyler explained. "Can you see me doin' Shakespeare with this accent? That's one of the reasons I wanted to transfer to a northern school —

most of my friends back home sound just like I do!"

"So, Lex, how's life?" Austin asked. "What are your plans for the summer?"

Getting you to fall in love with me, Lexi thought. *After Fawn dumps you.*

"Oh, you know," Lexi said casually, "hanging out."

"Totally not true," Juliet said. "She's really busy doing volunteer work for PETA — you know — People for the Ethical Treatment of Animals."

"Really?" Austin asked. "Cool! I admire you for that, I really do."

"Thanks," Lexi said, flushing at his compliment.

"Lexi Mundy?" Greg asked. "As in Fawn Mundy?"

"She's Fawn's little sister," Austin explained, putting his arm around Lexi in a brotherly fashion.

Lexi's heart sank.

"Although tonight you don't look like anyone's little sister," Austin added, giving her a hug.

Lexi's heart soared.

The band began to play Wynonna's "No One Else on Earth." Ty grinned at Juliet. "Want to dance?"

"Sure!" Juliet said, thrilled to be asked by a cute college guy. She shot her friends a look of glee as Tyler led her toward the patio.

"Way too hot to dance," Greg said, shaking his head. "This is upstate New York! We're not supposed to have this kind of weather till August!"

"Well, I think you ought to do something about that!" Paris said with mock outrage. "Buy off the weatherman! Do what you have to do!"

Greg laughed. "A cute girl with a sense of humor — my, my, my."

He just called me a cute girl. Not that I care. Paris shook her hair off her face. "What, someone told you a girl can't be cute *and* funny?"

"I don't run into it all that often," Greg replied.

"Am I supposed to care?" Paris shot back.

Greg laughed again. "Hmmm, you're a prickly one. Would you bite my head off if I suggested we get something to eat from the buffet?"

"Take your chances." Paris shrugged.

Greg scratched at his chin. "Okay. I'll risk it," he decided. "See you two later," he added, as he and Paris headed for the food.

Lexi looked over at Austin. *I'm alone with*

him, she thought. *It's exactly what I wanted. I can't blow this.*

She turned to Austin and gave him her most dazzling smile. "So, Austin, I haven't seen you in a while. What's been going on?"

"You know," Austin said easily, brushing the hair out of his eyes. "School, frat stuff, the usual."

He didn't even mention Fawn the Perfect, Lexi realized.

"Oh, and I got a new horse," Austin added with excitement. "Did Juliet tell you?"

"No!"

"She's a beauty," Austin said eagerly. "Want to go meet her?"

"I'd love to!"

They walked across the endless expanse of lawn toward the stalls where the horses were kept. The horses began to whinny with happiness when they heard them coming. Austin opened the paddock gate and they walked into the cool darkness of the barn.

"Hey, girl, hey there," Austin crooned to a beautiful horse. She was all black with white feet and a white spot on her nose. "This is Binky," Austin said. "Bink, this is Lexi."

"*Binky??*" Lexi echoed, reaching out to pet the animal.

"It was my first girlfriend's nickname," Austin admitted with chagrin. "She dumped me at the end of first grade for Greg, actually."

Lexi looked at him. "Touching story," she teased. "But why did you name your horse after her?"

Austin shrugged. "I still remember her, I guess. Isn't that dumb? She had the cutest little chipped tooth in the front . . ."

"Whatever happened to her?" Lexi asked.

"The last I heard, she joined some right-wing militia in Montana," Austin admitted.

"Oh, great!" Lexi said, shaking her head ruefully. "I think I like this Binky better!"

She kept petting the horse. Silence filled the stable. Lexi could hear the beating of her own heart.

Say something, she commanded herself. *This is your big chance. Don't blow it.*

"You know, I can't imagine any girl choosing Greg over you," Lexi said softly. She couldn't look him in the eye.

Austin smiled. "Thanks, but lots of girls have chosen Greg over me. There's just something about him . . ."

"Like what?"

Austin shrugged. "He's rich — "

"So are you," Lexi said.

"Yeah," Austin agreed reluctantly. "It's

never meant very much to me, you know?"

"It would if you knew what it was like to be poor," Lexi pointed out.

"True," Austin allowed. "Anyway, Greg's wild — a lot of girls go crazy for that. And he looks like a movie star."

"So?" Lexi asked. "Some girls don't like guys who look like movie stars. There's a lot more to liking a guy than that!"

"Like what?" Austin asked, as he ran his hand across Binky's flank.

"Intelligence, and . . . and integrity," Lexi said firmly. "And character."

"Integrity," Austin mused.

"Standing up for things you believe in," Lexi qualified. "Being your own person."

"That's a little tough when you're a Stanfield."

"Why?"

"It's hard to explain," Austin began. "For example, my dad just expected me to be a business major. And once I graduate, he expects me to go to law school so I can handle the family trust."

"Isn't that what you want?" Lexi asked.

Austin stopped petting Binky and leaned against the wall of the barn. "I used to think I did. I mean, why would I want anything else, you know? But . . ." his voice trailed off.

"But what?" Lexi asked, leaning next to him against the wall.

"But there's something else I really want to do," he admitted. "I haven't told anyone. God, it's probably stupid . . ."

"What is it?" Lexi asked.

"It's crazy — "

"You can tell me," Lexi prompted.

Austin picked up some hay and twirled it between his fingers. "It's . . . I know it's crazy, but I want to be an actor. Jeez, it's so lame — "

"It's not!" Lexi cried. "You were wonderful when you played David in *David and Lisa* in high school — "

"A dumb high school play . . ."

"It wasn't dumb!" Lexi insisted. "Juliet and Paris and I came to see you in it every night! You were fantastic!"

Austin crossed his arms. "Can you even imagine me telling my parents I was going to become an actor? Leave Stanfield and try to make it in Hollywood? They'd have me committed. I haven't even told Fawn. She'd have a fit."

Lexi reached out and touched Austin's hand. "Austin, it's your life, not theirs."

He looked at her for a long moment. "Maybe you're just braver than I am, Lexi."

"No," she insisted. "You *are* brave. I know it."

He reached out and touched Lexi's hair. "You've always been a great person, Lex. Have I ever told you that?"

"No," she whispered.

"Well, you are. And you're not a little girl anymore."

"No, I'm not," Lexi agreed.

Now their faces were so close that Lexi could feel his breath on her face. His hand was still touching her hair. Then his face came closer.

This was it. At last. All her dreams were coming true. Lexi raised her face to his and closed her eyes, and then —

Neighhhhhhhh!

They were startled apart by Binky's loud whinny as someone stepped into the barn.

Two someones. A girl in a long, flowery dress and a guy in jeans. They stumbled in, almost spilling their glasses of champagne.

"Hey, Ken, Jennie," Austin said, quickly pulling away from Lexi. "What's up?"

"We came to visit the aminals!" the girl said drunkenly. "Oops, I mean, animals. You know. Horses."

"Have a blast," Austin said. "We were just leaving."

"Hey, swell party, dude!" Ken called as Austin and Lexi hurried out of the barn.

"I guess the two of them got around my mother's no-champagne-for-my-friends rule," Austin said dryly.

"I guess," Lexi agreed.

They stood there staring at each other, the sounds of the party in the distance.

"Well, I guess we'd better get back," Austin said.

"I guess."

"Hey, Austin, man!" Ken yelled, sticking his head out of the barn. "I forgot to tell you. Fawn is looking for you and she's ticked!"

"Thanks for the message," Austin called back to him. He looked at Lexi. "Hey, forget everything I said in there, okay?"

"Is that what you really want?" Lexi whispered, her eyes searching his. "Deep in your heart, is that what you want?"

Austin sighed and he gave Lexi a quick hug, then he held her at arm's length and smiled sweetly. "Lex, the truth is I don't know what I want. But I'd better figure it out pretty soon. Or I'm going to hurt a lot of people I love."

"No you won't," Lexi insisted, "you'll just — "

"Austin? Are you in there?"

Lexi froze.

Oh God. My sister just caught me with Austin.

Red-handed.

Chapter 4

"Austin, there you are!" Fawn cried. Austin walked toward her a little guiltily. But Fawn didn't seem to notice. She hooked her arm through Austin's in a proprietary way and kissed his cheek.

"I was introducing Lexi to Binky," Austin explained.

"That's sweet," Fawn said, smiling at her younger sister. "Lex, you look so pretty!"

"Thanks," Lexi mumbled, hardly able to look her sister in the eye as the three of them drifted back toward the main house.

"Did I really see Paris with Greg," Fawn asked, amused, "or did I imagine it?"

"He was flirting with her big-time," Lexi said, her voice a little too loud. "Why do you find that so hard to believe?"

"Well, I just meant . . ." Fawn's voice trailed off.

"Because she's not thin?" Lexi prodded. "Or because she's my friend?"

Fawn gave her sister a curious look. "I didn't mean anything by it, Lex."

"Then why did you say it?" Lexi crossed her arms defensively.

"What's wrong with you?" Fawn asked, confused.

"Nothing. Forget it," Lexi snapped.

"Hey, I hate to see you two fight," Austin said, his arm going around Fawn's tiny waist. "You're two of my favorite people in the world!"

"Thanks," Fawn said, kissing his cheek again.

The band began to play a slow song, and Fawn turned to Austin. "Oh, let's go dance!"

"Sure," he replied. "Uh, Lexi — ?"

"Oh, I'm perfectly fine," Lexi assured him breezily. "Have fun."

Lexi watched them walk away, Fawn's dainty hand in Austin's. When they reached the patio she watched Austin take Fawn into his arms. They swayed to the music.

That should be me, Lexi thought miserably. *Austin was going to kiss me. I know he was.*

Juliet weaved her way across the now crowded lawn area and walked over to Lexi. She, too, watched Austin and Fawn dancing on the patio. "Your sister looks perfect," Juliet admitted.

"What else is new?" Lexi sighed.

Fawn always managed to look perfect. It wasn't even that she and Lexi looked so different, because they didn't. But Fawn always looked better — at least that's what Lexi thought. They both had brown hair, but where Lexi's was kind of wispy, Fawn's was thick and shoulder-length with natural hints of gold. Lexi's eyes were just plain brown, but Fawn's were brown with green and gold in them, like some rare marble a little kid would save in his top drawer. And while they both wore a size eight, Fawn's bust was bigger and her waist was littler. Her nose was straighter. Her lips were fuller.

She was just . . . better.

Tonight Fawn had on a royal blue silk slip-dress that moved seductively over her curves. Her hair fell in perfect waves to her shoulders. A slender gold bracelet graced her arm.

Suddenly Lexi felt plain and dowdy in her white minidress.

"Why do you always compare yourself to her?" Juliet asked Lexi.

"I didn't say a word!" Lexi protested.

"Yes," Juliet agreed, "but I know what you were thinking."

"How does she do it?" Lexi asked with a sigh.

"It's a gift, I guess," Juliet replied, still gazing at the dancing couple. She turned to her friend. "But look, Austin really likes you. That's obvious!"

"You think?" Lexi asked nervously.

"Absolutely!" Juliet insisted. "Didn't he just tell you how great you look?"

"Maybe he was just being nice."

"You know this thing with Fawn won't last," Juliet decreed. "This is the summer you get Austin."

"I don't know . . ."

"I do!" Juliet insisted. "I am wise in the ways of love, as you know — "

Lexi laughed. "Very funny. You've never even *been* in love!"

"Totally false," Juliet said, flipping her hair back over her shoulder. "I've been in love about a thousand times."

"Exactly my point," Lexi replied. "None of that was real. What I feel for Austin is . . . well, it's everything."

Juliet squeezed Lexi's hand. "Don't give up."

"Hi, girls!" Mrs. Stanfield said, coming up to them. "Having fun?"

Mrs. Leonia Stanfield still looked as lovely

as the day Lexi had first seen her twelve years ago, when she had brought Juliet to preschool. Her blond hair was in a neat bun at the back of her head, and she wore an understated peach silk suit of total perfection. From a gold chain around her neck hung one perfect diamond of at least ten carats. Peach silk heels completed her outfit.

"Hi, Mrs. Stanfield," Lexi replied. "The party's great!"

"It did turn out lovely, didn't it?" Mrs. Stanfield agreed happily. "I'm just so thrilled the weatherman was wrong and it didn't rain!" She turned to her daughter. "Juliet, honey, please be sure you take the time to greet all the guests, not just the young people."

"I will, Mom," Juliet assured her.

"Thanks, sweetie." Her mom kissed her on the forehead. "Your dad and I have a little surprise planned for you later." She winked at her daughter and walked away.

"I guess I'd better go play well-mannered little rich girl," Juliet said.

"Go ahead," Lexi urged her. As Juliet started to walk away, she reached for her hand. "You really think there's a chance? With Austin?"

"Absolutely," Juliet assured her. "It's your summer."

* * *

". . . So I'm in the professor's office, right? She's going on and on about my grade, what I didn't do, why I don't deserve a B, and then she gets up and shuts the door, wham!" Greg told Paris between bites of caviar. "The next thing I know she's standing behind my chair, leaning over, whispering in my ear, something about how there were ways I could improve my grade . . ."

"Are you sure you aren't borrowing heavily from some movie you saw?" Paris asked him. She took a sip of the peach juice from her crystal goblet.

The two of them were sitting on folding chairs that had been set up under a huge oak tree. They had been talking, eating, and laughing together for quite a while — Paris had lost track of the time. She kept expecting Greg to blow her off so he could go flirt with some thin college girl, but he kept staying with her, talking, laughing . . .

Flirting.

"This story is totally factual," Greg insisted, holding his hand up as if taking an oath.

"So what did you do?"

"What do you think I did?" Greg asked, a sly grin on his face.

"I think you stood, puffed up with righteous

indignation, and told her that she was suggesting you compromise your principles for a mere grade."

"A mere passing grade that I needed desperately so I wouldn't get kicked out of school," Greg added mischievously.

Paris gave him a jaded look. "I'm young, I'm not stupid."

Greg threw his head back and laughed.

"Anyway, you totally made up that story," Paris insisted. "It never happened. And if it did, it would be sexual harassment, which is disgusting and illegal whether it's done by a male or a female."

"Oh, God, you're not political, are you?" Greg groaned.

"Depends," Paris said.

"I hate politics," Greg said. He popped the last bite of caviar on a toast point into his mouth and set his empty plate under the tree. Instantly a tuxedoed waiter came by and whisked it away.

"So what don't you hate?" Paris asked, crossing her legs.

"Having fun," Greg said. "Pretty girls." A wind came up and blew a few strands of Paris's hair onto her face. Greg gently pushed them off.

"Gee, I like a guy with depth," Paris quipped sarcastically.

Greg laughed again. "You just won't cut me any slack, will you?" He cocked his head, studying her. "Paris is a great name. Sexy. How'd you get it?"

"Guess where my parents went on their honeymoon?" Paris asked.

"Romantic couple," Greg said with a smile.

"Not for long. Mom split when I was, like, three. I think she went out for groceries or something and then neglected to find her way back home."

"No kidding?" Greg asked. "So you live with your dad?"

Paris nodded. "He's pretty cool. He teaches Jewish theology at Stanfield. He's always got his head in some book."

"Do you miss your mom?" Greg asked.

Paris shrugged. "Miss her? I don't even remember her."

"Tough girl, huh?"

She shrugged again. "Hey, the way I figure it is if she didn't want me, I don't want her, either."

Greg nodded, then he pulled a pack of cigarettes out of his pocket and offered one to Paris.

"Gross habit," Paris said.

"You're right," Greg agreed easily, dropping the pack back into his pocket. He stood up and reached his hand out for Paris. "Want to dance?"

She looked up at him. "You said it was too hot."

"I changed my mind."

She put her hand in Greg's and stood up. But Greg made no move toward the patio where everyone was dancing.

"Uh, didn't you just ask me to dance?" Paris asked him.

"Yeah," Greg said.

He was only a couple of inches taller than her. She was looking right into his gorgeous, deep brown eyes.

"Well, that sort of entails our going over there," Paris said, cocking her head toward the patio.

"Hey, you're a rebel," Greg said, just a hint of a smile on his lips. "Live dangerously."

Then he put his arms around her and began to sway to the music.

"Lovely party," a well-dressed African-American woman told Juliet as she walked by.

"Thanks, Dr. Avnet," Juliet said politely. "We're really glad you could come."

"Juliet, dear, how nice to see you," Mr. Kushner said as he and his wife passed by Juliet with their dessert plates piled high.

"Nice to see you, too," Juliet replied. "Thank you for coming."

It was a couple of hours later, and Juliet was, frankly, getting tired of playing the dutiful daughter.

What I'd really like to do is to send everyone home but my friends, put on some good rock 'n' roll, change into my new bikini and jump into the pool.

The sky had grown dark, and at that moment someone flipped a switch, and thousands of tiny white lights went on all over the yard. It looked magical. Everyone oohed and ahhed. A few people applauded.

The band began to play "I Wanna Dance With Somebody" and many couples took them up on it. Juliet craned her neck, looking for Tyler, Austin's friend from Tennessee. He had been quiet during their one dance together earlier that evening, and she hadn't seen him since.

But she wanted to. She thought he was darling.

"Juliet, sweetie, come and give me a big kiss!" a robust man with white hair said in a booming voice.

"Hello, Mr. Butler," Juliet said evenly, but she was wincing inside. Mr. Butler was a very rich man on the board of the college. He was very nice when he was sober, but when he drank . . .

And Juliet could tell he'd already had one too many glasses of champagne.

Since Juliet hadn't moved from her spot near the buffet tent, Mr. Butler crossed to her and gave her a hug. "Your parents have outdone themselves tonight, sweetie!"

"Thanks," Juliet said.

Mr. Butler held her at arm's length. "Such a pretty girl!" he boomed out. "You look like a little China doll!"

Juliet tried to smile, but couldn't. Mr. Butler was too drunk to notice. He just stumbled away to get another glass of champagne.

A little China doll. *I'm not even Chinese, you stupid, ignorant drunk!* she wanted to scream after him.

But she didn't. That wasn't something a well-bred Stanfield would ever do.

But I am the only one here who is Asian, she realized. *I do look different.*

I certainly don't look like a Stanfield . . .

This was a thought Juliet had had many, many times over the past few years. There was only one other person of Asian descent at Stanfield High, the son of a math professor at the college. People were forever trying to fix them up.

No one seemed to realize that they didn't particularly like each other, and they had absolutely nothing in common.

Except the color of their skin.

"You look as sad as a turkey the day before Thanksgiving," Tyler said, loping over to her.

Juliet laughed, immediately jolted out of her musings. "Did you just make that up?"

"Oh, I've got a million cute little country sayings," Tyler assured her. "They'll wear on you real quick. You did look kind of lost in thought, though."

"It's nothing important," Juliet said lightly. "Are you having fun?"

"Sure," Tyler said. "Great!" He looked around the backyard, then he pulled at the collar of his denim shirt under his tie. "Well, to tell you the truth, I'm more comfortable at a jeans-and-flannel-shirt kind of thing. I'd love to get a hold of the sadist who invented the necktie."

"But it looks so nice!"

"Thanks," Tyler said morosely. "But I'd rather be in some cutoffs swimming around in that pool, with some rock 'n' roll on the box."

"That's exactly what I was just thinking!" Juliet exclaimed.

"Really?" Tyler asked, a grin spreading across his face. "But you look like a girl who's real at home with all this formal stuff."

"I am," Juliet admitted. "But frankly, it gets old fast."

"Amen," Tyler agreed. He leaned close to her. "You think anyone would notice if we just peeled out of these clothes and jumped on in?"

"Yes," Juliet said with a laugh. "I think my mother would faint. No. She'd murder me and then she'd faint."

"Too bad," Tyler said. "It would have been fun."

"Why don't you come over tomorrow? We can swim then," Juliet asked impetuously. "With Austin, I mean," she added quickly.

"Well, now," Tyler began, "who's invitin' me, you or Austin?"

Juliet gulped hard. He was a college guy. And so cute. And he had only danced with her that one time, but . . .

"I am," Juliet managed to get out.

"Well, then, I'd love to," Tyler said, a big grin spreading across his face.

"Juliet! I have to talk to you!" Lexi exclaimed breathlessly, running over to her friend.

"I think I'll go try some of those desserts," Tyler said. "See you tomorrow, Juli."

Juliet grabbed Lexi's arm. "He's coming over swimming tomorrow! Don't you think he's darling?"

"Juli, I have the greatest news!" Lexi said, barely hearing what her friend had just told her. "I was in the house using the ladies' room, and I ran into Austin. Without Fawn. And he told me he had something really important to tell me about him and Fawn!"

"What is it?" Juliet asked.

"I don't know," Lexi admitted. "But he said it in such a romantic way — oh, Juli, I think he's breaking up with her! You were right all along! He really *does* care about me!"

"That's fantastic!" Juliet cried, hugging her friend. "When is he supposed to tell you?"

"He said later tonight, after the party," Lexi reported. "That's kind of like a date, isn't it?"

"It's so romantic!" Juliet said, her voice full of excitement. "This means that — "

"Can I have everyone's attention, please?"

Juliet and Lexi turned to the sound of the voice. It was Juliet's mom, talking through the lead singer's microphone on the patio.

"Gather 'round, everyone!" Mrs. Stanfield called out. Her husband, a tall, handsome, silver-haired man, stood proudly next to his beautiful wife.

The crowd buzzed and moved to stand near the patio. Juliet stood toward the back of the crowd with Lexi. Paris stood with Greg. There were perhaps two hundred people waiting expectantly.

"I'd like to ask our wonderful children to join us up here," Mrs. Stanfield continued.

Juliet shrugged at Lexi and made her way up to her mom and dad. Austin, who stood with Fawn just a few feet from his parents, moved closer. His dad put his arm around him.

Mr. Stanfield moved closer to the microphone. "We're so pleased that all of you could join us this evening for this wonderful party. Friends and family are what make life worth living."

Everyone applauded.

"As you know my mother hasn't been well lately, but she wanted to come out and say hello to all of you tonight."

The crowd looked behind them, where a tuxedoed waiter was wheeling the frail, elderly Mrs. Stanfield toward the group. Her son broke away from the microphone and hurried toward his mom's wheelchair, taking over for the waiter. He wheeled the woman up onto the patio. Juliet bent over and kissed her grandmother's cheek. The old woman reached for her hand and held it tight.

Everyone applauded again.

"We have a couple of surprises for the kids tonight," Mr. Stanfield continued, "and we wanted to share them with all of you." He turned to his daughter. "Juliet, honey, in honor of your terrific report card, and just because you're an all-around wonderful daughter . . ."

There was a loud honk, then from around the house came a silver Jaguar convertible, driven by one of the waiters.

"Don't mess up any more of my lawn than that!" Mr. Stanfield yelled. He turned to his daughter. "Honey, that's for you."

"Oh my gosh, it's fantastic!" Juliet cried. She ran over to the car as the waiter held the door open for her, and she jumped into the driver's seat, waving to the crowd.

Everyone applauded again as Juliet ran back over to her family. "Thank you so much!" She kissed both of her parents and her grandmother.

"You deserve it, honey," her father said. "Now I'm going to turn this back over to my wife."

Mrs. Stanfield stepped back to the microphone. She smiled at Austin, who smiled back. "Austin, honey, your father and I decided that tonight was the perfect time to announce some very special news. I know we had all agreed to wait on this, but Grandmother Stanfield wanted so badly for us to do this tonight, so . . ."

Austin looked confused at first, then he just looked wary.

Mrs. Stanfield reached for Austin's hand. "Tonight, I am pleased and proud to announce the engagement of our son, Mr. Austin Baylor Stanfield, to Miss Fawn Elizabeth Mundy." She turned and gave Fawn a dazzling smile. "Come on over here, sweetheart," she said. "You're family now."

Chapter 5

"Lex, are you awake?" Paris whispered.

It was the next morning, quite early. Paris and Lexi had slept over at Juliet's house. Juliet had slept in one twin bed, Lexi in the other. Paris had slept in her sleeping bag on the floor.

"I didn't sleep," Lexi replied in a flat voice.

Paris sat up and stared at her friend, who was staring up at the ceiling. "Not at all?"

"No," Lexi said in that same flat voice.

Paris looked over at Juliet, who was actually snoring quietly, the pillow over her head. "We should go out to talk, and let her sleep."

"I'm awake," Juliet said, her voice muffled by the pillow. She pulled it off and reached blearily for the clock on her nightstand. "Why are we awake? It's only seven o'clock. And we didn't get to bed until three!"

"That means we got four more hours of

sleep than she did," Paris said, cocking her head at Lexi.

"I must be the biggest fool in the entire universe," Lexi said, still staring at the ceiling. "I thought Austin wanted to tell me that he and Fawn were breaking up so he could be with me, and all the time he just wanted to tell me that they were in love, and they were going to get engaged."

Juliet and Paris traded looks. When they'd finally gone to bed that night, Lexi had been saying the exact same thing.

"You're not a fool," Juliet insisted, just as she had insisted the night before. "You had no way of knowing Austin and Fawn were going to get engaged!"

Lexi turned her look at Juliet. "If he's so in love with Fawn why was he going to kiss me, answer me that?"

"I can't," Juliet admitted. "Maybe he wasn't really going to kiss you — "

"But he was!" Lexi insisted. "I know he was!"

"So maybe he's just a jerk," Paris offered. Juliet and Lexi both gave her sharp glances. "Okay, not a jerk," she amended. "But why would he and Fawn want to get married, anyway? I mean, they're only twenty! They haven't even finished college yet!"

"So?" Juliet asked. "Don't you think you can fall in true love at a young age?"

"Whose side are you on?" Lexi asked plaintively.

Juliet swung her legs over the side of the bed. "Lex, you and Paris are my best friends in the entire world. But I love my brother, too. And if he's in love with Fawn and she's in love with him and they want to get married, well then, I'm going to be happy for them!"

"But what about me?" Lexi asked.

Juliet went to Lexi and hugged her. "You're going to meet someone else, I'm sure of it," she promised.

"There isn't anyone else."

"Horse dooky," Paris said. "There are lots of guys around, you know."

"And this is the summer we're going to meet them all!" Juliet added, nudging her elbow into Lexi's ribs.

"It won't be any use," Lexi said. "Every guy I meet I'll just compare to Austin." She put her hands over her face. "I can't believe he's going to be my brother-in-law forever!"

"I'm telling you, the only cure for this is to meet other guys," Juliet insisted.

"Guys are highly overrated, if you ask me," Paris said, snuggling back down into her sleeping bag.

"Oh, really?" Juliet asked. "You didn't seem to think so last night. You spent just about every minute with Greg!"

"Yeah, well, I'm a guy magnet, what can I tell you?" Paris deadpanned.

"Did he ask for your phone number?" Juliet asked eagerly.

"No," Paris admitted.

"Well, maybe he's going to ask me for it," Juliet considered.

"Yeah, right," Paris snorted. "I'm sure he dates a lot of chubbos."

"Don't put yourself down like that!" Lexi said sharply.

"I'm not!" Paris replied. "I'm just being honest! What's the problem? Greg could get any girl at Stanfield College. He's a total babe, he's rich, he's fun to be with, he's . . . way out of my league."

"Then why did he spend so much time with you last night?" Juliet asked.

Paris shrugged. "I think I made him laugh."

"Because he really likes you," Lexi told her firmly.

"Hey, I've got a great idea!" Juliet said, her eyes shining. "Tyler is coming over to swim this afternoon. How about if I call him at the frat house and ask him to invite Greg? And another guy, too!"

"Have you lost your mind?" Paris shouted. "Do you think I'm going to appear in front of him in a *bathing suit??*"

"Well, I just thought — " Juliet began.

"I look like Orca the Whale in a bathing suit!" Paris cried.

"A barbecue, then?" Juliet asked. "We'll keep our clothes on! And we'll tell him to bring someone really cute for you, Lex — "

"Juliet, guys are not interchangeable," Lexi explained. "I don't want another guy. I want Austin."

"Well, you can't have him," Juliet pointed out gently. "And the sooner you realize it, the better off you'll be."

"Lexi, is that you?" her mother called, as she let herself into the back door of the family's private apartment attached to the rear of the Stanfield Inn.

It was a few hours later. Lexi felt irritable and out of sorts, partly because she hadn't slept, and partly because of what had happened the night before. She kept playing the scene with Austin in the barn over and over in her head.

He was going to kiss me, she thought for about the zillionth time. *I'm not crazy.*

"Hi, Mom," Lexi said, as she came into the

kitchen. Her mom was sitting at the kitchen table doing some bookkeeping for the inn.

"Fawn told us what happened last night!" her mother said, her face animated. Lexi realized how pretty her mother was, with her thick chestnut hair, green eyes, and lithe figure in jeans and a No Nukes T-shirt.

But, of course she's pretty, Lexi thought. *Fawn looks just like her. The only difference is that Mom's in her forties — although she doesn't look it — and Mom never wears makeup.*

"Yeah," Lexi said noncommittally. She pulled out a chair and sat down, her elbows on the table, her chin in her hands.

"I can't believe Fawn and Austin are engaged!" her mom said, shaking her head. "They're so young . . ."

"I agree with you," Lexi said. "Too young!"

"Well, I don't know," her mom said. "Your dad and I were only a year older when we got married."

"But Fawn's so fickle!" Lexi cried.

"Maybe she's changing," her mom said.

"She's way too immature to be getting married," Lexi insisted. "I mean, she didn't even tell any of us!"

"Fawn told me they weren't planning to announce it for another few weeks. She was as shocked as Austin was when his mother made that announcement last night!"

Lexi sighed with irritation. "Well, I just don't get it. I think she's making a major mistake."

"It's possible," her mom agreed.

"So, talk to her, then!" Lexi cried. "She's your daughter! Tell her not to do it!"

"You know I can't do that, honey," her mom said gently. "Fawn has to make her own decisions."

Lexi sighed again. Sometimes she wished her parents, Sheila and Michael, weren't so . . . so *understanding* about everything! They had met when they were both college students at the University of Michigan in Ann Arbor, both very politically involved in many causes — anti-nuclear power, antisexist, antipesticide, etc.

Anti-everything except Fawn getting married, Lexi thought.

The two of them got married the day after they graduated and informed their conservative parents they were off to see America. So they purchased an old school bus, painted it bright colors, tore out the seats and put in mattresses, and traveled around the country for three years. It was only when Sheila got pregnant with Fawn that they settled down —

picking Stanfield because they had good friends who were teaching at Stanfield College.

Also Stanfield was very reminiscent of Ann Arbor, which they liked just fine.

With an inheritance from Michael's grandmother, they had purchased the run-down Stanfield Inn, doing all the fix-up work themselves. For twenty years now they had owned and operated the inn, as well as the small health food store and restaurant they had opened right next door.

The Mundys had raised Lexi and Fawn to be independent people, concerned about others and concerned about the planet. They had never set down harsh rules for the girls, nor forbidden them to do anything. They just offered counsel and guidance. And Lexi and Fawn had done well with that kind of trust. Both girls had always been good students with lots of friends. They didn't drink or smoke or do drugs.

None of that, Lexi thought bitterly. *We just fall in love with the same guy, that's all.*

"Hey, Lex," her father said easily, as he came into the kitchen. He was wearing faded jeans, a T-shirt and Doc Martens on his feet. His thinning blond hair was pulled back into a neat ponytail. He kissed her on the top of her head. "Cool news about Fawn, huh?"

"She's too young," Lexi said sourly.

Her father shrugged as he looked through a pile of bills on the table. "I couldn't say. That's a decision she's got to make for herself." He looked over at his wife. "Hey, remind me to bring some more granola brownies over from the store, okay? We've got some repeat guests who are crazed for them."

"Did we pay this electric bill yet?" Lexi's mom asked, holding it up to her husband.

Granola brownies. Light bills. How can they be talking about such stupid, mundane things while my life is falling apart? Lexi thought miserably.

Lexi got up and started out of the kitchen.

"So, what's up for you today, sweetie?" her mom asked, lifting her head from the bills.

"I don't know," Lexi said. "I didn't sleep much — I guess I'll go take a nap."

"We could go on a picnic later and celebrate Fawn's engagement," her dad suggested. "Out by the falls, get some rubber inner tubes, what do you think? I've got someone to cover dinner at the restaurant."

"Yeah, okay," Lexi agreed, because she couldn't think of a way to say no.

She padded upstairs, so tired she felt as if she could barely make it into bed. But just as she was pulling her oversized sleeping T-shirt over her head, there was a knock on her door.

It was Fawn. She looked so happy — lit from within. And beautiful.

"What?" Lexi snapped.

"Oh, Lex, isn't it wonderful?" Fawn breathed, giving Lexi a hug. She sailed into Lexi's room, oblivious to her sister's mood.

"I think you're too young," Lexi said, padding back over to her bed. She sat down cross-legged.

"But how can you say that?" Fawn cried.

"It's what I think."

"But I love him, Lex," Fawn said earnestly. "I've never felt this way before in my entire life!" She came and sat next to her sister.

"You've said that before," Lexi reminded her. "It never lasts."

"No, no, this is completely different," Fawn explained earnestly. "Austin is . . . well, he's everything I've ever wanted in a guy. And he loves me, Lexi! He really does!" She reached for Lexi's hands and held them tightly. "Please say you're happy for me!"

Lexi stared into her sister's shining eyes and gulped hard. *I love Fawn. It's not her fault if she's perfect and I'm jealous. And if Fawn really loves Austin and Austin really loves Fawn, then how can I be so small about it?*

"If . . . if you're really happy, then I'm happy for you," Lexi managed to say.

"Oh, thank you!" Fawn said, hugging her younger sister hard. "Last night you seemed so strange . . . and then I realized it was just because Austin's mom made that announcement, and I hadn't even had a chance to tell you yet!"

"It was . . . unexpected," Lexi agreed carefully. She couldn't quite look her sister in the eye.

"I still can't believe his mother did that," Fawn said, brushing her thick hair off her face. She held up her left hand. "I don't even have an engagement ring yet!"

"When does Austin plan to give you one?"

"Oh, it's so wonderful! Mrs. Stanfield — oh, I guess I have to get used to calling her Leonia — she says there's a family diamond in the vault that is Austin's to use for my engagement ring. It's a perfect four-carat diamond that belonged to Austin's great-grandmother!" Fawn stared at her ring finger, picturing how it was going to look adorned by the huge diamond ring.

"That's nice," Lexi said lamely.

"I guess I'll have to get it insured," Fawn murmured, still looking at her finger. "And listen to this — how incredibly sweet and wonderful Austin is — he said I should have the chance to pick out my own engagement ring, so eventually we're going to New York to look at diamonds, and when I get that ring, I'll wear the family heirloom on my right hand!"

"Wow, two engagement rings," Lexi said, trying hard to sound enthusiastic.

Fawn gave a little laugh. "There's so much I need to do. It's kind of . . . kind of overwhelming!"

Lexi picked up some lint from her bedspread. "So . . . when's the wedding?"

"In the fall," Fawn replied.

"In the fall!" Lexi repeated, startled. "So soon?"

"I know, it seems crazy!" Fawn agreed. "Austin's family wants this huge wedding. How can you plan something like that in just three or four months?"

"So why don't you plan it for a year from now or something?" Lexi asked. "Isn't that what most people do?"

And wouldn't that give the two of you a chance to realize you really aren't in love after all? she added in her mind.

"It's Grandmother Stanfield," Fawn explained. "She's very ill — they don't think she has long to live. And she said it would mean the world to her to see Austin married before she dies. I couldn't say no to that!"

"No, you couldn't," Lexi agreed. She pushed some hair behind her ear. It still felt sticky from all the spray and gel Juliet had used on it the night before. "So, this is going to be a really big wedding, huh?"

"Huge."

"You shouldn't have a huge wedding if it's not what you want," Lexi said.

"I guess it *is* what I want," Fawn said softly. "I've had this fantasy wedding in my mind ever since I was a little girl, you know?"

Lexi didn't answer. She had never fantasized about her wedding. About falling in love, yes, about being in Austin's arms forever and ever . . .

"Do you know what Mrs. Stanfield told me?" Fawn asked, her voice hushed. "She said there will be about two hundred and fifty guests from her side alone! The Stanfields know a lot of rich and famous people, Lex!"

Lexi cocked her head to the side. "But who's going to pay for this? I mean, I thought the bride's family always paid . . ."

"Not in this case!" Fawn exclaimed. "Can you imagine? If Mom and Dad paid for it I'd get married in front of the inn and we'd have the reception at the Beansprout!" Fawn shuddered at the thought.

"I don't think that would be so terrible," Lexi said defensively.

"But, Lex, Austin is a *Stanfield!* The wedding has to be spectacular!"

"If he really loves you that isn't important," Lexi maintained.

Fawn got a faraway look in her eyes. "Maybe not," she said. "But I have a chance to have a storybook wedding. The kind of wedding most girls only get to dream about. Only in my case, the dream can actually come true!"

"I guess that's right," Lexi agreed, trying to sound happy for her sister.

Fawn bit her lower lip. "They're so rich, Lex! It's kind of . . . well, it's kind of scary!"

"It'll be fun for you to be rich, I suppose," Lexi said.

"I know!" Fawn exclaimed. "I hate to admit it, but . . . I think it'll be a blast! You know how Mom and Dad are — they don't care much about money and they never did. But can you imagine being able to afford *anything* you want anytime you want it?"

"Frankly, no," Lexi said.

"Well, I'm going to be able to do that . . ."

"Gee, swell," Lexi said, her voice sounding sharper than she had intended.

Fawn's eyes grew wide. "Hey, I didn't fall in love with Austin for his money, you know!"

"Not even a little bit?" Lexi asked.

"No," Fawn insisted. "I would love him just the same if he didn't have a penny. It's just . . . it's everything about him . . ."

Fawn gazed out the window, as if she could see Austin's reflection in the blue sky and fleecy clouds. Then she pulled herself away from her reverie and took her sister's hands, her eyes shining. "You'll be my maid of honor, won't you, Lex?"

No, no, don't ask me to, a voice inside her screamed. *But she's my sister and I love her,* another voice said. *I can't turn her down.*

"Of course I will," Lexi finally murmured.

Fawn hugged her again. "Oh, Lex, I'm so happy! Oh, and I want to ask Juliet and Paris to be bridesmaids — Juliet's going to be my sister-in-law, and I used to babysit for Paris! I'm going to have ten bridesmaids — can you imagine?"

"Wow," Lexi managed.

"You'll help me plan everything, won't you?" Fawn asked, bubbling over with excitement. "You know how laid-back Mom is, and I don't want Mrs. Stanfield — I mean Leonia — to just plan the whole thing. I mean, I know they're paying for it, but it's still my wedding, right?"

"Right," Lexi replied, attempting a small smile.

Fawn jumped up and spun around in a circle, hugging herself tight. "I feel like the princess in some wonderful fairy tale!" she said. "I'm going to marry my prince. I must be the luckiest girl in the world!"

At that moment, Lexi, her heart heavy, knew she couldn't disagree.

Chapter 6

"Hi, dear," Paris's dad said when she walked into the kitchen. He was standing at the counter making himself a tuna fish sandwich.

"Hi, Dad." Paris kissed her dad on the cheek and wrinkled her nose, because he hadn't shaved. After spending the morning rehashing the party and the big announcement with Juliet and Lexi, she was just arriving back home.

"Home" was an old clapboard house built in the 1800s that her parents had bought as newlyweds. They got it cheap — it really was dilapidated — and their plan had been to fix it up themselves.

Only Paris's dad had gotten so involved in studying and teaching theology that he never seemed to have time for the house. And her mother had quickly learned that she was not a house-fixer-upper type person.

At least that's what Paris *thought* had happened. She had no way of knowing for sure, since it was very difficult to get her father to talk about those years, and she had been too young to remember . . . or had blocked it all out.

According to the photo on my nightstand I look just like my mother, weight problem and all, Paris thought to herself. *But I bet I wouldn't recognize my mother now if she were standing in front of me at the grocery store. Well, that's what happens when you run out on your kid when she's only three.*

Anyway, no one ever did fix up the house. The roof still leaked when it rained, and the floors all sagged in one direction. Still, with all its secret little nooks and crannies, Paris loved it.

"So, you'll never guess what happened last night," Paris said.

"Uh-huh," her father agreed, as if he didn't really hear her.

She took out some rye bread and scooped a large portion of tuna fish onto the bread, closed it up, and brought it to the table. "Ask me what happened last night, because you won't believe it," Paris prompted him.

Her father didn't seem to hear, he just stared off into the distance, his sandwich mid-way to his mouth.

"Dad? Are you okay?"

He blinked twice and focused on her. "What?"

"I asked if you were okay," Paris said. "You're, like, zoning out on me."

"Oh, I'm fine," he said absently. He put his sandwich down.

"I was just saying that last night Lexi's older sister, Fawn, got engaged to Juliet's older brother, Austin. Isn't that wild?"

"Very nice," her father said, getting that absent look on his face again.

"Oh, and by the way, Dad, I'm about to give birth to Michael Jackson's love child," Paris added, taking a bite of her sandwich.

"Very nice," he said again, staring into the distance.

Paris waved her hand in front of her father's face. "Dad! You're not listening to me at all!"

He did that weird blinking thing at her again. "What?"

Paris put her sandwich down. She got a terrible feeling in the pit of her stomach. "Something's wrong."

"No — "

"Yes," Paris insisted. "I always know when something is wrong with you. Are you sick? Do you have cancer?"

Paris had dreamed the same nightmare

many times. Her father got very sick and left her, just like her mother had left her, and then she was all alone.

Forever.

"I'm not sick," her father said.

"So what is it, then?"

He reached for her hand. "Yesterday I . . ." He couldn't seem to finish what he had started to say.

"What?" Paris asked, her voice cracking. "You're really scaring me!"

"I'm sorry," her father said. He took a deep breath. "Yesterday I got a postcard . . ."

"You're upset about a *postcard?*" Paris asked incredulously.

". . . from your mother," he finished.

"You're kidding."

"No, I'm not," he said. He put his hand on hers. "She's in Europe. In Belgium. She . . . she just remarried."

Paris's face grew hot with rage. "Hold on. You're telling me that after all these years, when we haven't heard from her at all, she sends a cute little postcard saying she's in Belgium and she just *remarried??*"

"That's right."

"But . . . but that's crazy!" Paris cried. "Where the hell has she been for the past thirteen years?"

"I don't know," her father admitted.

"And this postcard was addressed to you?" He nodded.

"Did I get mentioned at all in this chatty little missive, or did she forget that I even exist?"

Her father got up wordlessly and went to the small table in the front hall. He picked up the postcard that lay there and brought it to Paris.

Dear Joseph (Paris read),
It's been a long time. I'm living in Belgium and I've just remarried. He's a great guy. I hope you're well and happy, and that things have turned out for the best. Paris can write to me if she wants.
Lauren

Paris turned the postcard over. On the front was some famous church in Belgium surrounded by a riot of red and purple flowers.

"Gee, this is rich," Paris said bitterly. "After all these years, this ridiculous card. I can write to her if I *want??*"

"Maybe I shouldn't even have told you." He reached for the postcard.

"Oh, believe me, I can handle it," Paris said

breezily. "I'm not upset. I mean, I couldn't care less."

"I don't believe that," her father said gently. He sat back down at the table. "Come on, sit with me and talk."

"There's nothing to talk about!" Paris insisted. "She's a crazy witch and she split, you're my cool dad and you're here. End of story."

"You know, the Ten Commandments tell us to honor our father *and* our mother — " her father began.

"Please, Dad, I'm not one of your theology students," Paris reminded him. "As far as I'm concerned a person has to act like a real parent for that rule to apply. Which lets her out."

Her father wiped his hand wearily over his face. "It's hard for you to understand, I know, because you never knew your mother."

"Well, whose fault is that?"

"You're right," Mr. Goldman agreed. "But people are complex, Paris. No one is all good or all evil. And people do the things they do for reasons — "

"What?" Paris asked. "What reasons? Let's see, did you beat her up? Psychological abuse, maybe? Or was I just such an awful baby that she couldn't stand to be around me?"

"No, no, nothing like that — "

"What then?" Paris asked. "What could be so horrible that a woman would walk out on her kid without looking back?"

"I'm . . . I'm not making excuses for her," Mr. Goldman began. "But your mother was . . . she was both very beautiful and very insecure. She thought I couldn't possibly find her beautiful because of her weight . . ."

Paris blushed. It felt as if her father were talking about *her* instead of about her mother. "Dad, I don't want to hear this — "

"She needed so much attention, to prove to herself that she was attractive, I think," her father continued. "But there was no amount of attention that could fill the emptiness she felt."

"Whoa, would you look at the time," Paris said loudly, jumping up from the table. "Too bad we have to end this deep little chat about Mumsy — "

"I'm just glad that you're so different from her, Paris. You know how beautiful and wonderful you are." Her father smiled at her.

But the rest of his unspoken statement echoed in Paris's head anyway: *Even though you look just like her.*

When Paris went into her room she shut the door and put a Tori Amos tape in, cranking it up loud. Then she picked up the photo of her mother and stared at it.

In the photo her mother had two tiny braids on the front of each side of her head. The rest of her long hair fell to her shoulders. Her mother had a pretty though too full face, with great eyes and a sparkling smile. She was wearing an oversized T-shirt with Marilyn Monroe's picture silk-screened on it, and she struck a Marilyn-type pose for her fiancé — later on her husband — who had taken the picture.

Her father had taken that photo the day they had gotten engaged.

Impetuously Paris held the photo up to the large mirror on her dresser, staring at the reflection of both herself and her mother's photo. She affected the same pose, and realized again just how much they looked like each other.

"Only I'm nothing like you," Paris said out loud, as if hearing the words could prove that it were so. And then, to further prove it, she took the framed photo and dropped it into the wastepaper basket.

Just then the phone by her bed rang. She threw herself across the bed to answer it, reaching over to turn down her music at the same time.

"Hello?"

"Hi, it's Juliet. You'll never believe who's over at my house right now."

Paris quickly vowed to put all thoughts of her mother out of her mind. "Brad Pitt?" she replied breezily.

"I wish."

"Bigfoot?"

"Greg, silly girl!" Juliet cried. "I'm on the extension by the pool. Greg just dove into the deep end."

"So?" Paris asked, wrapping the phone cord around her finger.

"So he came over with Tyler!" Juliet exclaimed. "I'm sure he was hoping to see you again!"

"And just what are you basing that on?" Paris asked.

"The fact that he asked if you were still here," Juliet replied.

"Really?" Paris asked, forgetting about her mother for the time being, thrilled in spite of herself.

"Really! You ought to get back over here!"

"I can't — "

"It's the bathing suit thing, right?" Juliet asked. "Well, maybe I was wrong about . . . you know, what I said yesterday. Maybe Greg likes voluptuous women!"

"And maybe he'll run screaming into the woods if he sees me in a bathing suit!"

"You can't take that attitude!" Juliet insisted.

"Easy for you to say," Paris said. "You can wear a bathing suit the size of three postage stamps and look cute."

"So come over and make up an excuse for why you aren't swimming," Juliet suggested. "Just come!"

"Nah, I can't," Paris decided.

"But — "

"I've got . . . some stuff to do. I'll call you later, okay?"

"You're missing out on the guy opportunity of a lifetime, Paris!"

"I'll risk it," she said before saying goodbye and hanging up.

Paris leaned back on her bed and stared up at the ceiling. Greg. He was so fine. And even though it seemed impossible, he really *had* spent just about the entire evening with her. He laughed at her jokes. He flirted with her. He acted as if he thought she was cute.

Paris stood up and pulled her T-shirt over her head, staring at herself in the mirror once again. She figured her bra was similar enough to the top of her bathing suit for her to get an idea of what Greg would see — if she were actually to allow herself to be seen by him in a bathing suit, that is.

"Ugh," she grunted. "Never happen."

It didn't seem fair that she had to hate her body, or try and hide it.

But then, who ever said life was fair?

So if you don't like it, what are you going to do about it? a little voice in her head asked.

"Nothing," she said out loud. "I'm perfectly cool the way I am." Then she opened the drawer on her nightstand and reached in to pull out the candy bar she knew she had left there.

But instead of reaching for the candy, she saw something else. Something she had torn out of the newspaper a couple of weeks earlier.

Diets Don't Work! (the headline screamed) You can get lean and fit. You can take control of your life. You can do it without starving. You can be in control of your destiny.

Then it gave a phone number to call, at an organization called Fit Forever.

Impulsively, Paris picked up the phone and dialed the phone number. *Just because I'm calling doesn't mean I have to do it,* she told herself. *And if it turns out to be some stupid scam I'll just hang up.*

She got a recording, telling her where she could go that week to a Fit Forever seminar, which stressed low-fat, healthy eating and a regular exercise program. Quickly she scribbled all the information down on a piece of paper.

She told herself that she wasn't doing it for Greg, or for any guy, for that matter. And she wasn't even doing it so she would look less like her mother.

If I'm going to do it, she vowed, *I'm going to do it for myself.*

But it wouldn't hurt to look absolutely spectacular at Fawn's wedding, she admitted to herself, *and for Greg to think I was the most gorgeous girl there.*

It wouldn't hurt at all.

Chapter 7

"What do you think?"

Fawn walked into Lexi's room and twirled around to show off her new dress. It was the palest pink and fell just above the knee, with a pink silk slip under a layer of paler pink chiffon. Tight chiffon sleeves were fitted at the wrist with tiny pearl buttons.

It was the following Friday, and the Mundy family was dressing for a dinner at the Stanfields' mansion. Although the parents had met each other a few times over the years, they certainly traveled in different circles and really didn't know one another at all. This was supposed to be the opportunity for them to "get to know our new family," as Mrs. Stanfield had told Lexi's mom on the phone, "and we can begin to make plans for this wonderful wedding!"

Everyone involved seemed thrilled about all this. Except Lexi, that is.

Lexi was sitting on her bed in her bra and panties, lost in thought. About Fawn and Austin. About how she should act around him. About how she could ever live with the fact that he was marrying her sister.

The only good thing is that I'll finally be able to get a pet, Lexi thought glumly. *Fawn and her allergies will be out of the house.*

She forced herself to stop obsessing about her problems, and turned to look at Fawn, posed in the doorway. "Fawn, that dress is incredible!" Lexi exclaimed. "Where did you get it?"

"The French Shoppe at the mall," Fawn replied, looking happily at her reflection in the mirror on Lexi's dresser. "I wanted to make sure I looked absolutely perfect tonight."

"But everything at The French Shoppe costs a fortune!" Lexi said, eyeing her sister.

"I know," Fawn agreed dreamily, still staring at her reflection. "This is a Carolina Herrera. She designed Marla Maples's wedding gown."

"Well, Marla can afford her," Lexi pointed out. "How did you?"

"How did I what?" Fawn asked. She turned

to look at the back of her dress. The silk slip dipped to nearly her waist and the pale chiffon covered her to the neck.

"Afford that dress?" Lexi asked bluntly. "It must have cost a mint!"

"Oh, it was . . . on sale," Fawn said brightly.

"It still must have cost a fortune," Lexi said. "How could you possibly afford it?"

"What is this, an inquisition?" Fawn asked sharply.

Lexi was taken aback. "No, I just thought — "

"Everything has to be perfect tonight," Fawn went on, her face etched with anxiety. "You understand, don't you?"

"Sure," Lexi replied. She'd never seen her sister quite so tense before. "And I'm sure everything will go fine. I guess I was just concerned that you'd emptied out your college bank account, that's all."

"Oh, stop thinking about money," Fawn insisted. "Soon I'll be rich and I'll never have to think about money again! So, what are you wearing?"

Lexi padded to her closet and pulled out the white designer minidress Juliet had given her.

"You can't wear that!" Fawn objected. "You wore it to the party last Saturday!" She examined it more closely. "Besides, you got a tiny spot on it." She pointed to a spot near the neckline.

"I guess I have to get it dry-cleaned," Lexi said, hanging it back up. "Oh, I guess it doesn't matter what I wear. It's you that matters."

"I want the whole family to look fantastic tonight," Fawn said. "It's really important to me." She began to paw through Lexi's clothes, finally pulling out an ankle-length sleeveless dress in a floral print. Lexi's grandmother had given it to her last Christmas, and she had never actually worn it.

"*That?*" Lexi asked, aghast.

"It's perfect," Fawn said, thrusting the dress at Lexi. "You'll look demure. Demure is good."

"I'll look twelve years old," Lexi protested.

"Wear it, okay?"

"But will I be allowed to eat at the big table with the grown-ups, that's what I want to know," Lexi said with a sigh as she pulled the dress on over her head. "Well?" She looked at her reflection in the mirror.

"Very cute," Fawn decreed.

"Gee, thanks," Lexi said in a flat voice.

There was a knock on Lexi's doorframe. The door was open. There stood Fawn and Lexi's parents, dressed for their dinner at the

Stanfields', bright, expectant smiles on their faces.

"Well, do we pass inspection?" Mr. Mundy asked.

Sheila Parker-Mundy wore an ethnic print gauze skirt over a brown leotard. Around her neck hung many strands of ethnic beads and symbols. Michael Mundy had braided his ponytail. He had on a white shirt from the Philippines, black jeans, and his best Birkenstock sandals.

With black socks.

Fawn looked as if she was going to faint.

"Dad, what is that shirt?" she gasped, her face pale.

Michael Mundy looked down at himself. "It's my Filipino wedding shirt, honey! You remember, when your mother and I went on that trip to the Philippines when you were in high school — "

"You . . . you can't wear that," Fawn managed to get out in a strangled voice.

"Why not?" her father asked. "I thought it looked festive!"

Her mother looked concerned. "Did you want us to get more dressed up, honey?"

"Mom, the Stanfields are kind of . . . conservative," Fawn said carefully.

"Yeah, and we're not," her father said with

a shrug. "Come to think of it, it would probably be a good idea if we don't bring up politics . . ."

Fawn had to sit down on Lexi's bed. She buried her head in her hands.

"I think what Fawn means," Lexi began, taking over for her sister, "is . . . she'd feel more comfortable if we all wore more . . . conservative clothes."

"Is that what you want, Fawn?" her mother asked her.

Fawn lifted her head from her hands. "I don't want to hurt your feelings, but . . ."

"I get the picture," her father said.

"Are you mad at me?" Fawn asked meekly.

"Just don't ask me to cut my hair," her father warned, grabbing his ponytail protectively.

"We're not mad at you," Sheila assured Fawn. "We understand. You're nervous. You want everything to be perfect — "

"Exactly!" Fawn exclaimed. "I want everyone to feel comfortable. You know, get off on the right foot and everything . . ."

Michael sighed and scratched his head. "I do own a suit, you know. I haven't worn it since my mother's funeral three years ago, but it probably still fits."

"Thank you, Daddy," Fawn said gratefully. She turned to give her mother a pleading look.

"But I like this skirt," Sheila objected mildly. "I'm comfortable in it."

Fawn went over to her mother. "I want you to be comfortable, Mom," Fawn agreed. "But this is so important to me . . ."

"I suppose I could wear that navy dress with the white collar and cuffs that my mother gave me . . ." Sheila began. Then she noticed what Lexi was wearing. "Come to think of it, she gave you that dress, too, didn't she?"

Lexi nodded. "She gives us all the stuff we never wear."

"Well, see, now you'll have an opportunity to get some use out of it!" Fawn said brightly. "Isn't that great?"

Sheila turned to her husband. "I think we've just been sent back to our room to change, young man." She hooked her arm in his and they left.

"That is incredibly nice of them," Lexi said.

"I know."

"I think you should have let them dress like they wanted."

"But don't you see?" Fawn asked. "This way everyone will be much more comfortable."

You mean you'll be more comfortable, Lexi

thought to herself. But she decided to keep her mouth shut.

"More dessert?" Mrs. Stanfield asked everyone at the table. The uniformed maid who had served the dinner stood at the sideboard, ready to bring whatever anyone wanted to the table.

"I couldn't eat another bite," Sheila Mundy said. "Everything was just delicious."

It was a few hours later, and the Mundys and the Stanfields had just finished an elaborate meal — cold cucumber soup, followed by roast duck, baby asparagus, and tiny roasted new potatoes. Dessert was a velvety lemon mousse, and fresh strawberries hand-dipped in chocolate.

Lexi had barely eaten a thing.

She could not bring herself to look at Austin, who was sitting across from her, Fawn on his right, his mother on his left.

She was too afraid she would see pity in his eyes.

Except for Lexi's misery, so far everything had gone really well. Grandmother Stanfield had made a brief appearance to congratulate the happy couple, then she had adjourned to her guest cottage. The Mundys had changed into "conservative" clothes that met with

Fawn's approval. Mr. and Mrs. Stanfield were gracious and charming, telling wonderful stories about Stanfield College and their plans for the school in the future. The Mundys listened with interest. No one talked about politics.

When the duck was served, Juliet kicked Lexi under the table, and bit her lip to keep from laughing. She knew that Lexi's parents were vegetarians. Fawn's face silently begged her parents to keep their mouths shut about this, which they did. They both just sort of cut the duck and moved it around on their plates.

"I hope the duck isn't too rare," Mrs. Stanfield had said at one point.

"Oh, no," Sheila insisted. "It's . . . perfect!"

While they were eating dessert, Juliet told a story about how wonderful the food was at the Stanfield Inn's health food restaurant. Her parents replied that they'd have to eat there some time. Sheila and Michael said that of course the Stanfields would be their guests.

On and on and on.

But nothing about the wedding.

"Well, perhaps this would be a good time to adjourn to the study and talk about our happy event," Mr. Stanfield suggested, getting up from the table.

"Great idea," Mrs. Stanfield said. "I plan to devote my entire summer to this!"

Juliet's eyes met Lexi's, and Lexi gave her a look that said "uh-oh." Mrs. Stanfield had a tendency to be extremely controlling.

Fawn looked both happy and nervous. She took Austin's arm as they all strolled toward the study.

Austin turned to look at Lexi, who was deliberately lagging behind them. "You okay?" he asked her.

"Sure," she said, trying to sound as nonchalant as was humanly possible. "Why wouldn't I be okay?"

"You were so quiet at dinner," Austin said.

Lexi shrugged diffidently.

"She's just busy thinking about . . . her new boyfriend!" Juliet invented. "Right, Lexi?"

"Lexi, I didn't know you had a new boyfriend!" Fawn exclaimed. "How sweet!"

"I didn't even know you had an old boyfriend," Austin added with a chuckle.

Lexi wanted to kill both of them. "I do have a social life, you know," she told them coolly.

"Oh, Lexi, don't be so sensitive," Fawn admonished her.

"So, who's the lucky guy?" Austin asked.

"Well, uh . . ." Lexi began.

"Hey, Mom, did you know Lexi has a new boyfriend?" Fawn asked her mother.

"Really?" Sheila exclaimed. She put her arm

around Lexi's shoulders. "We haven't even heard about this yet! Who's the guy?"

I'm going to kill Juliet, Lexi thought.

"He's . . . in college!" Juliet invented. "Very cute. And smart!"

Fawn laughed. "That sounds like Austin!" She hugged his arm close to her. He kissed her on the cheek.

Fortunately at that moment everyone started to talk about what the actual date of the wedding should be, so they dropped the topic of Lexi's mystery boyfriend.

Lexi pulled Juliet back and leaned close to her. "Thanks a lot!" she hissed at her.

"I was just trying to help!"

"You call that help?" Lexi yelped.

"You want to seem like you don't care about Austin, right?" Juliet replied in a whisper. "So I just invented a guy for you!"

"But there is no guy!" Lexi pointed out.

"I don't think anyone is going to ask for proof!" Juliet exclaimed.

"This is such a lovely study," Fawn said as they walked into the room.

The study was bigger than the Mundys' entire apartment.

Everyone settled down on the lush taupe leather furniture, and Mrs. Stanfield brought out a calendar and an appointment book.

"I've got my eye on Saturday, September seventh," Mrs. Stanfield said briskly. "I've already checked about the availability of the chapel and the ballroom at our country club, and miracle of miracles, they've had a cancellation for that night and both rooms are available. And of course, we'll do hors d'oeuvres in the Opal Room before the sit-down dinner in the ballroom."

Fawn's mouth opened, then shut again. "We . . . we hadn't decided yet where the wedding would be . . ."

"But I just assumed . . ." Mrs. Stanfield began. She took a deep breath. "Forgive me. You're absolutely right. What did you children have in mind?"

"It sounds . . . fine," Fawn agreed, her voice a little dazed.

"Wonderful," Mrs. Stanfield said, marking something on her calendar. "Now, we can expect, say, three hundred from our side — "

"I thought you said two-fifty!" Austin reminded her.

"Frankly, son, I'll be relieved if we're able to hold your mother down to three hundred," Mr. Stanfield said jovially.

"Oh, stop, Gerald," Mrs. Stanfield remonstrated. "Many of the people we'll invite are important business connections through the family trust and you know it."

"Yes, dear," Mr. Stanfield said, a grin on his face.

Mrs. Stanfield made a face at him, then looked expectantly at Sheila and Michael Mundy, her pen poised over her appointment book. "So, what's your best guesstimate for how many we can expect from your side?"

Sheila and Michael looked at each other, then they looked back at Mrs. Stanfield.

"Well, you'll be relieved to know we don't even *know* three hundred people," Michael said, a smile playing around the corners of his mouth.

Fawn made sure everyone else laughed before she allowed herself to join in.

"Really, you should be asking Fawn," Sheila pointed out.

"Oh, I think about . . . forty of my friends," Fawn said nervously.

"And maybe forty for us?" Sheila asked, looking at Michael.

"Sure," he agreed easily. "Our families aren't that big. And I don't plan to invite old friends from our Woodstock days or anything."

"Wow, you were at Woodstock?" Juliet asked in awe. "I never knew that!"

"Oh, yeah," Michael said. "Sheila and I were both there. And we're talking the original Woodstock, the real thing, back in the sixties. What an experience. See, we had to hitchhike in, and . . ."

Fawn caught her father's eye and gave him a look that begged him to shut up.

"But we'll talk about it some other time," Michael told Juliet.

"They've changed a lot since then," Fawn assured the Stanfields nervously. "They're very . . . responsible now."

"I'm sure they are, dear," Mrs. Stanfield said soothingly. "Not to worry. All right. So, we're talking about roughly eighty from your side and three hundred and fifty from ours — "

"Mom! The number just went up again!" Austin pointed out.

"Better to plan high, I always say," Mrs. Stanfield decreed. "There is just so much to do — we'll have to make a detailed list, Fawn, and — "

"I would like to bring up something," Sheila said in a calm voice.

"Please, don't think twice about the expense," Mr. Stanfield assured her. "This is something we really want to do for the kids.

And we're honored that you're allowing us to do it."

"That's up to Fawn and Austin," Sheila said. "I do think we should be careful, though, to remember that it's *their* wedding, not ours."

Mrs. Stanfield stiffened slightly. "I really think of it as a family affair."

"Yes, but Fawn and Austin are the ones who are getting married," Sheila said gently.

"Yes, of course," Mrs. Stanfield agreed. Her voice had an edge of frost to it.

"Come on, Mom, no one can plan a big event like you can," Austin said, smiling at his mother. "No way could we get this together in just a few months without you!"

"And I'm really happy that you want to be so helpful," Fawn told Mrs. Stanfield. "I mean, I'm grateful . . ."

Mrs. Stanfield smiled at her, her good graces restored. "I know you are, dear. Now, we have to talk about the menu — we'll go with red meat, I think, but with an alternate seafood choice — the flowers, the photographer, the orchestra — there's really only one top group and I've already got a call in to them. I should think a string quartet during the hors d'oeuvres. Your gown, of course, and the outfits for the bridal party, and — "

"Mom, Mom, come up for air!" Austin said. "I think Fawn wants some input into all this!"

Fawn's eyes were the size of Frisbees. She looked completely overwhelmed.

"I'm so sorry, dear," Mrs. Stanfield said. "Am I going too fast for you?"

"It's just that it's all kind of . . . overwhelming," Fawn admitted.

"I understand totally," Mrs. Stanfield said. "But I'm used to planning large events — Gerald always says I should have been a brigadier general — so you can leave everything to me."

"I just wish we had a little more time — " Fawn began.

"I wish we did, too," Mrs. Stanfield agreed. "But it's so important to Mother Stanfield that we do this quickly, I'm sure you understand — "

"Oh, I do," Fawn agreed. She twisted her hands anxiously in her lap. "My sister will help me. You know, with the bridesmaid's dresses and things like that — "

"We can't pick the bridesmaid's dresses out of one of those tacky wedding magazines," Mrs. Stanfield said with a shudder. "Now, I've already called Madame Renaud — no one designs like Madame Renaud, and I was thinking of either all white for the bridal party, perhaps with shades of beige and eggshell — "

"But I . . . I like pink," Fawn said meekly.

"Oh, no, dear," Mrs. Stanfield said. "This isn't a baby shower. Pink just isn't done!"

"Fawn, honey," Sheila said, reaching for her daughter's hand. "You don't have to make all your decisions tonight, okay?"

"But there's so little time . . ." Fawn began.

"We'll all help," Sheila said soothingly.

"And I think you should have whatever colors you want," Juliet added.

"Me, too," Lexi put in.

"Oh, well, Mrs. Stanfield knows so much more about all of this than I do . . ." Fawn said.

She's afraid to stand up to her, Lexi realized. *I've never seen Fawn act like this in her entire life. It's like all her spirit is gone!*

"I'm telling you, my wife could plan the invasion of Europe and color coordinate it, too," Mr. Stanfield said proudly.

"Thank you, dear," Mrs. Stanfield said. She turned back to Fawn. "I've arranged the first fitting for your gown," Mrs. Stanfield steamrolled on. "And believe me, I had to beg to get you in only two weeks from now — the very best seamstresses are booked a year in advance, and — "

"Yo, I have something to add here," Michael broke in.

"Yes?" Mrs. Stanfield asked.

"Sheila and I would like to give an engagement party for Fawn and Austin. At the Stanfield Inn."

"How lovely!" Mrs. Stanfield exclaimed. "I know a wonderful caterer — "

"Mother, they have their own restaurant," Juliet reminded her. "Remember, I was just telling you about it?"

"Well, yes, but health food . . ." Mrs. Stanfield began.

"Our food happens to be great," Michael said. "Just keep your guest list down to twenty-five, because the restaurant only seats fifty. Hey, we'll party outside on the lawn if the weather is nice. It'll be a real T-shirt-and-jeans kind of gig. We were thinking about this awesome country-bluegrass band, the Beavers — they're friends of ours that Fawn has known forever. Beer in kegs, megacasual . . . Oh, and by the way, if your buds want meat, they're out of luck." He gave her a huge grin. " 'Cuz us old hippies are strictly vegetarian."

"Tell me Chris O'Donnell wasn't the cutest in that scene where he finally kissed her," Juliet sighed as she, Lexi, and Paris walked out of the movies the next night.

"You say that about every movie star under

the age of thirty," Lexi reminded her.

"Well, cute guys get to be movie stars, so it makes sense," Juliet pointed out. Two guys in Stanfield College sweatshirts walked past them. "Oh, gosh, that guy is so fine!" she cried.

"Does the term 'guy-obsessed' ring any bells with you?" Paris asked her.

"Love makes the world go 'round," Juliet said with a shrug. "Hey, I'm starving. Let's stop at Mario's for a pizza."

Mario's was the most popular pizza place in Stanfield. It was just down the block from the movie theater, which was right across the street from the Stanfield College student union.

"Gee, this wouldn't have anything to do with the fact that those two cute guys just disappeared into Mario's, would it?" Lexi asked her friend.

"Cute guys and great pizza," Juliet replied, as they pushed open the door to Mario's. "Tell me life isn't great."

The jukebox was blaring out a tune by the Stone Temple Pilots, and the girls made their way through the crowded restaurant to the only empty table in the back.

"A large with everything, right?" Juliet asked. It was what they always got.

"I'm not really hungry," Paris said casually.

"Ha ha," Juliet said, rummaging around in her purse for something. "Big joke."

"I'm serious," Paris said. "I'll just have a diet Coke and a small salad."

"Are you on a diet?" Lexi asked.

"No," Paris snapped.

"Ah, here it is," Juliet exclaimed, bringing some fabric swatches out of her purse. "I promised Mom we'd give her our opinion on the fabric for our bridesmaid's dresses."

"Yeah, what do you want?" a young waitress asked, appearing at their table. Clearly she was a college student, and clearly she hated her job.

"A large pizza with everything," Juliet said.

"Uh, I just said I don't want any," Paris reminded her.

"Oh, I know you don't mean it," Juliet said breezily.

Paris shook her head. "I'd like a small green salad, no dressing. And a diet Coke, please."

"We're out of salad," the waitress said in a bored voice.

Paris just stared at her. "How can you be out of salad?"

The waitress shrugged. "Easy. There's no more lettuce." She looked at Lexi. "You want anything to drink?"

"Iced tea, please," Lexi said.

"Make that two," Juliet added. "Oh, and extra cheese on the pizza, please."

"Yeah, yeah," the waitress mumbled and walked away.

"Geez, if she hates her job that much, she should quit!" Juliet exclaimed.

"Easy for you to say, you've never had to work a day in your life," Paris pointed out.

"True," Juliet acknowledged. She spread the fabric swatches out on the table. "Okay, what do you guys think?"

"How can we pick out fabric when we don't even know what the dresses are going to look like?" Lexi asked.

"Oh, that's right, you haven't seen the sketch yet." Juliet reached into her purse again and pulled out a piece of paper. She laid it out on the table. "This is the bridesmaid's dress."

On the paper was a sketch of a very tall, very thin model-like figure wearing a simple, sleeveless dress. It was very fitted through the torso, then fell in graceful folds to the ankle.

"This is a joke, right?" Paris said, pushing the drawing back to the center of the table.

"Nope," Juliet said. "This is it."

"Wait, is she asking us or telling us?" Paris queried.

"Well, you know my mother," Juliet said. "Supposedly she's asking us, but really she's telling us."

"Fine," Paris said. "Then I'm not a bridesmaid."

"But Fawn will be so hurt!" Lexi exclaimed.

"Frankly, this sounds more like it's Mrs. Stanfield's wedding than Fawn's," Paris said. "I mean, which one of them picked this monstrosity out, answer me that!"

"My mother," Juliet admitted. "But Fawn agreed to it."

"She's afraid to stand up to your mother, Juli!" Lexi cried. "You know it's the truth!"

"I know," Juliet agreed. "Mom means well, but she can be kind of . . . overbearing."

"That's an understatement," Lexi agreed. Then she laughed. "You have to admit, my father was hilarious when he told your mom about the engagement party."

Juliet laughed, too. "I thought Mom was going to faint at first. But after that, you have to admit, she was a good sport about the whole thing."

"The engagement party sounds like a blast, if you ask me," Paris said. She had heard the whole story of the family dinner. "How does Fawn feel about it, though?"

Lexi sighed. "That's the problem. No one

can really tell how Fawn feels! I think she's so worried about making a good impression on her future in-laws that she's scared to venture an opinion about anything."

"Well, that sucks," Paris said bluntly.

Lexi nodded in agreement. She looked over at Juliet. "Listen, we have to help her. If the three of us support Fawn, maybe it'll help her."

"Fine with me," Juliet agreed. "I'm used to my mother, Fawn isn't. And I want Fawn to have the most romantic, perfect wedding in the entire world — except for mine one day, of course." She looked over at Lexi. "You're okay about Austin now, aren't you?"

"Sure," Lexi replied, even though deep in her heart she knew that wasn't entirely true.

And maybe it never will be, Lexi thought to herself. *But I am not going to ruin my sister's wedding.*

Juliet gazed down at the sketch her mother had given her. "You know, my mom might be a pain in the neck, but she does have good taste. The dress is beautiful."

"Juliet, let me explain something to you," Paris began slowly. "The dress is beautiful in the sketch because the girl in the sketch is six feet tall and weighs maybe a hundred pounds. I would look like the fat lady in the circus in that dress, which is why I am not wearing it."

"Maybe it would look good — " Juliet began.

"Earth to Juli," Paris called. "It's sleeveless. I don't do sleeveless. It's fitted. I don't do fitted. End of report."

"One diet Coke, two iced teas," the waitress said, putting their drinks on the table. "Oh, by the way," she told Paris, "there actually is some lettuce back there. It looks like it's left over from a previous decade, but if you want to waste your money, I'll bring you some."

"I'll skip it," Paris said.

"Paris! I just realized what you're doing!" Juliet yelped. "You're trying to lose weight for Fawn's wedding!"

"Bull!" Paris snapped.

"Oh, come on!" Juliet cried. "No pizza, salad with no dressing?"

"Look, maybe I decided to lose weight, okay?" Paris asked. "But if I do, it doesn't have anything to do with the wedding!"

"Or with Greg?" Juliet asked slyly, the dimple in her cheek showing as she grinned.

"You are crazed about this guy and romance stuff!" Paris said with disgust. "It's really obnoxious!"

"No, I'm not, I'm just — "

"You guys, don't argue," Lexi interrupted.

"And Paris, you don't have to answer to us about what you eat or don't eat."

"She's right," Juliet agreed. "I'm sorry. Hey, you know Heather Frazier? The cheerleader with the black hair?"

Lexi and Paris nodded.

"Well, remember how chubby she was getting, and everyone was making jokes about how she was going to bust out of her cheerleading skirt?"

"Not everyone," Lexi said mildly.

"Well, I ran into her at the mall yesterday," Juliet said. "She was so much thinner, I couldn't believe it. She told me she was doing something called Fit Forever and she's already lost ten pounds."

"Oh, I know all about Fit Forever," Paris said. "I went to their seminar."

"What is it?" Lexi asked.

"It's just your basic eat-low-fat-and-exercise plan," Paris said with a shrug. "But I hate to exercise. It would never work for me. And besides, it takes forever. Just like its name. It's really slow."

"So, what are you doing?" Lexi asked. "I mean, if you want to tell us, that is."

"I'm only eating one meal a day," Paris confided. "Other than that I just drink diet Coke or eat salad without dressing." She leaned close to her friends. "I started three days ago, and I've already lost five pounds!"

"That's fantastic!" Juliet exclaimed.

"It's water," Lexi said bluntly. "It's impossible to lose five pounds of fat in three days."

"Who cares?" Paris asked. "The scale says five pounds less, and the scale doesn't care if it's water or fat or Doritos!"

"One large pizza with everything," the waitress said, depositing the pizza on their table. "And three plates." She put a plate in front of each of them.

"I don't need one, thanks," Paris said, handing the plate back to the waitress. She took the plate, shrugged, and walked away.

"You really can sit there and smell pizza, and watch us eat it, and not have any?" Lexi asked.

"Yep," Paris said. "Can you imagine how cute I'm going to look in the fall when we go back to school? And every guy who ever ignored me when I was fat is going to get ignored by me when I'm thin."

Lexi shook her head in amazement. "What brought all this on? I mean, I thought you didn't want to lose weight."

"I changed my mind," Paris said casually.

Lexi took a big bite of her pizza, and Paris's

stomach growled with hunger. She had last eaten at lunchtime, many, many hours earlier. And even then all she'd eaten was a turkey sandwich and a banana.

I can do this, Paris thought to herself. *It's just like that guy on TV said — I have to love the idea of being thin more than I love food. I just have to have willpower, that's all.* She took a huge gulp of her diet Coke and hoped it would stop the hunger pangs in her empty stomach.

"I'm so proud of you, Paris," Juliet said. "I knew you could do it!"

"I didn't do it yet," Paris pointed out.

"You are going to be such a fox," Juliet predicted.

"I think she's a fox now," Lexi said.

"I'm a fat fox, okay?" Paris asked.

"Well, one thing is for sure," Lexi said. "We won't hang out here anymore until you reach your goal, right, Juliet?"

"Absolutely," Juliet agreed. "But wouldn't it be good if you exercised, too? I'd go to an aerobics class with you — "

"Thanks but no thanks," Paris replied. "I'm not ready to see myself in surround-around mirrors dressed in a leotard, bouncing around with all those little size-five girls screaming 'I'm so fat! I'm so fat!' "

Lexi laughed. "We could get a videotape and

work out with you," she offered, polishing off her first slice of pizza.

"I'm allergic to exercise," Paris said.

"But if you exercise your metabolism will speed up," Lexi began.

"Listen, Lex, I read that you can spend an hour on a treadmill and only burn up, like, two hundred calories," Paris explained. "I'd have to spend my entire life sweating to get rid of five pounds! I'd rather just not eat!"

"If you're sure," Lexi said cautiously.

"I'll buy you mountains of sugar-free gum," Juliet promised. "And I'll do this incredible makeover on you when you reach your goal. Oh, it's going to be so cool at the wedding, Paris! Just think, Greg won't even recognize you, you'll be so gorgeous!"

"But Greg likes her now!" Lexi reminded Juliet.

"Maybe," Juliet said. "But think how much more he'll like her when — oh my gosh!" she exclaimed, staring in the direction of the front door of the restaurant. She was the only one facing in that direction — Lexi and Paris sat opposite her in the booth.

"Speak of the devil," Juliet hissed. "Guess who just walked in? Greg, Tyler, and Austin! And they're headed this way!"

Chapter 8

"Hi!" Juliet said brightly when the guys reached their table. "How did you know we were here?"

"We didn't," Greg said.

"But we're glad you are," Tyler added.

Juliet's heart did a happy little dance. She really, really liked Ty. But it was difficult to tell how he felt about her. She was glad she had on her favorite white cotton, open-crocheted summer sweater over a camisole and her most perfectly faded jeans.

I know he likes me as a person, Juliet thought to herself, *but I can't tell if he likes me as a girl!*

Juliet flashed Tyler her most dazzling smile. She couldn't help but notice how darling he looked, in his jeans and white T-shirt and suede vest. "Want to sit here?" She scooted over so that he could fit into the booth next to her.

"I'll find some chairs and we can stick them on the end of the booth," Lexi offered, sliding out of the booth. She was careful not to look at Austin.

"I got it," Austin said. He grabbed two chairs and pulled them up to the booth, sitting in one. Greg slid into the booth next to Paris, which left Lexi to sit next to Austin.

"How you doing, big bro?" Juliet asked Austin. "I haven't even seen you in a while."

"I've been busy," Austin said.

"Don't feel bad, Juli," Greg said. "I haven't seen him, either. Fawn is the only one who sees him."

"I'm starving," Austin said, ignoring Greg's comment. He looked around for a waitress.

"Not me," Tyler said with a sigh. "When I get nervous air seems like a big meal!"

"What are you nervous about?" Juliet asked.

"It's nothing, forget it," Austin said quickly. He looked around. "It's a zoo in here tonight. I don't even see the waitress."

"It ain't nothin'," Tyler drawled. "And you did real good up there, buck-o."

"Wait, let me guess," Paris said. "The three of you just auditioned to be male exotic dancers — "

"The girl is psychic," Greg said. He casually draped his arm across the back of the booth.

Meaning around Paris.

She tried very hard to pretend it was no big thing.

"Have y'all heard about the new summer stock company that just took over the old theater on Hillwood Road?" Tyler asked. "It's a producer out of New York, and today he held a casting call for the whole summer season."

"And you auditioned?" Juliet asked.

"Sure did," Tyler said. "Me and Austin."

Juliet stared at her brother. "You?"

"What, you don't think it's possible?" Austin asked defensively.

"It isn't that," Juliet said. "It's just that you haven't been in a play since high school . . ."

"Look, it was probably a stupid idea," Austin said. "I mean, I probably suck. So don't say anything to Mom and Dad, okay?"

"But what if you got a part?" Juliet asked.

"I doubt that I did," Austin said.

"I don't know," Tyler said. "I think you're on the money for Brick in *Cat on a Hot Tin Roof*."

"Man, I'd love to play that part . . ." Austin admitted.

"Yeah, what do you want?" the same surly

waitress who had waited on the girls asked, pulling her pencil out from behind her ear.

"A large double mushroom," Greg replied, "and three beers."

"Yeah, right, like I'm not gonna card you," the waitress snorted.

Greg pulled out his fake ID and showed it to her.

"Please," the waitress said. "I'm a poli sci major. Credit me with a little intelligence, okay?" She walked away.

Austin laughed at Greg. "Don't sweat it, man. I heard Mario got fined big-time last week for taking fake ID here."

"Being twenty is the pits," Greg said.

"Being sixteen is worse," Juliet pointed out.

Austin reached over the table and picked up the drawing of the bridesmaid's gown. "This from Mom?"

Juliet nodded. "You like it?"

"Sure, whatever she wants is fine with me," Austin said, tossing the drawing back down on the table.

"What about what Fawn wants?" Lexi asked sharply.

"Well, that's what I meant," Austin said.

"No, you said whatever your mother wants. And it isn't her wedding."

"I'm sure Mom and Fawn will work it out,"

Austin said with a shrug. "I'm really not into all this wedding stuff."

"Well, I don't think that's very fair to my sister," Lexi said.

"Hey, you think Fawn is ticked at him now, wait until she hears he's going to be in a play while she's trying to pull their wedding together!" Greg said.

"Oh, thanks, man, that's very supportive," Austin said.

"I calls 'em like I sees 'em," Greg said.

"He's right, actually," Juliet said. "How can you be doing summer stock while the wedding is being planned? And what about Mom?"

"Whoa, what is this, beat-up-on-Austin night? Mom'll be glad I'm occupied," he said. "I'm going to put some coins in the jukebox, so you can all just chill out while I'm gone." He got up. "And I wouldn't worry about all this too much. I'm not getting cast, anyway."

"It's pretty lame if you ask me," Paris said. "He didn't tell his parents *or* Fawn . . ."

But he told me, Lexi thought. *He told me he really wanted to be an actor more than a week ago. Why did he do that?*

"So, Paris," Greg said, "what's up with you?" He casually let his hand touch her shoulder.

"Oh, you know," Paris said casually, "not much."

The waitress laid the guys' pizza on the table.

"Maybe I can eat after all," Tyler said, reaching for a slice.

"I really could use a brew with this," Greg said, biting into his steaming slice of pizza.

"Suffer," Paris quipped. It was everything Paris could do not to drool on the table, she was so hungry.

"Hey, listen, I heard about this wild party over on the West Side tonight," Greg said. "You guys up for it?"

"I'd love to," Juliet said with a sigh. "But I promised my mother I'd be home by eleven o'clock."

"So call and tell her you'll be late," Greg said.

"She'll never go for it."

"What if you tell her your brother's gonna be there," Tyler suggested. "That ought to make your momma feel better."

"What will make Mom feel better?" Austin asked, coming back over to the table.

"If Juliet tells your mom that you're gonna be at Shannon Michner's party tonight," Greg said.

"Except I'm not," Austin said, reaching for a slice of pizza.

"Why, because Fawn won't be there?" Greg asked derisively.

"You have a problem with that?" Austin asked.

"Austin, you're engaged, not joined at the hip," Greg said.

"No can do, bro," Austin said, taking a bite of his pizza.

Greg turned to Paris. "You're not going to blow me off too, are you?"

"Yep," Paris said. "I hate wild parties."

"Get out of here," Greg said with a laugh.

"It's the truth," Paris insisted. "People get wasted and then they think they're being incredibly cool when really they're acting so incredibly stupid."

"Not me," Greg said.

"What, you don't act stupid or you don't get wasted?" Paris asked archly.

Greg laughed and hugged her shoulders. "You're a quick one, you know that?"

"I've heard rumors."

"Okay, so if you won't go to the party with me, how about if I give you a ride home?" Greg asked Paris.

"No, I don't think so — " Paris began.

"What is it?" Greg asked. "Did I turn ugly overnight or something?"

"I'm with my buds," Paris explained.

"Oh, I think you should go," Juliet said quickly. "He's got a great car!"

"Am I supposed to care?" Paris asked. "So do you."

"Look, how about if I drive to the party," Juliet said, "and then we can all go. But we'll only stay a few minutes."

"I don't think that's a very good idea, Juli — " Lexi began.

"It's only ten o'clock," Ty said, looking at his watch.

"Yeah, and I say we drag Austin's butt out with us," Greg said.

"No way — "

"Yes way," Greg insisted. "Come on. You're too young to curl up and die!"

"Yeah, okay," Austin said. "Just to shut you up, Greg."

"Once a party animal always a party animal," Greg said, wiping some tomato sauce off his fingers. "Let's get out of here and par-tay!"

"I thought you knew where this party was," Paris told Greg, as they circled the same area for the fourth time.

"Can I help it if the girl gave me lame directions?" Greg asked irritably.

It was almost an hour later, and they were still driving around, trying to find the party. Greg was driving his jet-black BMW, and Paris sat next to him holding the directions to the party. In the backseat were Austin and Lexi. She sat as far from him as she possibly could. Tyler had gone with Juliet in her car, and they were right behind, following every false turn that Greg made.

"Why don't you call her on your mobile phone?" Austin suggested from the backseat.

"I don't have it with me," Greg said. "Are you sure it says a right turn at the third stop light after Cannon Drive?"

"That's what it says," Paris confirmed.

"I'm gonna kill Shannon," Greg said. "The girl is too dumb to live."

"Maybe she gave you bogus directions on purpose," Austin said. "Did that ever occur to you?"

"Hey, Shannon and I never really had anything going, okay?" Greg said.

"Look, let's just forget it," Lexi suggested. "Juliet has to be home in ten minutes, and it'll take longer than that for her to get there from here."

"So, what's her mom going to do if she's late, send her to jail?" Greg asked, stopping for a red light. "Man, this really eats my lunch. I'm gonna kill Shannon."

"Let's just bag it," Austin said.

Juliet pulled her car up next to Greg's at the light.

"Hey, y'all sure know how to have a blast!" Tyler teased, calling to Greg from Juliet's car.

"You guys, I have to get home soon," Juliet called.

"We're all the way out here," Greg began, "let's at least stop at Point Lookout and chill out before we drive back, okay?"

"My dad's going to worry — " Paris began.

"Don't you girls ever loosen up and have fun?" Greg asked her. "Oh, that's right, I forgot. You're only sixteen. You've probably never been to Point Lookout."

Actually that's true, Paris thought. *Everyone calls it Point Make Out instead of Point Lookout. And I've never, ever been up there with a guy. But I have no intention of telling him that!*

She leaned over toward Juliet's car. "We're gonna stop at Point Lookout, okay? For just five minutes!"

"All right!" Greg approved, grinning at her. The light changed and he pressed on the accelerator, moving into the right lane. Then he popped a Hootie and the Blowfish CD into his player and turned it up loud.

"Uh, excuse me," Lexi called up to Greg, trying to be heard over the wind and the music blaring from the CD player, "does my vote count here?"

"Sure," Greg called back.

"Well, I have no desire to go to Point Lookout!" Lexi said.

"I second that." Austin folded his arms and stared at the back of Greg's head.

"Okay," Greg said. "Well, that makes it two in favor, two against. But the driver gets an extra vote — Greg's Rules of Order — which means I break the tie!"

"Real funny, Greg," Austin said. "And just what are we supposed to do at Point Lookout?"

"Do what it says, man," Greg replied, as he turned right. "Look out."

"Great," Austin mumbled sarcastically. "Just great."

They took a couple more turns, Juliet's car right behind them, and headed up a steep dirt road. Soon they were at the highest point of the hill overlooking the small town of Stanfield. There were four or five cars parked there already. Juliet's Jaguar pulled up next to Greg's

BMW, and she cut the engine. The lights of Stanfield glittered below them.

"Fine, terrific, awesome view," Austin said. "I've only seen it a hundred times before. So can we go now?"

"Hey, Austin, I think you're turning into an old man on me," Greg said, turning around to contemplate his friend. "I am deeply disappointed in you, bro. You used to know how to have fun."

"Dang, great view!" Tyler said, getting out of Juliet's car. She got out, too, and stood next to him.

"Greg, this isn't funny — " Austin began.

"Hey, *I'm* laughing," Greg said with a shrug. He turned to Paris. "Come on, take a walk with me." He playfully pulled on the ends of her hair.

"Five minutes," Austin warned him. "I'm serious."

"Yeah, I'll set my watch," Greg replied lazily.

He and Paris got out of the car, then Paris looked back at Lexi. "We won't be long," she said. "I promise." Her eyes begged Lexi to understand.

Lexi nodded reluctantly. Paris and Greg walked away. Juliet and Tyler strolled off in the other direction.

Which left Lexi Mundy sitting in the dark, alone, at Point Make Out with the guy she loved.

Who just happened to be her sister's fiancé.

"It's nice up here," Tyler said, kicking at a stone with his red lizard-skin cowboy boot. "Peaceful."

Juliet, who was walking slowly beside him, nodded. "It's the best view in Stanfield, too. Not that anyone comes up here for the view."

Oh, now why did I say that, she asked herself, wincing with embarrassment. *Now he's going to think I'm asking him to kiss me or something.*

"We just did," Tyler said with a small smile. Juliet could just make it out by the light of the full moon.

"So, you're an actor," Juliet said, wanting badly to change the subject.

"Well, I wanna be one," Ty said, his hands in the pockets of his jeans. "Wantin' ain't the same as bein'."

"It's a start," Juliet said. "Have you been in plays?"

"Oh, sure," Tyler replied. "High school, one in college." He leaned against a huge oak tree and folded his arms. "So, Juliet Stanfield, what's your deal, girl?"

"What do you mean?"

"I mean . . . this may come as a shock to you, but you don't exactly look like a Stanfield."

Juliet laughed and picked some bark off the tree. "Well, it's either very, very weird genetics, or I'm adopted."

"From?"

"Viet Nam," Juliet said. "I was only six months old when I came to America. It was a closed adoption, so I really don't know anything else."

"Don't you want to?"

"Want to what?"

"Know," Tyler said, cocking his head at her. He was so much taller than she was that he had to stretch his neck down to look into her eyes.

Juliet shrugged. "I haven't really thought about it."

That's a lie, she admitted to herself. *You have too thought about it.*

"So, you don't know anything about your own culture," Ty said.

"I'm American," Juliet said sharply. "This is my culture."

Ty reached out to touch her arm. "Hey, I didn't mean anything by that — "

"I just get tired of people making assumptions about me because I look different!" Juliet exclaimed. "I'm tired of well-meaning adults trying to fix me up with the only Asian-American guy at our high school. I don't even like him! But it's like people think we should have something in common because he's Chinese and my birth-parents were Vietnamese! It's ridiculous!"

Ty rubbed his chin. "That was quite an outburst."

"I'm sorry," Juliet began, "it's just that . . . no, I'm not sorry. I don't have anything to apologize for!"

"You're right," Ty agreed.

"I know!" Juliet said.

They looked at each other, then they both broke out laughing. When Juliet could catch her breath she leaned next to Ty, against the tree. "Wow. I guess that was building up and I didn't even know about it!" she realized.

"I guess," he agreed, looking at her out of the side of his eyes. "You might want to find out more about where you came from, sometime."

"I might," Juliet allowed.

He was facing her now, still leaning against the tree.

He looks so handsome in the moonlight, Juliet thought. *And I like him so much. Why doesn't he just lean over and kiss me?*

"So, do you . . . do you have a girlfriend?" Juliet asked as casually as possible.

"Nope," Ty replied. "I went out with a girl Austin introduced me to, from Sigma Sigma Pi, that sorority across the street from the frat house? Real pretty girl."

"So I guess you'll go out with her again, then," Juliet said, her heart sinking.

"Yeah, when it rains beer," Ty said with a laugh. "I'm sure she's a nice girl, but she put the *bore* in *boring*. Of course, she probably felt the same way about me."

"I doubt it," Juliet said softly.

He leaned his head back against the tree. "I guess your momma and daddy would have a fit if you went out with some ol' southern boy with more nerve than brains, huh?"

"They don't tell me who to go out with," Juliet said, her heart beating fast.

"I don't know," Tyler said, "from what I've seen your momma runs a pretty tight ship."

"She doesn't tell me who I should like," Juliet insisted. "She's not like that."

"So, who do you like?" Tyler asked casually.

"Who do *you* like?" Juliet raised her face and looked him in the eye, her heart beating a tattoo in her chest.

And when his lips touched hers, she got her answer.

"Too bad we missed Shannon's party," Greg told Paris. He picked up a stone and threw it into the distance. They had walked in the opposite direction from Tyler and Juliet, and were now far enough from the car that they couldn't see it anymore.

Paris was thrilled to be with Greg. He was by far the cutest and oldest guy who had ever paid attention to her. As they walked along she looked down at her clothes — the baggy, khaki-colored shorts and oversize Stanfield College sweatshirt she had worn to the movies — and she marveled that Greg seemed interested in her.

It wasn't like the five pounds she had already lost showed that much. Her stomach growled from hunger, and she quickly cleared her throat to cover the sound.

"So, you and Shannon were an item, huh?" Paris asked, walking slowly beside Greg.

"Like I said, it was no big thing," Greg replied. "She's a party girl."

"Sounds perfect for you," Paris pointed out dryly.

"She partied with everyone, if you know what I mean," Greg said.

"Oh, and you don't," Paris snorted.

Greg laughed, but he didn't say either way. He reached for another stone and sent it sailing into the air. "Ever wish you could fly?"

"When I was a kid I thought I really *could* fly," Paris said, remembering. "Wow, I haven't thought about that in years . . ."

"Me, too," Greg said with a grin. "I was totally convinced. My parents used to argue a lot, and I thought I could just fly away, zoom out the front door and soar above the whole thing, never go back."

"My dream was that I could lift my arms and I would kind of float up, you know?" Paris told him.

"Great idea." Greg spread his arms, closed his eyes, and waited to take off.

Paris stared at him, earthbound. "I guess it doesn't work," she said.

"Nah, it works," Greg said, dropping his arms. "When I was seven I flew away to boarding school."

"Did you like it?"

Greg shrugged. "Beat being home," he admitted. "Austin went there, too, for high school."

"Why didn't he go to Stanfield High?" Paris asked.

"A better question would be how come Juliet doesn't go to boarding school?" Greg said.

"Got me," Paris replied. "But I'm glad she doesn't. I mean, we fight, but I love her to death. I'd miss her."

They walked quietly for a little while, then Greg sat down on a large boulder, staring out at the lights. Paris sat next to him.

This is it, she thought. *He's going to kiss me. This might be the single greatest moment of my life thus far. I just hope he doesn't expect to go too far too fast . . .*

"I'd like to just take off from this cliff and fly . . ." Greg said, staring out into the distance.

"But not to boarding school," Paris said. The wind blew some hair in her face and she tucked it back behind her ear.

He gave her a wry smile. "It kind of sucks to grow up," Greg said.

"You think?" Paris asked. "I can't wait! When I was a little kid all I wanted was to be twelve. Then I thought sixteen would be everything, because I'd be able to drive. Now

I'm sixteen and I hate it. I can't wait to go away to college and really live . . ."

"And then you'll probably feel like you can't wait to get married," Greg said, disgust coloring his voice.

"You've definitely got the wrong girl there," Paris said.

"Oh, yeah, right," Greg said. "Every girl I know has been planning her wedding since she was a little kid."

"Juliet, maybe," Paris said. "Not me." She hugged her knees with her arms and stared down at the twinkling lights. "I plan to have a million adventures before I get married."

"Austin used to say that," Greg murmured.

"Did he?"

"Yeah. We were going to go to Europe together next summer, and just bum around . . ."

"But now he's marrying Fawn the Perfect, so that's out, I guess," Paris said.

Greg shot her a look. "She's not so perfect. You think she's not after the big bucks?"

"Fawn's not like that," Paris said. "I've known her my whole life — "

"Hey, I know girls, okay?" Greg said.

"That's a totally stupid thing to say," Paris shot back. "This may come as a shock to you, but we're not all alike."

"You think Fawn would be so hot to marry Austin right now if he was poor?"

Paris thought for a minute. "I don't know," she finally said. "Maybe she'd want to wait until they both finished school or something. But I'm sure she really loves him."

"He's throwing his life away," Greg whispered.

He said it so softly Paris wasn't sure she had heard what she thought she had heard. "Did you say — "

"Yeah," Greg said with disgust. "He's throwing his damn life away. And he doesn't even know it."

Greg stared out into the distance for a long time. He didn't even seem to know Paris was there.

"So, you're ticked at him, right?" Paris finally said.

"You got it," Greg replied. He looked at his luminous watch. "How long you think we've been out here?"

"I don't know — fifteen minutes, maybe," Paris replied.

"Good," Greg said. "I say we stay fifteen more."

A terrible feeling welled up in Paris's throat. "Listen, this is just a wild guess, but did you leave Austin stuck at Point Lookout with Lexi because you're ticked off at him?"

"Austin's been to Point Lookout with dozens of girls in the past," Greg said. "He always thought it was a blast. I don't see why things should change now."

He doesn't want to kiss me at all, Paris realized. *This isn't even about me. He's just trying to punish Austin. I was so stupid to think he liked me. So stupid . . .*

And he is such a moron.

Paris got up quickly. "Excuse me for not wanting to be a pawn in your stupid little game," she said sharply, and she turned on her heel and headed back toward the car.

Lexi folded her arms over her chest and looked over at Austin. "This is stupid."

"No kidding," Austin agreed. He drummed his fingers on the side of the car. "I'm gonna kill Greg."

"Me, too."

Silence.

"He did it on purpose," Austin finally said.

"What do you mean?"

"I mean he's mad at me because Fawn and I got engaged," Austin explained.

"Why should that make him mad?" Lexi asked.

"He thinks I'll get over her," Austin admitted. "And he's ticked off because I didn't tell him I was going to ask her to marry me. He found out when my mom made the big announcement at the party."

"That's when everyone found out," Lexi said.

"Mom wasn't supposed to say anything," Austin explained. "I didn't want it to happen like that . . ."

"So how did you want it to happen?" Lexi asked, her voice sharp. "Announce it from a billboard on the highway?"

"I wanted to tell Greg first, at least," Austin said. "He's my best friend, I owe him that."

"Uh-huh," Lexi murmured, eyeing Austin carefully.

"And . . . I wanted to tell you," Austin added in a low voice.

Lexi gulped hard. "Why?" she asked casually. "You don't owe me anything."

"It's not about owing, Lexi, it's . . ." He sighed and drummed his fingers on the car again. "Just forget it."

"No, I don't want to forget it," Lexi insisted. "When we went to the barn I thought that — "

I thought that you were going to kiss me, she wanted to tell him. *Why don't you just admit it?*

But she could not make the words come out of her mouth.

"I thought that you . . . wanted to say more than you did," she managed to get out. "And then you told me you wanted to talk to me after the party — "

"To tell you about me and Fawn," Austin said, nodding.

Lexi looked away. "I don't see any reason I should hear about it before anyone else."

She could feel his eyes on the back of her head. "You've always been special to me, Lexi," he said quietly. "I can really talk to you . . ."

Her eyes filled with tears, and she was just grateful that her face was turned away and he couldn't see. "You should be talking to Fawn," she said, trying to keep the pain out of her voice. "After all, she's the girl you're going to marry."

"Things just get so complicated with Fawn — "

"You can talk to her," Lexi said. "She loves you. And you love her."

"So why is it so much easier to talk to you, then?" Austin asked.

Lexi wiped the tears off her cheeks with the back of her hand, and turned to face him, careful not to give away the aching in her heart.

"I wouldn't know," she told him. "I'm just the little sister, remember? I'm not the bride."

Chapter 9

THE MUNDY FAMILY INVITES YOU TO JOIN US
FOR A PARTY AND BARBECUE
IN HONOR OF THE ENGAGEMENT OF
FAWN ELIZABETH MUNDY AND
AUSTIN BAYLOR STANFIELD
DRESS: AS INFORMAL AS YOU CAN BE AND
STILL HAVE ON CLOTHES!

As Lexi put the little pearl studs into her ears, she glanced down at the engagement party invitation that lay on her dresser. Made from recycled rag paper and printed with sepia soy ink, it featured a watercolor drawing of trees and flowers around the border. A family friend of the Mundys, Linda Lipski, who had her own art gallery on Main Street, had volunteered to make the invitations herself.

When Sheila and Michael saw the finished invitations, they thought they were charming.

But Fawn practically had a heart attack, Lexi recalled. *She did not appreciate Linda's method of telling people to dress down.*

The engagement party was set for Saturday night, and Lexi only prayed for her sister's sake that the combination of artsy, politically left friends of her parents and the wealthy, politically right friends of the Stanfields could all get along at a vegetarian barbecue with a bluegrass band.

It was ten days after Lexi's terrible experience with Austin at Point Lookout. She tried hard not to think about it. What would be the point, except to rub salt into her wounded heart?

Fawn never seemed to be home, which meant that Lexi served breakfast to the guests in the inn every morning by herself. She wasn't too thrilled about it, but she tried to understand. After all, Fawn was trying to plan the world's most lavish wedding in just two and a half months.

The summer wasn't turning out the way Lexi had hoped at all. She'd only seen Juliet twice in the past ten days and she hadn't seen Paris at all. Paris had left suddenly to visit some relatives in Connecticut that Lexi had never even heard of before. She would be back in time for Fawn and Austin's engagement party.

Juliet was crazy about Ty, they were dating, but since Ty had gotten a part in the summer stock company's production of *Cat on a Hot Tin Roof* he was very busy with rehearsals and couldn't spend much time with Juliet. Juliet wanted to talk about him endlessly with Lexi. And frankly, in Lexi's current state of mind, having her best friend madly in love was kind of depressing.

Lexi kept herself busy doing stuff at the inn, and working for People for the Ethical Treatment of Animals, which met on the Stanfield College campus. It killed her that she couldn't have a dog or a cat, but Fawn was very allergic to both. Animals were Lexi's favorite thing in the universe. PETA was planning a demonstration against a cosmetics company that used animals to test the ingredients in their makeup, and Lexi wrote letters and made phone calls to help plan the event.

It beats sitting around feeling sorry for myself, Lexi thought, reaching for her hairbrush. *And I will get a cat out of all this, at least.*

"What do you think about this outfit?" Fawn asked, hurrying into Lexi's room.

Lexi turned around. Fawn wore perfectly

fitted beige pants and a matching double-breasted jacket, in a material that looked to Lexi to be raw silk.

"It looks like something Austin's mother would wear," Lexi said, putting down her brush.

"Really? Too old?" Fawn asked anxiously. She studied her reflection in the mirror on Lexi's dresser.

"I didn't mean it like that," Lexi said. "I just meant it looks like some designer outfit that cost a mint."

"It did," Fawn admitted, turning around to study her reflection from the back. "Should I put my hair up?"

"Fawn, we're only going for your first gown fitting," Lexi said, "not to lunch at the White House. Why should you be dressed up?"

"Because I have to have the guts to stand up to Austin's mother, that's why," Fawn said, sitting on Lexi's bed. "She'll be dressed impeccably. The scarf around her neck will be worth more than my entire wardrobe."

"So?" Lexi asked. "She's a middle-aged rich woman who chooses to spend her money on her clothes. That's not you."

Fawn sighed. "You don't understand, Lex. When I'm wearing jeans and sneakers I feel like this little kid and I can't even have a conversation with her, much less insist that I have the wedding gown that I really want!"

Lexi sat down next to Fawn and felt the material of Fawn's jacket between her fingers. "This really is raw silk, isn't it?"

"Yeah," Fawn said.

"How could you afford this?" Lexi asked.

"Oh, don't start with that again — "

"I'm not trying to be nosy, Fawn," Lexi said.

"What would you call it?"

"Is Austin giving you money for clothes, is that it?" Lexi asked.

"I would definitely categorize that question as 'nosy,' " Fawn said. "Now let's talk about something important. Like how you can help me get the bridal gown of my dreams."

"What is the bridal gown of your dreams?" Lexi asked.

Fawn reached into the pocket of her jacket and brought out a folded page from a magazine. "I got this out of *Brides* magazine," she said, unfolding the photo. She handed it to Lexi.

"Wow," Lexi said, staring at the picture. A beautiful blond-haired model wore a white gown covered with antique lace and tiny seed pearls. Hundreds of white sequins were sewn here and there into the lace, creating a sparkling effect. The sweetheart neckline was filled in with sheer, delicate lace, and the same lace made up the sleeves, which came to points over each wrist. The gown was fitted to the waist, then fell in yards and yards of silk and lace. There were bows on each sleeve, and bows down the back.

"It looks like the dress my wedding doll was wearing when I was a little girl," Lexi murmured.

"Exactly!" Fawn agreed. "I had that doll first! It got passed down to you!"

"Well, if this is what you want, all you have to do is show it to Mrs. Stanfield's seamstress — "

"Ha," Fawn barked, folding the photo up and slipping it back into her jacket. "This gown will not be to Mrs. Stanfield's taste — I can tell you that already. It's not elegant enough. She'll want me in something plain and impeccably designed, without a bow or a sequin in sight. She'll say this gown is tacky."

"Maybe she won't — "

"You're right," Fawn agreed. "She won't actually say it. She's too well bred for that. She'll just think it, and make me feel like I have the taste of a gnat for wanting this."

"So what's our game plan, then?" Lexi asked.

"I'm not sure," Fawn admitted. "I'm hoping that two against one will help me stand up to her."

"Listen, I don't blame you for being intimidated by her," Lexi said. "She intimidates me, too. But you should discuss this with Austin, shouldn't you?"

"How can I?" Fawn exclaimed. "It's his mother!"

"I know that," Lexi said. "But it's your marriage — yours and Austin's. You guys have to be able to talk to each other, to tell each other how you really feel, right?"

Fawn sighed and fiddled with a button on her jacket. "It's not so easy."

"I know that, but — "

"He doesn't care about the wedding," Fawn blurted out. "I mean, he cares, but he doesn't really want to be involved!"

"I'm sure that's not true," Lexi said, even though she strongly suspected the same thing herself.

"It is true," Fawn said. "He's perfectly happy to leave it up to his mother and me. Evidently his father's mother planned his parents' wedding — this is how he thinks it's done."

"But he can change," Lexi insisted. She reached for Fawn's hand. "You just have to tell him how you feel."

"He's so busy now with that stupid play, he couldn't even focus," Fawn admitted in a low voice.

Much to Austin's shock and joy, he had been cast as Brick, the male lead, in *Cat on a Hot Tin Roof*. When he told his mother, her attitude had been actually one of relief — he would stay out of her hair and out of trouble until the wedding.

Fawn, on the other hand, just felt lonely and deserted.

"I . . . I guess acting is important to him," Lexi said carefully.

"Oh, it is not," Fawn said crossly, pulling her hand away from Lexi. "He's just a big baby sometimes. He wants to play around and do whatever he feels like doing without having any responsibility!"

Lexi bit her lower lip. "Well, if you feel that way, why are you getting married?"

Fawn's eyes grew huge with alarm. "Because I love him!"

"But . . . you're only twenty," Lexi said. "Maybe you're not ready!"

"I'm ready," Fawn insisted. "It's going to work out fine. You'll see."

"But — "

"Don't!" Fawn exclaimed. "Don't say anything negative. Promise?"

Lexi sighed. "I promise," she said reluctantly.

"So, back to my wedding gown," Fawn prompted.

"Right. Well, it's your wedding and you should have exactly the gown you want," Lexi said firmly. "Maybe we should take Mom with us — then it'll be three against one."

"Oh, no!" Fawn said, getting up quickly. "Mom will stand up to Mrs. Stanfield, you can count on it, and they'll get into a huge fight!"

"Come on, Fawn, Mom isn't going to fight with her — "

"She'll stick up for me and tell Mrs. Stanfield she has no right to dictate to me. She'll tell her she's being overbearing — you know Mom. She's too honest for her own good!"

"I suppose," Lexi said.

"You have tact," Fawn told her sister, "sometimes Mom doesn't." She looked at her watch. "We've got to kick it or we'll be late." She gave Lexi a distressed look, suddenly realizing that Lexi was wearing jeans and a plain navy cotton sweater. "You're wearing that?"

"Hey, I don't have to impress Mrs. Stanfield," Lexi said, reaching for her purse on the dresser. "I'm not the one marrying her son."

"You're late, dear," Mrs. Stanfield admonished gently as Fawn and Lexi flew into the small, private studio on Decanter Street where Fawn's wedding gown would be designed.

"I'm so sorry," Fawn said, kissing the air

near Mrs. Stanfield's cheek so as not to muss her perfectly applied lipstick, "we got caught in traffic."

"Well, you're here, that's the important thing." She turned to the middle-aged, slender, austerely dressed woman who stood patiently behind her. "Madame Renaud, may I present Alexis Mundy and my future daughter-in-law, Fawn Mundy. This is Madame Anais Renaud, perhaps the finest seamstress in the world."

"Madame, you flatter me too much," Madame Renaud said, with a heavy French accent.

"Nonsense," Mrs. Stanfield said. "I speak only the truth." She turned to Fawn. "Madame Renaud occasionally teaches master pattern design classes at the college," Mrs. Stanfield explained. "Most often she is flying around the world, creating wedding magic. The only reason we are fortunate enough to have her here in Stanfield is because her husband is head of the French department at the college."

"Yes, I've heard of you," Fawn said softly. "I'm honored that you're going to do my bridal gown."

"It is my pleasure," Madame Renaud said graciously. "You will make a most beautiful bride."

"Thank you," Fawn began. "I — "

"Of course, normally I require nine months to a year to do ze wedding gown," Madame Renaud sniffed. "Zis is very unusual, to do a gown in zis amount of time!"

"I really am grateful — " Fawn said.

"I do zis for my friend Mrs. Stanfield, eh?" Madame Renaud said, interrupting Fawn again.

"So kind," Mrs. Stanfield murmured. "So, shall we sit down and discuss our ideas for the gown?" Mrs. Stanfield suggested.

"Come into ze salon," Madame Renaud said, ushering them into the next room. "I zink much better in ze salon."

"Ze salon" was a small room furnished with rich, tapestry-covered love seats surrounding a beautiful, worn rug in shades of rust and burgundy. Bolts of fabric lined the room. On a large board on the wall were tacked sketches of wedding dress designs on long-necked models carrying small bouquets in front of them. Next to the drawings were small swatches of white or off-white fabric.

"I can offer tea?" Madame Renaud asked.

"No, thank you," Mrs. Stanfield said, answering for all three of them. They sat on the love seats.

"So, Fawn, have you any ideas about the

kind of gown you want?" Mrs. Stanfield asked pleasantly.

This is good, Lexi thought, pleasantly surprised. *She's actually giving Fawn a chance to tell her what she wants!*

"I, uh . . ." Fawn stammered. She gave Lexi a panicked look.

"Fawn has some great ideas," Lexi prompted.

"Well, you know, just some suggestions," Fawn murmured.

"It is your wedding gown, no?" Madame Renaud asked. "You must say what you want, what is, how you say, your *rêve,* your dream."

"Right," Fawn agreed. She took a deep breath. "Well, I was thinking of something like . . . like this." She reached into her pocket, pulled out the photograph, and handed it to Madame Renaud. Mrs. Stanfield leaned over to look at it.

"Rather . . . lavish, isn't it?" Mrs. Stanfield asked.

"Yes," Fawn said nervously, "but I always dreamed of having a gown that would belong on a princess . . ."

"But dear," Mrs. Stanfield said, looking up from the photograph, "a real princess would never, ever wear a gown like this!"

"But I like it," Fawn said in a low voice.

"I do, too," Lexi added, her voice a little too loud. "I think Fawn will look fantastic in it!"

Mrs. Stanfield smiled. "That's very sweet of you, Lexi. I'm sure Fawn will look lovely no matter what style of gown she chooses. But I'm sure she wants the absolute perfect thing. Something that shows taste and breeding, right?"

Fawn's face burned with embarrassment.

"Why don't we get Madame Renaud's opinion," Mrs. Stanfield suggested, turning to the seamstress. "What do you think, Madame?"

"Zis will never do," Madame Renaud decreed simply.

"You see, darling," Mrs. Stanfield said, "you must bow to those with more experience, don't you think?" She stood up and walked over to the board where the wedding gown sketches were mounted. "I took the liberty of asking Madame to sketch a few things out for you."

"How thoughtful," Lexi said sarcastically under her breath. Fawn elbowed her in the ribs.

"This gown is high-necked and simple," Mrs. Stanfield said, gesturing to a sketch. "I was thinking in re-embroidered French Alençon lace, with an understated silk charmeuse braid."

She pointed to the next drawing. "Now, this is lovely, too — a very different look, but also understated and marvelously elegant. No lace, just the perfection of the material and the pattern. Clean, simple lines, I'd say done in a rich Italian matte satin and organza. The draped crossover bustline would be finished in covered buttons imported from Paris."

"Those are lovely," Fawn said politely.

"Aren't they, though?" Mrs. Stanfield agreed. "Madame is truly a genius."

"You are too kind," Madame murmured.

Fawn took a deep breath. "Perhaps we could . . . incorporate some of the elements of the gown I like?"

Madame Renaud's thin lips smiled. "Mademoiselle, zat would be like asking Van Gogh if he could perhaps just pencil in a few comic strip characters." She pronounced the word "strip" like "streep."

"I . . . I'm sorry," Fawn said, turning red again. "I didn't mean to insult you."

"Oh, it's fine, Fawn, dear," Mrs. Stanfield said in a soothing voice. "Madame Renaud understands that you are very young."

Fire came into Fawn's eyes. It was a fire

Lexi hadn't seen there in quite a while.

"It's true that I'm young," Fawn said. "And I'm sorry if I haven't developed wonderful taste in clothes yet. But it's my wedding and I don't want a bridal gown like those. I want a bridal gown like this." She tapped her finger on the photo from *Brides* magazine.

"Zis I cannot do," Madame Renaud said, throwing her arms into the air. "Not even for you, Mrs. Stanfield — "

"I understand, Madame, truly I do," Mrs. Stanfield said. She turned to Fawn. "Dear, perhaps you don't understand — "

"I understand," Fawn said calmly. "Madame Renaud doesn't want to make the gown I want. So I guess we'll just have to go elsewhere."

The color drained from Mrs. Stanfield's face. "Fawn, there is neither a designer nor a seamstress worth her salt who will design and sew a wedding gown for you in two months. Madame Renaud agreed as a very special favor to me."

"Then we'll go to New York," Fawn insisted. "And we'll find a gown."

"Off-the-rack?" Mrs. Stanfield gasped, growing even paler.

"There's a place in Bay Ridge, Brooklyn — Buchbaum's — that has the largest selection of bridal gowns in the world," Fawn said.

"I suppose you learn zis from *Brides* magazine, too," Madame Renaud said dryly.

"That's right," Fawn said, her chin jutting up a little higher. "Girls from all over the world go there to find their wedding gowns."

"But you're not just another girl," Mrs. Stanfield said sharply. "Stanfields just don't do things this way!"

Lexi reached over and squeezed Fawn's hand for support, and Fawn managed to smile at her future mother-in-law.

"I'm not a Stanfield yet," she reminded her. "This is how Mundys do things."

Chapter 10

"I feel great that I stood up to her, Lex, I really do!" Fawn said, as she finished spraying herself with French perfume Austin had given her. She stopped to enjoy the light from the window playing on the heirloom diamond ring on her left hand.

"I do, too," Lexi agreed. She laughed. "The look on her face when you said you were going to buy a gown off-the-rack! It was priceless!"

"Where are you guys?" Juliet called from down the hall.

"In Fawn's room!" Lexi called back to her.

It was three days later, and Fawn, Lexi, and Juliet were on their way to the Stanfield Country Club to look over the facility and choose a menu for the wedding.

And Fawn had just lucked out. Mrs. Stanfield had called at the last minute and said she had an emergency trust board meeting she had to go to, so Juliet would go in her place, Lexi recalled with a grin.

As if Juliet were anything at all like her mother! Lexi thought.

"Wow," Juliet said when she saw Fawn. "You look beautiful — but you didn't have to get so dressed up to go pick out your wedding menu!"

Fawn had on tan suede trousers and a white silk blouse — yet more clothes Lexi had never seen before. When she'd tried to ask Fawn about them, Fawn had just gotten irritated.

"Every time Austin's taken me to your country club, people were dressed up," Fawn said defensively. "I just want to fit in."

Juliet hugged her spontaneously. "Oh, Fawn, you'd look beautiful in a paper bag," she said sincerely.

"You're sweet," Fawn said with a smile.

"Actually, Mom would scream with joy if she saw your outfit," Juliet admitted. She looked down at her own outfit, a gauzy yellow-and-white babydoll dress with combat boots. Her hair was braided down her back, with a daisy at the end of the braid. "She hates it when I dress like this!"

"Well, it's not national Let's-Please-Leonia-Stanfield-Day, so who cares?" Lexi asked. She was wearing overalls and a baby T-shirt that bared part of her stomach, and she was pretty sure Mrs. Stanfield would have been upset about her choice of clothing, too.

"True," Juliet agreed. "Anyway, I'm used to her, you guys aren't. So, we ready to jam?"

"Lead the way," Fawn said gaily. "Now that I've stood up to your mom once, I feel like I can accomplish anything at all!"

"... and then the wedding would move into here, the Emerald Room, which is our main ballroom, for the dinner and reception," said the elegantly dressed Mrs. Behmmann, the wedding planner for the very ritzy, very private Stanfield Country Club.

"It's beautiful," Fawn breathed, slowly turning to look around the vast room.

It was huge, with a fifteen-foot ceiling and hanging ornate chandeliers sparkling with emerald crystals. The walls were painted a deep forest green with borders of cream and green paisley. The cream-colored carpeting was so thick, Fawn felt as if she were walking on a cloud. And in the center of the room was a large dance floor, behind which was a huge stage that could easily accommodate a full symphony orchestra.

Mrs. Behmmann had already shown them the chapel — a lovely, long, narrow room decorated in shades of white, cream, and eggshell — the Opal Room, featuring a marble fountain hand-carved by the famous sculptress Andrea Opal, where a string quartet would play and hors d'oeuvres would be served while the bridal party prepared for their entrance into the main ballroom, and now, finally, this.

"It *is* lovely, isn't it?" Mrs. Behmmann agreed. "We are all so looking forward to a Stanfield wedding here at the club. So, all of this is satisfactory?"

"Oh, yes," Fawn said faintly, feeling a little overwhelmed.

"Wonderful," Mrs. Behmmann said. "Now, if you three ladies will have a seat, I'll get the books."

"Books?" Lexi asked.

"Colors, table service, menus — we have a lot of work to do!" Mrs. Behmmann exclaimed as she scurried off.

The three girls sat down at a large, round table.

"This wedding stuff is intense, huh?" Lexi asked.

"Too bad Paris isn't here to kind of lighten up the mood," Juliet said.

"I guess you're used to all this," Fawn said. "I mean, you're a Stanfield . . ."

"Yes, but I'm not a Stanfield who ever

planned a wedding before," Juliet pointed out.

"All right, ladies, let's start with colors," Mrs. Behmmann said, returning to the table. "Your colors are — ?"

"Pink and white," Fawn said firmly, though her voice was shaking a little.

Lexi squeezed Fawn's hand under the table. *No matter how I feel about Austin, I'm going to be there for Fawn,* she vowed. *And Fawn should have the colors she wants and the wedding she wants, no matter who is paying for it.*

"Pink and white, lovely," Mrs. Behmmann said, writing on a form with the heading "Stanfield Wedding." "Shall we go with white china and pink linens?"

"Fine," Fawn agreed.

"And who is your florist?" Mrs. Behmmann asked. "We'll need to coordinate with them for floral placement, delivery, et cetera."

"I . . . I don't know yet," Fawn stammered. "I mean, I guess I haven't selected a florist yet."

"That's fine, you'll let me know," Mrs. Behmmann said smoothly, checking something off on her list. "Let's move on to the menu for the Opal Room. We'll begin with the food, shall we, and then we'll move on to the wine selection." She handed Fawn a list of hors d'oeuvres that seemed to go on forever. "Select whatever you like."

Lexi and Juliet leaned over as Fawn scanned the list. Smoked salmon on Russian rye with crudités. Beluga caviar on toast points. Rock shrimp with arugula. Blue point oysters on the half shell with mango chutney. It went on and on and on.

And I don't know what most of it is, Lexi realized, still reading the list. *I'll bet Fawn doesn't, either, and she isn't going to want to admit it.*

"I'm . . . not really sure," Fawn said weakly.

"Why don't you suggest some things?" Juliet asked.

"You know, it just so happens that Mrs. Stanfield called me just a half hour ago and made some suggestions for you, since she found out she wouldn't be able to make this meeting."

"Figures," Fawn muttered so low that Mrs. Behmmann couldn't hear her.

"Here are her suggestions, and I must say, they're excellent," Mrs. Behmmann said, handing a handwritten list to Fawn.

"Yes, all right, this will be fine," Fawn said, clearly at a loss.

"Lovely," Mrs. Behmmann said. "Now, let's move on to the dinner. Mrs. Stanfield has suggested — "

"I'd like to select the dinner," Fawn said smoothly.

"Of course," Mrs. Behmmann agreed. "But perhaps you'd like to consider Mrs. Stanfield's suggestions?"

"All right," Fawn agreed reluctantly.

"Very good," Mrs. Behmmann said. "Well, now, since this is a summer wedding, she suggests we begin with a cold fruit soup, followed by a delicate baked oyster brulée in pastry puffs. Then the salad, of course, ten greens including the wonderful imported bitter Charteux which we'll fly in from France — "

"Of course," Juliet agreed with feigned seriousness. She had no idea what "bitter Charteux" was and she was sure Fawn and Lexi didn't, either.

Mrs. Behmmann smiled at Juliet's excellent taste. "Following the salad course we'll move on to a choice of rare prime rib, duck à l'orange or poached sea bass, as the guest chooses, with wild rice, baby asparagus, and carrot soufflé," she read. "How does all that sound?"

"Delicious," Fawn admitted. "It sure beats burgers and fries, huh?"

Mrs. Behmmann laughed and made a note. "Now, the desserts. Let me show you the wedding cake book." She brought out a spiral-bound book and turned to the back page.

"Let's start at the top of the line, shall we? This is a most wonderful cake — traditional white, twenty tiers, with an almond and raspberry filling and traditional vanilla frosting, hand-decorated with marzipan detail by our master baker!"

"It's huge," Fawn breathed.

"Well, you're having a very large wedding, I understand," Mrs. Behmmann said. "I just love this cake, myself. But if you want something less traditional, we have chocolate, lemon, anything you want!"

"No, no, I love this cake," Fawn admitted.

"And we can have the master baker hand-create the figurines for the top of the cake so that they look just like you and Austin," she added happily. "Will Austin be wanting a groom's cake?"

"I don't even know what that is," Fawn admitted nervously.

"It's actually a charming idea," Mrs. Behmmann said. "Usually it's a darker, somewhat smaller cake, chocolate or a rich fruitcake. Traditionally it's displayed during the reception, then sliced and distributed in pretty boxes to guests as take-home favors."

"That sounds nice," Fawn said.

Mrs. Behmmann smiled. "Legend has it that if a single woman goes to bed at night with a slice of groom's cake under her pillow, she'll dream of her future husband."

"You should definitely have a groom's cake, Fawn," Juliet said. "I want a slice under my pillow!"

"I'll have to ask Austin and let you know," Fawn said.

"It's too bad he couldn't come in with you today," Mrs. Behmmann said.

"He's . . . very busy," Fawn said, reddening.

"I'm sure he is, dear," Mrs. Behmmann said. She went into wines and champagnes, and Lexi's mind began to drift.

It doesn't seem right that Austin isn't here doing this with Fawn, she thought. *I'd feel terrible if it were my wedding. Now I wonder, what would make Austin act that way?*

"God, look at this list, Lexi, I'll never get everything accomplished!" Fawn told her sister.

"Yes, you will," Lexi said. "We'll all help."

It was the next day, and Fawn was spending every minute on the wedding. Lexi was helping as much as she could. She was also doing all the breakfast service at the inn. It didn't really seem fair to Lexi; on the other hand, she understood about how busy Fawn was.

And I also feel guilty, she admitted to herself, *since I'm green with jealousy that she's ending up with Austin.*

Austin. Just thinking about him was like a dagger in her heart. *So I won't think about him,* Lexi vowed. *I'll only think Austin-and-Fawn, like they're one entity. Then it won't hurt so much.*

"Okay, this band is called Mimi and the Screamers," Fawn said, reading the side of a cassette. She slipped it into her boom box. She and Lexi were listening to tapes of bands that had been recommended by various people. There wasn't enough time to travel around and actually catch all the bands playing gigs, so this was the next best thing.

The piercing sound of a high-pitched female voice screeched from the speaker:

"What's love, anyway?
 First it's here, then gone away.
 Just when you think love's here to stay
 You're all alone, your heart must pay . . ."

"A friend actually recommended them to play for your *wedding??*" Lexi asked incredulously.

Fawn clicked it off. "I think it was my friend Diana — you know, the one who doesn't think anyone should get married before the age of thirty? I guess it was her idea of a joke." She slipped the cassette out.

"Some friend," Lexi commented.

"This is the one Leonia wants us to use," Fawn said, slipping another cassette in place. "Frank De Vaughn's Orchestra."

The sound of strings filled the air, then brass instruments joined in. Then a male voice, singing an old Frank Sinatra tune, "Strangers in the Night."

"Over my dead body," Fawn vowed, clicking off the music. "I am not going to have that kind of music at my wedding!"

"What kind of music does Austin want?" Lexi asked casually.

"I have no idea," Fawn said, looking through the other cassettes.

"Have you asked him?"

"No, because I wouldn't get an answer," Fawn said with irritation. "Honestly, it's not like I'm forcing him into this wedding or anything!"

"No one thinks that — "

"He's always too busy, or else he says 'whatever you and Mom want, Fawn!' " Fawn exploded. "I'm not marrying his mother!"

"Maybe you guys need to talk . . ."

"Oh, I'm sick of hearing that," Fawn snapped petulantly. "You can't talk to a guy who doesn't want to talk to you now, can you?"

"I guess not."

Fawn sighed and reached for another tape. "I know he loves me, Lex. He's just never had to plan a wedding before. He thinks it's like organizing a birthday party. Anyway, he says it gives his mom a lot of joy."

She looked over at her sister. "That's it, isn't it?"

"Yeah, I'm sure," Lexi agreed, trying to be supportive.

"It's just . . . I have all these fantasies about my wedding, you know?" Fawn said softly. "I want everything to be so perfect . . ."

"I'm sure Austin does, too," Lexi said, trying hard to mean it.

"You think?" Fawn asked worriedly.

"Of course," Lexi said brightly. "Forget I even said anything. Come on, let's listen to some more tapes."

But even as they listened to tape after tape, Lexi couldn't get the lyrics from the Mimi and the Screamers song out of her mind:

What's love, anyway?
First it's here, then gone away.
Just when you think love's here to stay
You're all alone, your heart must pay . . .

You're all alone, your heart must pay.

Chapter 11

"Have a little chicken," Paris's father coaxed, holding the serving dish out to his daughter.

"No thanks, Dad. I'm not hungry," Paris lied, reaching for her glass of water. The truth of the matter was that she was so hungry she felt as if she could eat not only all the chicken on the platter but the ceramic platter as well.

You've lost seven more pounds in ten days, she reminded herself. *Twelve pounds gone. This is no time to give in to temptation. Besides, if you need to you can always take another one of those little pink pills.*

It was Saturday night, the night of Fawn and Austin's engagement party, and Paris planned to knock everyone dead when she made her entrance.

If I were thin Greg would have been all over me at Point Lookout, Paris thought. *But cute guys can always ignore fat girls. And fat girls marry guys they don't really love just because they're so grateful that someone decent proposed.*

Like my mother. And I am nothing like her. And I never will be.

And Greg Cambridge is going to want me desperately.

Now that Paris had decided to lose weight once and for all, she was completely single-minded about it. She pictured herself a size five, snubbing all the guys who had ever snubbed her, flirting with Greg until he was begging for her.

Maybe I'll become a famous actress, Paris thought dreamily. *Wait, I don't have any talent. Not that that ever stopped half the stars in Hollywood. How about a rock star? Too bad I can't sing. Okay, so I'll settle for being so gorgeous that I'll break a million hearts, and I won't look anything at all like my mother. Ever again.*

For the past ten days, Paris had been living at the Pershing Health Spa in Connecticut, where she had done nothing but exercise and sweat, sweat and exercise. Aerobics. Step class. Water aerobics. Yoga. Free weights. Nautilus. More aerobics.

For a girl who hated to exercise, it was a stunning commitment.

For the first two days, when it came time

to eat the healthy, low-fat meals served in the communal dining room, Paris had merely pushed the food around on her plate. By the third day she was so hungry from continuous exercise and no food that she thought she would pass out.

That night, after the dinner Paris hadn't eaten, her roommate Claire, from Toledo, told her about the little pink pills she took.

"I swear, they totally kill my appetite," Claire said eagerly. She hopped off her bed and grabbed the pills from her dresser drawer.

"What is it, speed?" Paris asked dubiously.

"Hey, speed kills," Claire said. "Everyone knows that."

"And what, this is supposed to be healthy?" Paris asked sarcastically.

"It's a prescription from my doctor!" Claire said. "It's so cool. I'm never hungry, and I have all this energy. Take one! I've got lots, and I can always get more."

"I don't know," Paris hesitated.

"Well, it's totally up to you," Claire said, tossing her head. "But I've been at this prison for two months now, and I've lost forty-two pounds. I only have another fifteen to go. I don't eat any of their crappy health food, and I've lost weight faster than just about anyone here."

"Yeah, but if it's so great, why isn't everyone taking this?" Paris asked.

"It's, like, this totally new thing," Claire said. "My doctor in Toledo is this famous diet guru."

Paris studied Claire. She really did look good, and she had even more energy than Paris in the exercise classes even though she never seemed to eat anything.

Paris's stomach rumbled. All she had eaten all day was an apple. Her dreams were filled with visions of freshly baked bread, Heath bars, sugar cookies, homemade lasagna. Sometimes she thought she would kill just for one bite of an onion roll . . .

She reached for Claire's pills. "Just one," she told Claire.

"Whatever," Claire said with a shrug.

The pink pills worked. It was like some kind of miracle at first. Paris had unbelievable energy and she didn't think about food at all. By the time she left the spa she was taking three of Claire's little pink pills per day. She felt irritable sometimes, and dizzy every once and a while, but she just kept losing weight.

The day Paris left the spa, Claire gave her twenty of the magic pills as a going-away present. What she would do when the pills ran out was something Paris had yet to figure out.

"Your hand is shaking," Mr. Goldman said, cocking his head toward Paris's hand on her water glass.

She was startled back to the present. "I'm probably just nervous about the party tonight," Paris said, trying for a light tone.

Her father frowned. "Honey, I don't think this weight-loss thing is such a good idea."

"Just because my mother was fat doesn't mean I have to be, okay?" Paris snapped.

"Is that what this is about?" Mr. Goldman asked, reaching for his daughter's hand on the table.

"No," Paris said, snatching her hand away. "That was just a comment. Forget it."

"I don't want to forget it, Paris. Please, we can talk about this."

"There's nothing to talk about."

"I know it upset you to hear from your mother — "

"It didn't upset me," Paris said, reaching for her water again. Her hand was shaking so much that she quickly put it back in her lap.

"Maybe you and I should go talk to someone about this," Mr. Goldman said. "Rabbi Kavner, or — "

"Please," Paris snorted. "Rabbi Kavner's kid had a nervous breakdown at Harvard last year and he isn't even speaking to his father.

I don't think Rabbi Kavner's exactly a model of mental health himself."

"A therapist, then. We probably should have gone before this, but I — "

"Dad, I'm fine," Paris said. "I'm fine, you're fine, so let's just drop this, okay?"

Mr. Goldman swallowed a mouthful of chicken and took a sip of his water. "Did you eat at that spa?" he finally asked.

"Of course," Paris said. "It wasn't a prison."

Mr. Goldman stared at his daughter. "You asked me to send you there, I sent you. You wanted to lose weight, you lost weight. But this not eating at all is not healthy, Paris — "

"I eat!"

"When?" her father challenged her. "You got home yesterday. I've seen you eat a plum and half of a bagel with nothing on it. That's not eating."

"Dad, please, I'm fine," Paris protested. "God, you'd think I was some little anorexic thing from the way you talk! I've only gone down one dress size!"

"If you want to lose weight, that's fine," her father said patiently. "But you have to do it healthfully."

"I will, I promise," Paris lied, getting up from the table. She kissed her father on the cheek. "Don't worry so much, Dad. It's bad for your health."

Juliet sprayed herself with her favorite perfume, then surveyed herself in the mirror on her dresser. She liked what she saw. She had on her favorite jeans, a white lace T-shirt, and a white suede vest. On her feet were brand-new white suede cowboy boots. But more than her outfit, she liked the way her eyes were shining and the smile at the corners of her mouth.

And it's all because of Ty, she thought, hugging herself happily. *I just knew I was going to fall in love this summer!*

"Tyler Finn," she whispered to her reflection in the mirror. "I love you."

Not that she'd told him that yet. It was way too soon. But she knew the right moment was coming. Tyler was so terrific — cute and smart and sweet and really talented. He was playing the preacher in *Cat on a Hot Tin Roof,* which was a small part, and understudying Austin's role, Brick, which was the lead. Sometimes he'd pick her up after rehearsal and they'd go to Point Lookout, and Ty would recite Brick's lines for her. He was memorizing them all, just in case he ever had to go on in the role.

Between the play and Ty's part-time job at the video store in town, Juliet didn't get to see him nearly as often as she would have liked. But every moment they had together was precious and magical. Sometimes she would spend hours just thinking about him, writing his name over and over in her diary.

"Maybe tonight I'll tell you how I feel," she told her reflection, as if she were speaking to Ty. "It doesn't matter that you're only eighteen and I'm only sixteen, because this is the real thing, and — "

"Hey, Juli?"

She swung around. Austin was standing in the doorway.

"Don't you believe in knocking?" she asked him.

"Sorry. Listen, Ty called — I forgot to tell you. He has to work tonight — he'll be late to the party."

"How late?" Juliet asked, disappointed.

Austin shrugged. "He didn't say." He folded his arms and regarded his sister. "Listen, I'm not trying to tell you what to do or anything, but Ty's kind of old for you — "

"He is not," Juliet said. "He's only eighteen."

"Yeah, but he's in college and you're still in high school — "

"So? What does that have to do with anything?" Juliet asked belligerently.

"It's just . . . Ty's at a different place in his life than you are," Austin said. "I don't want you to get hurt."

"People can fall in love at any age," Juliet told him.

"Come on, Juliet," Austin chided her. "Nobody's talking about love here — "

"How would you know?" Juliet asked. She got a terrible feeling. "Did Ty say something to you?"

"No," Austin admitted. "I just meant you guys haven't even known each other very long."

"Well, look at you and Fawn," Juliet said. "Look how quickly the two of you fell in love!"

"Yeah, but I've known Fawn practically my whole life!" Austin pointed out.

Juliet began to nervously braid a tiny plait of her hair. "Just because you were *aware* of her existence is hardly any different from not knowing her at all."

"Yes, it is — "

"No, it isn't." Juliet finished the braid and wrapped a tiny covered rubber band around the end. "For a guy who's romantic enough to propose to Fawn Mundy so quickly, I don't see why you're not happy for me and Ty."

"I am, but — "

"No 'buts,' big brother," Juliet said, kissing her brother's cheek.

"It's just weird, my little sister going out with my friend."

Juliet grinned. "Get used to it."

Austin rolled his eyes. "I'll try. But I make no promises."

Juliet hugged herself happily. "Love is so wonderful!"

"Just take it easy, okay?" Austin asked her with a look of concern. "Don't be in such a rush."

"You were — in a rush, I mean," Juliet said.

"That's different."

"Why?"

"It . . . just happened," Austin said crossly. "I can't explain it!"

"Right," Juliet agreed. "That's why they call it love! It's so wonderful that you just can't explain it!"

"Yeah, but Juli — no offense — you kind of fall in love with the *idea* of love, don't you?"

"I do not!" Juliet exclaimed. "I know exactly what love is and I — "

"So are you two ready for this party?" their mother asked, appearing in the doorway.

"Sure," Juliet said. She shot her brother a look that told him to keep his mouth shut, then turned back to her mother. "You look nice, Mom." She took in her mother's Halston white pants ensemble.

"Thanks, dear," Mrs. Stanfield said. "I thought about wearing jeans, I know this is a very casual party — "

"But you don't own jeans!" Austin said with a laugh.

"True," Mrs. Stanfield agreed with a smile. "And I am who I am. Now, when you see your father, don't laugh."

"What would we laugh about?"

"You kids ready?" Mr. Stanfield asked, coming up next to his wife. He put his arm around her.

Now Juliet knew what her mother was talking about. Her father, who also did not previously own a pair of jeans, wore some now. They looked painfully new and clean. He also had on a new, multicolored western-cut shirt and new snakeskin cowboy boots.

Juliet bit her lip to keep from laughing. "You look . . . nice, Daddy."

"Thanks," her father said. "I thought this would be fun. And I wanted to make the Mundys' friends feel comfortable."

"Good idea, Dad," Austin said, trying to keep a straight face.

"The only problem is that our friends might

not recognize you," Mrs. Stanfield said, but the smile on her face made it clear she was only teasing.

"We have a major crisis," Sheila Mundy said to her husband as she walked out onto the porch of the Beansprout, the Mundys' health food restaurant. Michael was squatting in front of a speaker, fiddling with some dials, getting everything ready for the band.

"Whatever it is, we can work it out," Michael said calmly, going over to the other amp.

"Felicity has food poisoning," Sheila announced.

Felicity was the head waitress at the Beansprout. She was supposed to be completely in charge of serving the food for the engagement party.

"Is she okay?" Michael asked, straightening up.

"If you mean will she live, the answer is yes," Sheila said. "However, she's as sick as a dog and there's no way she can be here to serve the food for the party. And Nancy is home taking care of her."

Nancy was Felicity's daughter. Together they were supposed to be handling all the food service for the engagement party.

"Well, we'll have to find someone else, then," Michael said.

"Michael, the party starts in an hour. Who are we going to get?"

"It's not such a big deal," Michael said, checking a mike stand. "We can do it ourselves."

"But Michael — "

"Hey, honey, chill out!" Mr. Mundy said, putting his arms around his wife. "We're in the service business. What's the big deal if we do the serving for the party?"

"The big deal is that Fawn will have a fit," Sheila explained, hugging her husband back. "The parents of the bride are not supposed to be the hired help at the engagement party."

"Well, Fawn is just going to have to get over it," Michael said mildly. "This jumping through hoops to impress the fascist Stanfields is getting a little ridiculous!"

Sheila laughed. "The fascist Stanfields?"

"Okay, that was a low blow," Michael acknowledged. "But I hate to see Fawn acting so insecure just because they have money."

"She's young, sweetie," Sheila said. "She'll get over it. Now, what are we going to do about this party?"

"Hey, Sheila, Michael," Gerald Littlefeather

called, coming out the front door of the restaurant. "I put the veggie burgers in the fridge,
and the eggplant and tofu is all cut up for the
grill. You want the quiche in the oven now or
later?"

Gerald Littlefeather was the chef for the
Beansprout. He was an American Indian from
the Cherokee tribe, a tall, handsome, muscular
man in his mid-forties, with a handsome face
and long, black hair. In addition to being the
restaurant's chef, he was also one of Sheila
and Michael's best friends. With him was a
handsome teenage boy who looked a lot like
him, except that his hair was parted in the
middle and chin-length.

"Later, I think," Sheila said.

"Hey, I want you guys to meet my nephew,"
Gerald said, putting his arm around the boy's
shoulders. "He lives in North Carolina with his
grandparents, but he's spending the summer
here with me. This is Ricky Littlefeather.
Ricky, Michael and Sheila Mundy — they own
this place. And they're good people."

"Glad to meet you, Ricky," Michael said,
shaking Ricky's hand. "We have a daughter
about your age, I'm guessing."

"I'm sixteen," Ricky said.

"On the money," Michael said with a grin.
"Why don't you hang out — Lexi should be

out in a minute. She can introduce you to the kids around here that are your age."

"That would be nice, sir," Ricky said politely.

"I appreciate the good manners, but don't call me 'sir' unless you want me to call you 'sir.' It makes me feel ancient! Call me Michael."

"Okay, Michael," Ricky said with a grin.

"Hey, you don't need to invite Ricky. I was going to take Ricky back to my place and then come back myself," Gerald said. "I know you're full-up for this party."

"We'd love to have Ricky," Sheila said. "That's not a problem. However, we do have a whopper of a headache at the moment." She quickly told Gerald what had happened to Felicity.

"So, no sweat," Gerald said in his usual easy way. "I'll serve."

"But you're supposed to be a guest at this party!" Sheila objected.

"It's no big deal, Sheila," Gerald said cheerfully.

"I'll help you if you want, Uncle Gerald," Ricky offered, shoving his hands in the pockets of his jeans.

"Oh, that would be a lifesaver!" Sheila cried. "If you wouldn't mind — "

"No problem," Ricky said with a shrug.

"It doesn't seem fair," Michael said. "You arrive in Stanfield and we put you to work!"

Gerald grinned. "What else you gonna do, bro? It's not like you've got a lot of options!" He looked over at his nephew, concern written on his face, but it quickly passed. "So you'll be careful, Ricky?"

"Yeah, sure," Ricky said. "I'm cool, Uncle Gerald."

"Hey, what can I do to help?" Lexi asked, bounding over to them. She looked darling in jeans and an embroidered denim shirt.

It was pretty clear Ricky thought so, too. He stared at her with huge, love-struck eyes.

"You could show Ricky around the kitchen," Michael suggested. He quickly introduced Lexi to Ricky, and explained how it was that Gerald and Ricky were going to be serving for the party.

"Welcome to Stanfield," Lexi said, shaking hands with Ricky.

"Thanks," Ricky said, still staring wide-eyed at Lexi. "I have a feeling this is going to be a great trip."

"I can introduce Ricky to everyone," Lexi said easily. If she was aware of Ricky's interest in her, it didn't show.

"First, could you go show Ricky around the

kitchen?" Michael reminded his daughter.

"Sure," Lexi replied. "Come on, we can sneak some of the best food while they're out here yakking," Lexi told Ricky.

Lexi and Ricky headed into the restaurant. When he reached the step that led to the porch he stumbled, righted himself, and went inside.

"Listen, I need to talk to you guys," Gerald said when Ricky and Lexi were out of sight. "Ricky is a great kid, but he's . . . how can I put this . . . he's kind of accident-prone."

"Oh, that kind of thing can be a self-fulfilling prophecy," Michael said. "He seems fine to me."

"No, no, I'm serious," Gerald said. "This is one of the few times I've seen the kid where he didn't have a limb in a cast."

"Seriously?" Sheila asked, sounding doubtful.

"Seriously," Gerald said. "It's weird, because the kid is a terrific athlete. He's fine when he's playing baseball or something, but he could kill himself and everyone around him just walking around the block. His coaches are just pulling their hair out."

"Come on, you're exaggerating," Michael said.

"I wish I were," Gerald said seriously. "I don't know if your guests are safe."

Sheila glanced at her watch. "Oh, God, speaking of guests, I haven't even showered yet. I've got to run. I'm sure Ricky will be a big help!" She ran toward the inn.

Gerald looked at Michael and shook his head. "Famous last words, man. Famous last words."

Chapter 12

"Rollin' in my sweet baby's arms.
Rollin' in my sweet baby's arms.
'Gonna lay around this track
Till the mail train comes back.
I'm rollin' in my sweet baby's arms!"

The Beavers, a country-and-bluegrass band consisting of Joanne Beaver on fiddle, Ray Beaver on lead guitar, Ray's sister Betty Beaver on ukulele, and their grandmother Miranda Beaver on drums, were playing a hot old country tune on the front porch of the Beansprout.

The engagement party was in full swing. Friends of the Mundys, dressed mostly in faded jeans and T-shirts with slogans like Save the Whales, were dancing to the raucous music. Friends of the Stanfields, dressed mostly in new jeans and button-down-collar shirts with designer labels under sports jackets, were tapping their feet on the sidelines and trying hard to look comfortable. The high school and college-age guests were all having a blast, no matter whether they were Austin's friends, Fawn's friends, or both. The fact that nobody was paying much attention to who was drawing beers from the huge keg on the lawn might have contributed to that.

Gerald had done a great job serving the food inside the restaurant, and Ricky had tripped only twice. Once he was carrying a tray of stuffed mushrooms, which ended up in the lap of Dr. Bertolucci, a visiting scholar from Naples, but other than that no disasters had occurred.

Ricky brought a tray of whipped cream–covered fruit tarts out of the restaurant and began to pass them around to the guests. His eyes, however, were glued on Lexi, who was dancing with Greg.

"So, what's the deal with Paris?" Greg asked Lexi, as he spun her around in a circle.

"I don't know why she isn't here," Lexi said. Greg swung her under his arm. "Hey, where did you learn to dance like this?"

"What, you think I'm too much of a snob to know how to do a Texas two-step?" Greg asked, executing another fancy step.

"Basically, yeah," Lexi answered with a laugh.

"Well, I had a girlfriend from Texas last year, okay?" Greg said. "The only way I could get next to the girl was to learn this stupid dance!"

The music came to a rollicking finish, and everyone applauded. Juliet came running over to Lexi. "Lex, I'm worried. I just tried Paris's house again and there's still no answer."

"I just don't get it," Lexi said. "I talked to her last night and she said she'd be here."

"Do you think I should call Stanfield General?" Juliet asked, referring to the hospital in town. "Maybe she was in a car accident."

"How about if I take a ride over to her place?" Greg suggested. "I could check things out."

"Greg, if she's not answering the phone that would lead me to believe she isn't home," Juliet said logically.

"Unless she's sick or something," Greg pointed out.

"But her dad would be there — " Juliet began.

"No, he wouldn't," Lexi said. "She told me last night he was the guest speaker tonight at something at their synagogue."

"Maybe I should go," Juliet offered.

"No, your mom would kill you if you left," Lexi said. "You go, Greg. And if she's not there, go by the hospital, okay?"

"Yeah," Greg said. "I'm on my way." He took off for his car.

From overhead there was a loud rumble of thunder. Lexi and Juliet both looked up. Huge clouds had blown in so quickly neither had even noticed.

"I have a feeling it's about to rain on Fawn's parade," Lexi said.

"Fruit tart?" Ricky asked, holding the tray of desserts out to Lexi.

"Oh, no thanks, Ricky," Lexi said. "How're you doing?"

"Fine," Ricky said. He stared at her dreamily, then caught himself. "Uh, nice party, huh?"

"I think it worked out fine," Lexi agreed. "Oh, this is my friend Juliet Stanfield — her brother is marrying my sister. Juliet, this is Ricky Littlefeather. He's in Stanfield for the summer visiting his uncle."

"You'll have to come over swimming sometime," Juliet said. "We have a pool in the backyard."

"Great," Ricky replied, but he couldn't tear his eyes away from Lexi.

"Excuse me, but the whipped cream on your tarts is melting," Juliet pointed out.

"Oh, wow," Ricky said. "Better go offer 'em around. Well, see ya." He stumbled off.

"He's very cute," Juliet told Lexi. "And I think he has a crush on you."

"He does not," Lexi said.

"Oh, no?" Juliet asked. "Then why is it that he can't take his eyes off of you?"

"You're imagining things," Lexi said.

"As I keep telling you, I know about love," Juliet decreed. "He's cute, he's available, and he's crazy about you. I say, go for it."

"I'm not interested," Lexi said firmly, watching Austin and Fawn across the lawn. He had his arm around Fawn's waist, and they were talking with some friends of Austin's parents.

And of course Fawn the Perfect looks absolutely gorgeous, Lexi thought. Her sister had on white jeans and a pink silk shirt unbuttoned over a white bodysuit. Her long, thick, wavy hair looked perfect, and the small diamond studs Austin had given her as an engagement present danced in her ears.

Juliet took in Lexi's wistful expression. "Lex, you've got to get over him."

Lexi forced herself to turn away from Austin. "I *am* over him!"

"Liar," Juliet said bluntly.

Another loud clap of thunder shook the sky,

followed by a streak of lightning.

"I see a definite problem here," Lexi said. "Too many people got invited to this party to fit inside the restaurant. There must be a hundred people!"

"You know my mother has a hard time limiting her guest list," Juliet said, staring up at the angry-looking sky.

The Beavers, who were on the porch underneath an awning, began to play another up-tempo tune. Sheila looked up at the sky and then hurried over to the band to stop them. "Excuse me, everyone!" she called into the microphone. "It looks like the weather is not going to cooperate here. Let's move the party inside!"

Slowly everyone began to move toward the front door of the restaurant. Ricky hurried to the door and held it open, the tray of whipped cream–covered tarts still in his hands. Juliet went to help Sheila and Michael take down the tiny lights that were illuminating the front yard. Guests streamed inside.

At that moment the sky broke loose and sheets of rain fell down. Even the Beavers ran into the packed restaurant, along with the rest of the guests. Lexi and Austin were the last ones in except for Ricky, who was still holding the door, watching Lexi.

"Hey, Lex, I didn't even get a dance with you yet!" Austin said, coming over to Lexi just as she reached the porch. He put his arm around her waist.

"Oh, well, it's your engagement party," Lexi said, striving for a light tone. "You're pretty busy."

"It's a great party, don't you think?" he asked her.

"Great," she agreed.

"And you look really cute," he added.

"Look, you don't have to be so nice to me, okay?" Lexi said in a low voice so no one but Austin would hear.

"Why wouldn't I be nice to you?" Austin asked.

"Forget it," Lexi said.

Austin stared at her a moment as people streamed by them. Ricky watched her, too, from a few feet away. "I wish things could be the way they used to be with us," Austin finally said.

"I don't even know what that means," Lexi replied.

"Friends," Austin said. "Really great friends."

"Sure," Lexi said tersely. "We're friends. So let's just drop it." She turned around and walked toward Ricky, who was still holding the door open.

"Lexi, I — " Austin began.

She turned back to him. "What?" She grabbed some paper plates with food that had been left on the porch, just to give herself something to do so she wouldn't have just to stare at him.

"Here, let me help you," Ricky said eagerly. He reached for the dirty plates with one hand while balancing the tray of tarts with the other. The tray slipped, and he steadied it, but he began to drop the plates, and then he kind of tripped forward. Food spilled all over Lexi's shirt, and the whipped cream–covered fruit tarts landed in her face.

And Austin witnessed the whole humiliating moment.

"I feel like a total idiot," Lexi said, as she buttoned a white cotton shirt and tucked it into a clean pair of jeans.

"Well, you shouldn't," Juliet said. "It's not like it was your fault."

It was a half hour later, and Lexi had just finished showering and washing her hair. She had been gunky with sticky food, fruit, and whipped cream. The only saving grace about the whole embarrassing thing was that she had been able to get to her room by going around the inn, thereby avoiding all the guests at the party.

Of course, being seen by Austin had been bad enough.

"I could just kill Ricky," Lexi said, grabbing her hair dryer and turning it on.

"He didn't do it on purpose," Juliet said.

"Stop being so reasonable about everything," Lexi said over the sound of her dryer.

"Okay," Juliet said. "I'll just bitch about the fact that Ty *still* hasn't shown up at this party, how's that?"

"Good," Lexi said, letting the hot air feather her hair. "I don't want to be the only one in a terrible mood. I can't believe this party. Pouring rain, no Paris, no Ty, and I get decked with whipped cream in front of Austin."

The phone by Lexi's bed rang, and she quickly turned off her hair dryer and snatched it up. "Hello?"

"Hi, it's Greg."

"It's about time you called," Lexi said, sitting on the bed. "Did you find Paris?"

"Yeah," Greg said. "She's home. I'm calling from her house."

"She's *home?*" Lexi echoed incredulously.

"Yeah, she's . . . not really feeling good, or something," Greg said. His voice sounded very odd. "I've been here for a half hour already, but Paris didn't want me to call. She keeps saying she'll feel better in a minute."

"What's wrong with her?" Lexi asked.

Juliet snatched the phone from Lexi. "Greg, is Paris sick?"

"Kind of," he hedged.

"Put her on the phone, please," Juliet said.

"Just a sec." Juliet could hear Greg talking to Paris, but couldn't make out what he was saying. "Juliet?"

"Yes?"

"She says she'll be at the party in a few minutes," Greg reported. "She says she's fine."

"That's crazy!" Juliet cried.

Lexi grabbed the phone back. "Greg, what's wrong with her? Put her on the phone!"

"What am I, a babysitting service?" Greg snapped. "I can't make her do what she doesn't want to do! Uh-oh . . ."

"What?" Lexi cried. "What happened?"

"I think I'd better run her over to Stanfield General," Greg said reluctantly.

"What happened?" Juliet screamed into the phone.

"She just passed out," Greg reported. "How did I get myself into this?"

"Into what? Call an ambulance or something!" Lexi yelled at him.

"Lexi, chill," Greg barked. "I'll take care of her, believe me, I know what to do. She's breathing fine. I know a drug overdose when I see one."

Chapter 13

"Mom, Juliet and I have to go over to Stanfield General," Lexi said in a rush as she ran into the Beansprout, Juliet right behind her. "Greg is taking Paris over there because — "

Lexi stopped speaking and looked around the restaurant. Dozens of people were sitting in chairs, silent and white-faced, some doubled over. Betty Beaver was barfing into a paper sack. Fawn was crying, helping people out into the rain, her mascara streaking down her cheeks.

"Did someone just die?" Lexi asked, horrified.

"I think we just found out where Felicity got her food poisoning," Sheila said wearily.

"*Here?*" Juliet asked, clapping her hand over her mouth.

"Here," Sheila confirmed. "Your parents already left for the hospital, Juliet. More than half the guests are sick as dogs."

"This is a disaster," Michael said, his voice dazed. "And it happened so fast. Just a couple of hours. Our kitchen is so clean. I just don't understand what could have happened . . ."

"Where's Austin?" Juliet asked.

"He went to the hospital with your parents," Sheila explained. "Can you guys help us get the rest of the people into their cars?"

Lexi and Juliet quickly assisted the rest of the sick guests to their cars. Fawn helped, too, crying the whole time, her beautiful hair plastered to her head by the rain, her eyes red.

She doesn't look so perfect now, Lexi thought, and then immediately felt guilty at having such an ugly thought.

"This is the worst day of my life," Fawn sobbed to her mother.

"It'll be okay, honey," Sheila said, putting her arms around her daughter. "Everyone knows it isn't your fault."

"Oh, sure," Fawn sobbed. "Just because half of Stanfield and my future in-laws were poisoned at my parents' restaurant, I'm *sure* no one will blame me!"

"Fawn, there's no time for that now," Michael said gently. "Why don't you head over to the hospital? I have to stay and wait for the county health inspector."

"Why aren't we sick?" Lexi asked. "It's bizarre."

"We were too busy and nervous to eat anything," Sheila explained.

"I guess that's right," Lexi realized. "I didn't eat, either."

"You guys want to go in my truck?" Gerald asked them.

"That would be great," Juliet said. "I came with my parents in their Mercedes — "

"And they just left in it," Gerald finished for her. "Come on, let's go face the music."

"Lexi? Juliet?"

"Paris! Oh my gosh, are you okay?" Juliet cried, as she and Lexi went running over to their friend, who was waiting in a small room off the emergency room lobby.

When they arrived, the emergency room was already full of guests from the party. Nurses hovered over them, taking vital statistics. A harried nurse at the front desk directed Juliet and Lexi to the room where Paris was resting.

"Yeah, I'm fine," Paris said, sitting up on the examining table. Her face was white and her hair was wet with sweat. "I'll never live this down, though."

"What happened?" Lexi asked.

"And where's Greg?" Juliet added.

"He went to get some coffee," Paris said. She buried her head in her hands. "God, I never, ever thought that something like this would happen to me. I can't believe it!"

"Me, either," Juliet agreed. "You were doing *drugs??*"

"No — yes," Paris stammered. "I mean . . . it's so stupid — "

"What?" Lexi asked, sitting in the plastic, orange-colored chair by the bed.

"You guys know I went to a spa to lose weight. Well — my roommate there gave me these diet pills," Paris admitted. "She told me her doctor was this big weight-loss guru and they were safe. So . . . I've been taking them. And not eating . . ."

"You do look thin," Juliet noticed.

"Don't tell her that like it's a good thing!" Lexi cried sharply. "So then what happened?"

"Well, I was sure the pills weren't speed, because you snort crystal meth, right? Yeah, right. The doctor here told me it was Dexedrine, which is just another form of speed." Paris sighed and rubbed her eyes. "I was nervous about eating at the party, so I took two extra pills — please don't tell me how stupid that was, okay?"

Her friends just silently stared at her.

"And . . . I haven't really eaten anything for days and days," Paris continued in a low voice. "I got unbelievably wired — it was scary. So . . . I took a couple of these Valiums my dad had in the medicine chest — "

"Are you crazy??" Juliet cried.

"Shhhh," Lexi remonstrated her.

"Look, I told you it was stupid, okay?" Paris said defensively. "I've never taken even one Valium before. I felt so weird and sick. I kept thinking I could get it together, but finally I just passed out."

"It's a good thing Greg came to look for you," Juliet said.

"Oh, right," Paris said sarcastically. "I really wanted him to see me looking like stoned roadkill."

"Paris, why . . . why did you do all that?" Juliet asked.

Paris sighed. "To lose weight, obviously. You don't need to tell me how dumb it was, either. And yes, I already threw out the rest of the little pink pills."

"Miss Goldman? How are you feeling?" a nurse asked from the doorway.

"Much better, thanks," Paris replied.

The nurse bustled in and took Paris's pulse, then she slapped a blood pressure cuff on her and took her blood pressure. "Your vitals are looking good," the nurse said. "The doctor said you can be released. And frankly, we're desperate for this room."

"Why, was there a car wreck or something?" Paris asked, searching for her purse.

"No, a whole bunch of guests at some party got food poisoning," the nurse reported, checking something off on her clipboard. "Okay, your brother, Greg, had signed for you, since you're under eighteen — "

"My bro — " Paris began.

"Yeah, sure, *Sis*," Greg said, striding into the room. "You know Dad put me in charge while he's away."

"Oh, right," Paris agreed.

"I'll just be taking my little sister home now," Greg said, taking Paris by the elbow.

"I can walk, thank you," Paris said, snatching her elbow back from Greg.

"I'm sure you can, *Sis*," Greg said cheerfully, since the nurse was still in the room. "Okay, thanks for everything."

"Why did you do that?" Paris hissed at Greg in the hallway.

"Because if I weren't your brother, and if your dad wasn't out of town, they would have called your father and told him everything," Greg explained. "I just saved your butt big-time, so a thank-you would be nice."

"Thanks," Paris said, and she meant it. "I don't know why you did this for me — "

"Me, either," Greg said. "And you owe me one."

Paris nodded in agreement. *I can't imagine having to tell my father about this,* she thought with a shudder. *He'd be so disappointed in me. And I can't believe I was stupid enough to —*

"What are *they* doing here?" Paris asked, interrupting her own thoughts. They had just entered the lobby, and sitting there were Sheila, Fawn, Austin, Gerald, and Ricky, looking shell-shocked. Fawn was sobbing, and Austin was white-faced with anger. The food-poisoning victims were all in examining rooms.

"Wow, Paris, looks like your little stunt really broke up that party," Greg commented.

"I am totally humiliated," Paris said, when she saw all of them. "You guys really didn't have to come over here for me — "

"They didn't," Juliet said. "You know that party the nurse mentioned, where all those unlucky people got food poisoning?"

"Whoa," Greg remarked, "I'm so glad I stuck to the beer."

Juliet hurried over to Austin. "Where are Mom and Dad?"

"Room three," Austin said. "Some intern is with them. Dr. Hutchison is out of town at some conference, but one of the partners said he'd be right over. Man, I can't believe this . . ."

Fawn reached out and touched Austin's arm, trying to choke back her tears. "Austin, I'm so sorry . . ."

"Why should you be sorry?" Austin asked in a cold voice. "Just because your parents happened to poison my parents?"

Fawn sobbed louder. "But it was an accident! It wasn't my parents' fault!"

"Hey, it's their kitchen, you tell me who's responsible!" Austin yelled.

"Come on, Austin, that's not fair — " Sheila began.

"I'm sorry, but I'm not much interested in 'fair' right now," Austin said. "My father has a heart condition, did you know that?"

"No," Sheila said quietly.

"Well, how do you think this is going to affect his heart?" Austin yelled.

"Austin, be fair," Juliet said, sitting down next to her brother. "This was just a terrible accident."

"Yeah?" Austin asked. "I wouldn't put it past them to do this just to break up the wedding plans."

"That's a terrible thing to say!" Fawn cried, jumping up from her seat and standing over Austin. "How could you say that?"

"What, you're gonna tell me your parents are happy that we're getting married?" Austin asked, jumping out of his seat to stare coldly into Fawn's eyes.

"They *are* happy for me!" Fawn insisted.

"Didn't they tell you we're too young?" Austin demanded. "Didn't they?"

"What does that have to do with anything?"

"I want to know the truth!" Austin said. "Is that asking too much?"

"My parents do not dictate to me," Fawn said, "unlike your parents — "

"My parents have been nothing but wonderful to you!" Austin insisted. "My mother is devoting every minute of her time to the wedding!"

Fawn's eyes seethed with fury. "Which is more than I can say for you!"

"You guys, please — " Lexi began, but they both ignored her.

"Just what is that supposed to mean?" Austin asked Fawn.

"That the stupid play you're in is more important to you than our wedding!" Fawn exclaimed.

" 'That stupid play' happens to be very important to me — "

"Obviously! More important than me!" Fawn cried. "How do you think I feel, planning our wedding with your mother instead of planning it with you?"

"You have all these ideas about how you want it to be, Fawn, so I — "

"Don't care!" Fawn finished for him. "That's it, isn't it?"

"Do we have to talk about this now? I mean, I'm just a little busy dealing with the fact that my parents — "

"Austin Stanfield, you just stop blaming my parents!" Fawn bellowed. "If you want to get out of the wedding, just say so! You don't need to use my parents as an excuse — "

"Look, you guys, this is silly — " Lexi began. "I'm sure we can — "

"Stay out of this!" Austin and Fawn both yelled at the same time.

"It's not me who wants to get out of this," Austin said, turning back to Fawn. "You give my mother a hard time when all she's trying to do is plan us a great wedding! You refuse to use her seamstress when she had to beg her to get her to — "

"I'm the bride!" Fawn yelled. "I'm allowed to pick out my own wedding gown! Maybe your mother is just so interfering and overbearing that she won't let me breathe!"

"Well, if that's how you feel, why the hell would you want to marry her son?" Austin thundered.

"That's a very good question!" Fawn replied.

"Oh, really?" Austin asked. "Then maybe we should be asking ourselves a few more questions, like why the hell we're doing this in the first place?"

"Fine with me!" Fawn cried.

"Fine with me!" Austin echoed.

"Good, then we agree," Fawn said. "The wedding is off! Have a nice life!" Then she turned and ran crying from the waiting room while everyone just sat there in stunned disbelief.

Chapter 14

Lexi parked the family Jeep in the circular driveway in front of the Stanfield mansion, and quickly sprinted to the front door. She knocked lightly and glanced at her watch. It was midnight, but Juliet and Paris were expecting her.

What an unbelievable night, she thought wearily. *Thank God no one died from the food poisoning. The only thing that died is Fawn and Austin's marriage plans. And I still can't believe it.*

She remembered an old saying she had heard long ago: beware of what you ask for — you might get it. *Well, I asked for Fawn and Austin to break up, and I got my wish,* she realized. *So why don't I feel wonderful and happy?*

After Fawn and Austin's fight, Lexi had left the hospital with her family. Fawn had cried hysterically all the way home. Sheila had tried to comfort her daughter, but Fawn just ran to her bedroom and slammed the door shut.

"I'll go try and talk to her," Sheila had said. "I'm sure neither of them meant the things they said. They'll kiss and make up by tomorrow morning." She went to tap on Fawn's door.

That's probably true, Lexi thought, as she'd wandered over to the Beansprout. *I mean, it's not like they had already been fighting or anything. Austin would never really hold the food poisoning against Fawn — it was such a stupid fight!*

When Lexi reached the front of the restaurant she had seen an awful sign: CLOSED BY ORDER OF THE BOARD OF HEALTH. She went back to the inn and found her father trying in vain to talk guests out of checking out. They were all very upset over what had happened at the restaurant and they planned to leave immediately, even though it was after eleven o'clock at night.

But nothing Michael told them seemed to help — four rooms that had been filled earlier were now empty.

"Man, this sucks," Michael told his daughter wearily, as he finished the paperwork on the retreating guests.

"It's not your fault, Dad," Lexi assured him.

"Did the health inspector figure out what food went bad?"

"Not yet," Michael said. "They're testing half of our kitchen right now. Where's your mother?"

"With Fawn," Lexi said. "I hate to add to your bad news, but here's some more. Fawn and Austin called off the wedding."

Her father stared at her. "You're kidding."

"I'm serious."

"Man, I never should have gotten up this morning," Michael said, bending back over his paperwork.

"Shouldn't we do something?" Lexi asked, watching her father work.

"What did you have in mind?" he asked wearily.

"I just mean that their fight was so stupid," Lexi said, leaning against the front desk. "Austin blamed Fawn for the food poisoning — but I know he didn't mean it. And then Fawn got all upset and said he was just looking for an excuse to call off the wedding . . ."

Michael put his pen down and rubbed his chin. "You're probably right — that they weren't really arguing about the food poisoning thing, I mean."

Lexi nodded.

"A lot of times people pick some stupid

thing to argue about, something really petty, you know? But that's not what they're really fighting about. It's something else completely, something bigger."

"Like what?" Lexi asked.

Michael shrugged. "I don't know, honey. I guess that's what Fawn and Austin have to figure out."

Lexi kissed her dad and left him to his paperwork. *What a great guy he is,* she thought as she walked back to their apartment. *And he's probably right — Austin and Fawn were really fighting about something else entirely.*

And I wonder if the something else is me.

Lexi went to her room, so tired that she just sagged onto her bed. Just as she closed her eyes, the phone rang, startling her.

"Hello?"

"Lex, it's Juli."

"Hi," Lexi said wearily. "Can you believe all of this?"

"It's terrible," Juliet said. "I suppose you're happy . . ."

"I'm not!" Lexi protested.

"But you wanted them to break up," Juliet accused her.

"Not like this!" Lexi cried.

"Okay, that was low of me," Juliet said. "Forgive me?"

"It's okay," Lexi assured her. "We're all just exhausted and stressed-out. Besides, they probably didn't really break up. They just had a fight."

"It sure sounded like they broke up," Juliet said.

"But you don't really believe they broke up because your parents happened to get food poisoning, do you?" Lexi asked.

"No," Juliet allowed. "That was stupid. But that fight sounded pretty final to me, anyway."

Lexi was silent for a moment. "So, how's Austin?"

"I have no idea," Juliet said. "He stopped home and made sure Mom and Dad were okay, then he left with Greg. Ty never even made it over to my house at all — I heard Austin on the phone telling Ty he'd meet him back at the frat house. Listen, do you think you could come over?"

"Oh, Juli, I am so beat — "

"Come on," Juliet said. "We're all in this together. Spend the night with me and Paris, please?"

"How's she feeling?"

"Tired but okay," Juliet reported. "We really need you here. My parents took some medicine they got at the hospital and they're passed out, so we won't have to deal with them. And Paris and I are both incredibly depressed. We can't sleep."

"Really?" Lexi asked. "I feel like I could sleep for days and days."

"So sleep later," Juliet said. "We really need to talk to you. Please?"

"Okay, I'll try," Lexi said. "I better make sure Fawn is okay first, though."

"Okay, see you soon," Juliet said, and hung up.

Lexi stretched, rubbed her eyes and got up from her bed. Then she slipped on some clogs and went down to Fawn's room. She knocked on the door.

"Go away," came Fawn's muffled voice.

"It's Lexi," she said, and gently opened the door a crack.

"I didn't say, 'who is it,' " Fawn mumbled, "I said, 'go away.' "

"And I ignored you." Lexi walked in and sat on the edge of Fawn's bed. Fawn was curled up in a ball, squeezing her pillow tightly. "Where's Mom?"

Fawn shrugged. "She was here and then she left."

"Do you want to talk about what happened?"

"No. I want to die."

"You don't mean that — "

"I keep thinking it's just some terrible nightmare and I'll wake up," Fawn said, dabbing a soggy Kleenex to her red-rimmed eyes. "But it isn't a dream. Austin doesn't love me. He called off the engagement. It's all true . . ."

"But Fawn, he didn't call it off any more than you did. I mean, you guys had a fight and said things that neither of you meant . . ."

"Oh, he meant it, all right. He was just looking for an excuse to say those things," Fawn said. "I tried so hard to be perfect so I'd fit in with him and his family — "

"You didn't have to do that — "

"Oh, didn't I?" Fawn asked. "Don't you think people find it odd that a Stanfield would marry a Mundy?"

"That's so ridiculous!" Lexi cried. "Austin loves you for who you are! He doesn't care about things like that!"

"His parents do."

"Maybe," Lexi said. "I really don't know. But you're not marrying his parents. And frankly it's pretty demeaning to our family to have you think that we're somehow . . . somehow less than the Stanfields just because we aren't rich!"

"You just don't understand," Fawn said, as tears cascaded down her cheeks again. She looked over at the phone on the nightstand. "He hasn't called. If he really loved me, he would have called by now. He was just looking for an excuse to end it. It's really over!"

Fawn began to sob in earnest and Lexi didn't know what to do, beyond pat her sister's shoulder and hand her more Kleenex. Finally Fawn said she just wanted to sleep, and she closed her eyes. At that point Lexi tiptoed out of the room.

And now she was at Juliet's front door. Austin's front door. She was glad that she wouldn't have to see him.

Only it was Austin who opened the front door.

"Hi," he said, his voice flat.

"I . . . I thought you went to the frat house," Lexi said. "I mean, that's what Juliet told me on the phone."

"I did. I came back," Austin said, stepping back to let her in. "I wanted to make sure Mom and Dad are okay."

"Oh," Lexi said. She stood in the massive front hall, hitching the strap on her shoulder bag further up on her arm. She was at a total loss for words. "So . . . where's Juliet and Paris?" Lexi asked.

"They went out to get something to eat." Austin laughed, a short, bitter sound. "That's pretty funny, isn't it? After what happened?"

"Yeah, I guess," Lexi said.

"They left a note for you — they're bringing something back for you."

"I'm not hungry."

"Funny, neither am I," Austin said.

"Well, I guess I'll just go upstairs to Juliet's room and wait for them — "

"Why don't you come on into the study with me," Austin suggested.

"You probably want to be alone," Lexi guessed.

"Frankly, Lex, I don't know what the hell I want anymore."

He walked slowly into the study, Lexi trailing behind. "Look, Austin, this is crazy. You're miserable, Fawn is miserable — "

"Well, misery loves company, right?" Austin said bitterly. He sat down on the leather couch.

"But both of you are feeling miserable alone!" Lexi pointed out. She sat down next to him and stared at him earnestly. "I think you both just felt stressed-out and . . . and had a fight and said things you don't mean — "

"It's bigger than that, Lex," Austin said.

"But it doesn't have to be!"

"Maybe it's for the best," Austin said with a weary shrug of his shoulders. "Fawn had everything all planned out for us, you know?

This perfect life, the perfect wealthy young couple doing charity work and getting our picture into the society column. But that's not what I want!"

"So tell her!"

"I can't, don't you get it?" Austin cried. "She doesn't want to know! She wouldn't even hear me!"

"But you never even tried — "

"Because I know just how it would turn out," Austin said bitterly. "I'm saving us both a lot of heartache, don't you see?" Austin got up abruptly and strode over to the window. He stared out at the night sky.

The room was so silent, Lexi could hear the antique grandfather clock ticking in the corner.

"I never really could talk to Fawn," Austin said, still facing away from Lexi. "It was always you, Lex. I could always talk to you."

Lexi felt as if she could hardly breathe. Her heart was pounding so hard in her chest she felt as if it might just burst out, with a life of its own, beyond her control, beyond reason . . .

But I do have reason, Lexi told herself. *I have to have reason.*

She took a deep breath. "Austin, I don't think — "

"You don't have to think," he said, striding

over to her. He sat down, his eyes searching hers. "You don't have to think because you know it's true."

"I . . . I . . ." Lexi stammered.

It was happening, just like she had dreamt it so many times. He was right there next to her, wanting her instead of Fawn. It was her dream come true at last.

But not like this, Lexi thought desperately. *Not like this!*

She tried to make herself pull away from him, to say that this wasn't right, that he really did love Fawn, that he was just upset and confused.

But she couldn't do it, even though she knew she should. No matter how much she tried, she couldn't pull away.

Instead, she raised her face to his and at long last felt herself pulled into Austin's arms.

Chapter 15

At the sound of voices in the front hall, Lexi and Austin quickly pulled apart. Austin jumped up, his eyes wide, like a deer caught in someone's headlights.

"Oh, God!" Lexi exclaimed, guilt and remorse suffusing through her. Instinctively she rubbed the back of her hand over her mouth as if she could erase the passionate kiss she and Austin had just shared.

"Hi," Paris said, walking into the study, Juliet right behind her. "Did you see our note?" She handed Lexi a paper bag containing a veggie burger and fries.

"Austin told me about it," Lexi said, setting the bag of food on the coffee table. She had never felt less like eating in her life.

"I thought you were staying at the frat house with Ty and Greg," Juliet told her brother.

"I changed my mind," Austin said. His voice sounded funny, sharp.

Guilty.

Juliet looked from Austin to Lexi, then back to Austin. *Something isn't right,* she thought. "How are Mom and Dad?"

"I looked in on them, they're sleeping."

Juliet cocked her head at Lexi, who looked away.

Very weird, Juliet thought. *Very, very weird.*

"So, Paris, how are you feeling?" Lexi asked, her voice a little too loud.

"I must have the constitution of an elephant, because I feel fine now," Paris said, flopping down in a leather chair. "The only thing that hurts is my ego."

"So . . . I'm going up to bed," Austin said nervously.

"You don't have to leave on our account," Juliet said. "What were you guys talking about, anyway?"

"Oh, you know . . ." Lexi said vaguely.

"Good night," Austin said, and he strode out of the room. He didn't look at Lexi at all.

Juliet watched him leave. "Okay, something very weird is going on here."

"What do you mean?" Lexi asked. She could feel her face turning red.

"I mean the vibe in this room was so weird when we came in — and don't tell me I'm imagining things, either."

"It's probably just exhaustion," Paris said, laying her head back on the chair. "Boy, this is one day I wouldn't repeat for any amount of money, I'll tell you that!"

"We should all just go to sleep," Lexi suggested, getting up from the couch.

Juliet walked over to her and looked into her eyes. "Lexi, this is us, your best friends. What's going on?"

Lexi couldn't help it — tears came to her eyes. She buried her head in her hands. "Oh, God, I hate myself!"

"What happened?" Paris asked.

"Whatever it is, it can't be that bad," Juliet added.

"Yes, it can!" Lexi cried, falling back on to the couch. "Everyone is going to hate me, and I deserve it! I hate myself!"

"Yeah, we hate you, too. You suck," Paris said cheerfully. "So now can we all just go to bed and talk about this tomorrow?"

"Paris, can't you see how upset she is?" Juliet chided.

"Yeah, okay, bad time for a joke," Paris allowed. "What's up? And whatever it is, we still love you, by the by."

Lexi took a deep breath. "I . . . I kissed Austin," she blurted out.

"You *what?*" Juliet asked.

"Or he kissed me, or we kissed each other or something," Lexi babbled. "It just happened! We didn't plan it!"

"How did it just happen?" Juliet asked, wide-eyed.

"I don't know!" Lexi exclaimed. "I was trying to talk him into making up with Fawn, but he . . . he told me it was really over with her, that I was the one he could really talk to, and then . . . it just happened!"

"Whoa, baby," Paris marveled. "This means you were right about him all along!"

"But I must be the worst sister in the universe!" Lexi cried. "How could I do that?"

Everyone was quiet for a moment, digesting what had happened.

"So, did you kiss a lot?" Juliet finally asked.

"Once," Lexi replied. "One long, incredible, sizzling kiss."

"Get down, Lexi!" Paris yelled.

"You don't seem to appreciate how serious this is!" Juliet said sharply. She turned to Lexi. "So what did he say after the kiss?"

"Nothing," Lexi admitted. "You guys showed up. And then, well, you saw, he went to bed."

"So you don't know what it means," Juliet mused. "Or how he feels."

"He told me how he feels," Lexi said, her eyes shining.

"What did he say, exactly?" Juliet demanded.

"That he could talk to me — "

"That's not exactly a declaration of love," Paris pointed out.

"He said I had always been the one," Lexi said in a hushed voice.

"Really?" Juliet asked, awed.

"Really."

"You and Austin . . ." Juliet began. "But it just doesn't seem right!"

"How can I ever tell Fawn?" Lexi asked.

"And how about your parents?" Paris asked. "They're going to have a fit. Austin is twenty and you're sixteen."

"That doesn't matter!" Lexi insisted.

"I'm not saying it does, and I'm not saying it doesn't," Paris said. "I'm saying that parents think it does."

"Oh, God, my parents don't even know they've called off the wedding," Juliet realized.

"Let's run right up and tell them the wedding is off and Austin is in love with Lexi," Paris suggested slyly.

"Let's not," Juliet retorted.

"Well, the only good news I can think of is that all three of us are miserable together. I made a complete ass out of myself in front of Greg, and Ty didn't even care enough about Juliet to show up at the party at all," Paris said.

"Nothing compares to calling off the wedding and Austin and Lexi being together," Juliet said, shaking her head. She looked over at Lexi. "I know we've always kidded around and called your sister Fawn the Perfect, but no matter how much you resent her, you can't just start dating my brother!"

"I know," Lexi agreed. "I feel so confused. I have to talk this all over with Austin tomorrow . . ."

"What I don't get is how Austin could be engaged to Fawn one minute and sucking face with Fawn's sister the next," Paris said.

"Maybe he was overcome by the force of his true feelings," Juliet guessed.

"That only happens in those dippy romance novels you read, Juli," Paris said with disgust. "In the real world a guy who does that is just plain lame."

"And so is the sister of the girl he was engaged to," Lexi added.

No one bothered to contradict her.

* * *

By the time the girls got up the next morning — afternoon, really, since they slept till 12:30 — Austin was long gone. Lexi was disappointed that he hadn't waited to talk to her or even left her a note. She knew they had to talk. And soon.

Juliet padded down to her parents' room. Mr. and Mrs. Stanfield, who were both weak but basically okay — at least they had stopped cramping and vomiting — said Austin had looked in on them at nine o'clock, and then he'd left. No, Mrs. Stanfield said, Austin didn't say where he was going.

"Did he say anything else about yesterday?" Juliet asked her parents, standing in the doorway of their room.

"No;" Mr. Stanfield said. "I expect yesterday is a day we'd all like to forget."

You don't know the half of it, Juliet thought.

"We must call the Mundys," Mrs. Stanfield said. "They must feel just terrible about what happened!"

Juliet smiled at her mother. Maybe she was kind of overbearing when it came to planning weddings, and she could be something of a snob, but she really was a nice person.

"Have they figured out what made everyone so ill?" Mr. Stanfield asked.

"I don't know," Juliet said. "So, Austin really

didn't say anything to you about . . . anything?"

"Is something wrong?" Mrs. Stanfield asked.

"Well, he and Fawn kind of had a fight," Juliet admitted.

"I'm sorry to hear that," Mrs. Stanfield said. "I'm sure it was just nerves. I'll bet that's where Austin went — over to Fawn's."

"Maybe so," Juliet said. *I can't be the one to tell them what happened,* she thought. *It should come from Austin. And Grandmother Stanfield is going to be so disappointed . . .*

"Honey, do go look in on your grandmother," Mrs. Stanfield said, almost as if she had been reading Juliet's mind.

"I will, Mom," Juliet promised. "Can I get you anything?"

"You're a sweetheart," Mrs. Stanfield said with a smile. "I don't think so — " She looked over at her husband. He shook his head no. "We'll just rest some more and take the pills the doctor gave us, and I'm sure we'll be up and around in no time."

"I'm sure, too."

"After all, we've got a wedding to plan, right?" Mrs. Stanfield asked.

"Right!" Juliet agreed, trying to make her voice match her mother's brightness. She walked over to the bed and kissed her parents.

"I'm going out for a while, okay?"

"Fine," Mr. Stanfield said. "We'll be here resting up."

After looking in on her grandmother, Juliet went back to her room. The radio was on, and a love song by Boyz 2 Men blasted sweet harmonies into the room. Juliet turned it down. "I couldn't tell them."

"About me and Austin?" Lexi asked.

"About Fawn and Austin," Juliet said. "I said they had a fight, and they just blew that off. We've got to talk to Austin!"

"You mean *I've* got to talk to Austin," Lexi said. "I can't believe he left here without saying anything to me."

"Maybe he just didn't want to wake you," Juliet said.

"And maybe he was being a wimp," Paris added.

"Look, it's possible that he's with Fawn right now," Juliet said. "Maybe he wanted to talk to Fawn before he said anything to you, Lex."

"I bet you're right!" Lexi exclaimed. "That has to be it!"

"So how about if we go over to your house and see what's up?" Juliet suggested.

They showered quickly, dressed, and scrambled into Lexi's Jeep for the drive back to the Mundys'. The sign was still taped to the

Beansprout door: CLOSED BY ORDER OF THE BOARD OF HEALTH. Lexi parked in the small lot at the rear of the inn, and the three girls ran up to Fawn's room. Lexi knocked softly.

"I told you I don't want any lunch, Mom!" Fawn called.

"It's me and Juliet and Paris," Lexi called in to her sister. "Can we come in?"

"If you want to."

Lexi opened the door. Fawn was sitting on the bed in the same clothes she had been wearing when Lexi saw her the night before. Her eyes were even more red-rimmed than they had been. She looked worse than Lexi had ever seen her, even worse than when she'd had a terrible flu that kept her in bed for a week.

"Hi," Lexi said. She, Juliet, and Paris all tried to smile at Fawn.

"Life stinks," Fawn said.

The three girls traded looks. Had Austin talked to her and told her it was definitely all over?

It doesn't seem as if he's said anything about Lexi, though, Paris thought, *or she'd be throwing things at Lexi instead of inviting her in.*

"So, have you talked to my brother?" Juliet asked gently.

"Not since our big moment at the hospital,"

Fawn said. She stared at the phone in an accusatory manner. "You think he forgot my number?" Her voice dripped sarcasm.

"Maybe you should call him," Paris suggested.

"When hell freezes over," Fawn said. "Did you hear the things he said to me?"

"You said some nasty things, too," Juliet reminded her.

"I know," Fawn admitted in a low voice. "He just made me so mad . . ." Tears welled up in her eyes again. "How could he break up with me? How?"

No one said anything.

"The really awful thing is," Fawn continued, her voice choked with tears, "I still love him. I love him so much!"

Lexi felt like the worst person in the entire world. *Right now I just hate myself,* she thought miserably. *Fawn loves Austin. How could I do it? How? But what if he loves me and I love him? Am I supposed to just give up everything for Fawn?*

"You and Austin really have to talk," Juliet said earnestly.

"You can't let pride stand in the way of calling him!" Paris said. "What difference does it make who calls who?"

Of course, Paris thought, *if you called him now, he wouldn't be home.*

"The difference is that he doesn't want to call me," Fawn said. "Because if he wanted to, he would have."

"How do you know?" Paris asked. "I mean, you want to call him, but you haven't called!"

Fawn shredded another Kleenex in her hands. "I keep asking myself . . . could it be that there's someone else?" Her eyes searched the other girls, finally landing on Lexi, who looked away.

"I . . . I think you guys need to talk," Paris said nervously.

"Oh my God, *is* there someone else?" Fawn cried. "Am I the last one to know? Please, tell me the truth!"

Lexi gulped hard. *I can't live with lies,* she thought. *I have to say something, even if it means she never speaks to me again.*

But just as she opened her mouth to speak, the phone rang.

Fawn snatched it up. "Hello?"

"Fawn?" came the deep, male voice through the phone. "It's Austin. We have to talk."

Chapter 16

"I can't stand it," Lexi said, pacing back and forth across her room for perhaps the hundredth time.

It was two hours after Austin had called Fawn. Lexi, Paris, and Juliet had gone to Lexi's room so Fawn could speak to Austin privately. Ten minutes later, Fawn had come by, saying she was going out to meet Austin. She sounded so hopeful, and she had finally changed clothes and washed her face — Lexi couldn't bear to face her.

"I'll let you guys know what happens," Fawn promised.

"Good luck!" Juliet called after her.

They hadn't heard a thing. Not from Fawn and not from Austin.

"How long could it take for him to tell her it's really over?" Juliet asked.

"Where would she go with a broken heart?"

Paris asked practically. "Who's her best girl-friend?"

"She doesn't really have one anymore," Lexi explained. "Her best friend transferred to Michigan State, so she's not around anymore." She paced the floor again. "She's going to kill me, you realize that."

"Maybe Austin will keep his mouth shut," Paris guessed.

"And maybe he won't," Juliet said. Her face grew even more concerned. "You don't think . . . I mean, Fawn wouldn't do anything . . . drastic, would she?"

Lexi's face paled, and she sat heavily on her bed. *If Austin told her about me, would Fawn want to end it all? Is that possible? No, it couldn't be . . .*

"Look, this is kind of flipping me out," Paris said uneasily. "Maybe we should go try to find her."

"My sister is way too stable to do anything drastic," Lexi said firmly, praying she was right.

"Who knows who's stable?" Paris asked with a shrug.

"We could go to the frat house," Juliet suggested. "Even if they're not there, someone might know where they went."

Lexi looked at her watch. "Okay, here's my

suggestion. We should put a time limit on just sitting here. It's two o'clock. If we don't hear anything by two fifteen, we'll go to the frat house. Agreed?"

"Agreed," Juliet said.

"Not agreed. I don't want to face Greg," Paris said, shaking her head. "God, I can't believe I was that stupid!"

"Frankly, I can't, either," Lexi said, relieved for just a moment to talk about something else. She sat next to Paris on the bed. "You never even wanted to diet at all. What made you do something so dumb?"

"I plead temporary insanity," Paris said, throwing herself back on the bed.

"It's great that you want to get thin, though," Juliet said, eyeing Paris.

"Thin is highly overrated," Lexi insisted.

"Easy for you to say," Juliet commented. "You don't have a weight problem." She scanned Paris's figure in baggy jeans and a T-shirt. "I can tell that you've lost weight, even in those baggy clothes."

"I'm down to a size twelve," Paris said. "Well, in pants, anyway. On the top I'm probably still a fourteen."

"Did you do it for Greg?" Juliet asked, idly braiding a tiny braid into her hair.

"Gag me," Paris muttered.

"Well, did you?" Juliet pressed.

"Never, ever, ever try to make yourself over for a guy," Paris decreed.

"You didn't answer my question," Juliet said, beginning a second braid.

"I don't know," Paris admitted. She dug her feet into the small throw rug on Lexi's floor. "When we were all at Point Make Out, he . . . this is totally embarrassing, you guys — "

"What?" Juliet asked. "You never told us anything about what happened that night."

"Yeah, because I was completely humiliated," Paris explained. "The truth is, he didn't try anything. Nothing. I could have been his kid sister for all the interest he showed in me."

"So why did he want to go up there with you, then?" Lexi asked, confused.

"To pay Austin back, that's why," Paris said. "He was so ticked at Austin for getting engaged to Fawn that he wanted to get back at him."

"Oh, come on, that can't be true," Lexi began.

"It is," Paris insisted. "He as much as admitted it to me. And I couldn't help thinking — if I were some devastating babe, he would be treating me differently, no matter how angry he was with Austin."

"So you *were* losing weight for Greg," Juliet realized.

"I'm not even into him," Paris protested. Her two friends looked at her. "Okay, I'm a big, fat liar. I want him. Bad."

"He's not the nicest guy in the world," Lexi said.

"Since when has any of us ever been interested in the nicest guy in the world?" Paris asked.

"Good point," Lexi said.

"My mom fell in love with the nicest guy in the world, and look where it got her!" Paris added.

"But . . . she's the one who left," Juliet said.

"Yeah," Paris acknowledged. She lifted her heavy hair and wound it around, then put an elastic band around the bun. "All I'm saying is, the nicest guy in the world still didn't make her happy."

"Ty is nice," Juliet said wistfully. "He's so nice . . ."

"Yeah, but he was too busy to show up at the party," Paris pointed out. "And he hasn't even called you today. In fact, I bet he cares more about *Cat on a Hot Tin Roof* than he does about you."

"I don't know if that's true," Juliet protested.

"It's true," Paris said flatly. "And you know what? You want him even more because he's not all over you. It's human nature."

"But I don't think — " Juliet began.

At that moment, the phone rang by Lexi's bed. All three girls stared at one another, unable to move.

Brrrrinnnng! Brrrrinnnnnng!

I don't know if I want it to be Fawn or Austin or . . . or what I want, Lexi thought desperately, her heart hammering in her chest.

Brrrrrinnnnnng!

"Go on, answer it!" Juliet cried. "At least we'll know something!"

Lexi lifted the receiver. "Hello?"

"Lexi?"

It was a male voice she didn't recognize. Definitely not Austin.

"Yes?" she asked.

"This is Ricky Littlefeather," came the voice through the phone. "Remember, from the party?"

Lexi sat on the bed, the adrenaline that had been rushing through her body suddenly spent. "Yes, how are you?" she asked politely.

"I'm okay," Ricky said. "Listen, I really wanted to apologize for spilling that stuff on you at the party — man, did I feel like a jerk!"

"It's okay," Lexi said, "no harm done."

"Who is it?" Paris hissed, but Lexi didn't have time to answer.

"So, I'd really like to make it up to you," Ricky went on. "I was wondering if maybe you'd like to go to the movies tonight? My uncle said I could use his truck."

"That's really nice of you," Lexi said, "but I'm busy tonight."

"Oh," Ricky uttered, disappointment coloring his voice. "How about tomorrow?"

"I have plans then, too," Lexi said.

"Oh. Well, that's cool," Ricky said.

Suddenly, Lexi felt terrible. After all, Ricky was new in Stanfield; he didn't know anyone.

"So, it was nice talking with you — " Ricky began, clearly ready to hang up.

"Wait, Ricky?"

"Yeah?"

"How about if I talk to Juliet and you come over to her house swimming with a bunch of us sometime soon?"

"You sure?" Ricky asked, his voice both eager and wary. "I don't want to impose or anything — "

"No, I'd really like that," Lexi assured him. "Give me your phone number, and I'll check it out with her and call you back, okay?"

Lexi quickly scribbled down Ricky's number, said her good-byes, and hung up the phone. She told her friends about the conversation.

"I told you he was nice and cute," Juliet said.

"Fine, you go out with him," Lexi said sharply.

"He didn't ask me," Juliet replied. "Besides, I'm in love with Ty."

"And Lexi's in love with Austin," Paris said. "Which leaves nice guy Ricky Littlefeather exactly nowhere, which proves my point about nice guys."

"What should we do?" Juliet asked.

"Go to the frat house," Lexi said, trying to sound more certain than she actually felt. She looked at Paris, who nodded weakly.

"But what if Fawn is there?" Juliet asked. "Maybe you need to talk with your sister alone . . ."

"I'll . . . I'll just have to play it by ear," Lexi decided, getting up from the bed. "But one thing is for certain — I can't sit here and do nothing!"

"So, they left together?" Juliet said, repeating what Greg had just told them.

"Yep," Greg said, shaking his head in disgust. "They were all over each other. I guess the storm has passed."

The Omega Pi fraternity was the oldest and most prestigious frat on the Stanfield College campus. Their house was an old, white-pillared mansion with a wide front porch filled with swings and rocking chairs. The huge living room featured shabby, mismatched furniture, but there was a big-screen TV and a top-of-the-line sound system to play the hundreds of CDs housed on a rack in the corner.

Normally, the girls loved to come to the Omega Pi house. Flirting with college guys was always fun, and Omega Pi college guys were the best.

The guys had even talked to the girls about how in the fall they hoped to nominate them as official little sisters of the fraternity house. Little sisters were always seniors in high school, and they were always the darlings of the fraternity. Paris said she had no interest at all, but Juliet and Lexi both suspected that what she really meant was she was afraid they wouldn't pick her.

When the girls arrived at the frat house, little sisters and fraternity parties were, for once, not on their minds. They found Greg and three other frat brothers in the living room watching the Yankees playing the Red Sox on the large-screen TV. Greg told them that Ty had gone to a rehearsal and that Austin and Fawn had left fifteen minutes earlier.

"You mean they . . . they made up?" Lexi had asked incredulously.

"Sure looked like it to me," Greg said. "Which is to say you couldn't have pried their bodies apart with a crowbar."

The three other summer-semester students in the room cheered as the Yankees scored a run.

"They really made up that fast?" Juliet wondered.

"Hey, could you take that somewhere else?" one of the guys called from the couch. "We're trying to watch the game here!"

"Sorry," Lexi whispered.

The four of them walked outside to the front porch. Paris sat in a rocking chair, not saying a word, not looking at Greg. *I couldn't care less about him,* she told herself.

"So . . . we should all be happy," Juliet said. "I guess the wedding is back on."

"Who knows?" Greg asked. "By tonight they could hate each other's guts again."

"Look, they just had a little fight," Lexi said, trying to sound normal even though she felt like the entire world was spinning dizzily out of control. "It was nerves, that's all."

Juliet and Paris stared at her.

"It's great that they're back together," Lexi said. "I'm happy for them."

Greg sat on the swing and rocked for a moment. "If you ask me, neither one of them knows what the hell they're doing."

"Why do you say that?" Juliet asked.

" 'Cuz it's the truth," Greg said darkly. "I've known Austin my whole life, right?"

"So have I," Juliet pointed out, shaking her hair off her face. "He's my brother."

Greg contemplated her a minute. "Let's just say you don't know everything, okay?"

"What's that supposed to mean?" Juliet asked.

"Forget it."

"No, I really want to know," Juliet pressed.

"Ask Austin," Greg said sharply. He turned to Paris. "So, how are you feeling?"

"Just ducky!" Paris said brightly.

"That was a really dumb stunt you pulled."

"Well, I'm just broken up that you disapprove," Paris said sarcastically.

"Hey, if you want to kill yourself with drugs, it's your funeral," Greg said with a shrug.

Paris stared daggers at him. *Why did I ever think I liked him,* she wondered to herself. *He's sarcastic and obnoxious!*

"Look, that was an accident, okay?" Paris said. "I wasn't doing it to party. And I didn't need you to come save me, either."

"Could have fooled me," Greg said.

"So, how late is Ty's play practice?" Juliet asked, wanting to change the subject.

"He didn't tell me," Greg said, getting up from the swing. "Look, I've gotta go. I was supposed to pick someone up fifteen minutes ago."

"Tell her we said hi," Paris sneered.

Greg jingled his car keys in his hand and regarded her. "You know, for a pretty, smart girl, you have quite a chip on your shoulder. She's a he, for your information. Catch you later." He walked briskly toward the rear parking lot.

"God, someone shoot me," Paris said, smacking herself in the forehead. "I acted like a total idiot just now!"

"What do you think he was talking about when he said I don't know everything about Austin?" Juliet wondered out loud.

"Who knows?" Paris asked. "It could be just nonsense to get you all upset. He just doesn't want to lose his partying buddy, if you ask me."

"I really miss Ty," Juliet said with a sigh. "Do you think I should go over to his rehearsal? Or is that too pushy?"

Lexi sat heavily on the porch step and buried her face in her hands. *They're back together. They love each other. Was Austin lying to me? How could he be back with Fawn and not say a single word to me? How?*

Tears cascaded down her cheeks, working their way between her fingers as a sob escaped from her throat.

"Oh, Lex, I'm so sorry!" Juliet cried, running over to her friend.

"Me, too," Paris said, coming to sit at her other side. "Here we are moaning about our own problems and ignoring yours." She put her arm around Lexi's shoulders.

"I . . . I just don't understand," Lexi sobbed. "How . . . how could he d-do this to me?"

"I don't understand it, either," Juliet said, her voice full of concern.

"He owes you an explanation big-time," Paris agreed.

"If I could just talk to him!" Lexi cried. "If he would just explain . . ."

Juliet looked up, and there were Austin and Fawn, walking toward the frat house, their arms around each other, Fawn's head leaning on Austin's chest. "Oh, God, Austin and Fawn are headed this way," she gasped.

"I can't face them, not together!" Lexi cried, jumping up from the step. And she ran back into the frat house as fast as her legs could carry her.

Chapter 17

"Lexi?" Sheila called as she strode toward her daughter's room. "Austin is here. He wants to talk to you."

It was that evening, and Lexi was more miserable than she had ever been in her life. She had actually run out the back door of the frat house that afternoon, and then had walked the five miles home. She had been in her room ever since, on her bed. Juliet and Paris called but she said she couldn't talk.

She felt as if she never, ever wanted to get out of bed again.

"Tell him to go away," Lexi told her mother.

Who cares if he bothers to come over now? she thought bitterly. *Who cares what he has to say? He and Fawn are back together. He just used me. Whatever he has to say, it's too late.*

Sheila came into the room and sat down on Lexi's bed. "What's wrong, sweetie?"

"Nothing."

"Clearly it's not nothing," Sheila said. "You're miserable, and I want to help."

"No one can help me."

Sheila smoothed the hair off of Lexi's hot forehead. "Why don't you want to talk to Austin?"

"Because I hate him," she said viciously.

Sheila sighed. "Honey, he's going to marry your sister and be related to you for a long time. Whatever kind of fight you had, you need to talk it out."

Lexi closed her eyes in pain. *How can my mother be so smart and so utterly clueless at the same time,* she thought.

"I guess he told you the wedding is back on," Lexi said in a tight voice.

"Fawn called and told me," Sheila said.

"Is she with him?"

"No, she's at the Stanfields' house meeting with a wedding photographer and a videographer."

"Gee, everything is sure back on track fast," Lexi said bitterly.

"So it seems," Sheila said. "You sure you won't come talk with Austin?"

"Positive. I have nothing to say to him. Ever."

"Well, that's your choice," Sheila said, getting up from the bed. "I'm going over to the Beansprout. The Board of Health says we can open up again tomorrow. Turns out it was the deviled eggs that made everyone sick."

"I'm glad you found out, at least," Lexi said in a muffled voice.

"Me, too," Sheila agreed. "That takes care of my immediate problem. I just wish I had a clue how to take care of yours."

Paris paced her bedroom, eyeing her phone nervously.

All you have to do is pick up the phone and call him, she told herself. *All you have to do is apologize for acting like an idiot. And then . . . and then . . .*

This was the part of the imaginary phone conversation with Greg that stumped her. She had no clear idea about whether or not he liked her and she didn't know how to find out.

Unless she picked up the phone.

At least, that had been Juliet's advice.

"Right now he thinks you detest him," Juliet had theorized. "Why would he pick up the phone and call a girl who loathes him, even if he were dying with love for her?"

"Good point," Paris muttered out loud. She eyed the phone again, then quickly strode over to it and dialed the number of the fraternity house, which she'd already scribbled on a piece of paper on the nightstand.

"Omega Pi," someone answered. In the background Paris could hear loud Grateful Dead blasting through the sound system, and over that voices laughing and carrying on.

"Uh, could I speak with Greg, please?" Paris said nervously.

"Hold on," the bored voice said. "Hey, anyone seen Cambridge?" the voice called into the din.

"He's in the living room with Christy, man!" someone called back.

Oh great, Paris thought with embarrassment. *Christy is probably a hundred pounds wringing wet and the cutest thing at Stanfield College.* She was about to hang up when Greg's voice came on the phone.

"Yeah?" he said abruptly.

Paris's hand was sweating on the receiver. "Hi, it's Paris."

"Oh, Miss I-Don't-Do-Drugs-to-Party, right?" Greg asked in an amused voice.

"Well, I don't," Paris said stiffly. "You got a problem with that?" She winced at the sound of her own voice.

This is how you got into this mess in the first place, she reminded herself.

"Hey, forget I said that last part," she said

quickly. "I'm starting again, okay? Hi, Greg, this is Paris. Wow, nice night out, huh? Hey, I hear you guys are listening to the Grateful Dead. Garcia was terrific, huh?"

Greg laughed. "See, you really are capable of being civil!"

"Super-civil," Paris agreed. "Some even call me ultra-civil! The civil-est!"

He laughed again. "Okay, so now that you've regained your sense of humor, what can I do for you?"

Oh, God. I have absolutely no idea what to say.

"I just called to . . . to apologize for this afternoon," Paris finally said. "And to thank you for what you did for me . . . you know."

"Cool," Greg said easily. "And you're welcome."

"Greggie!" a female voice whined. "I need you to make me another drink!"

"Just a sec, Christy," Greg said.

"Well, I guess you're busy," Paris said quickly.

"But Greggie, you're the only one who makes them strong enough!" Christy said with a giggle.

"Gee, I heard what ol' Christy had to say," Paris said. "And you're worried about *me* and drugs?"

"So she's had a couple of drinks," Greg said. "That's not the same thing!"

"The last I heard, alcohol was a drug!" Paris exclaimed.

"Oh, come on," Greg said irritably. "Everyone drinks!"

"Wrong," Paris said flatly. "I don't."

"Oh, no," Greg sneered. "Your body is a temple, right?"

Paris's face burned with embarrassment. "At least I don't expect you to pour alcohol down my throat, *Greggie!*"

"Christy is twenty-one," Greg said. "You're just a kid!"

"Greggie!" Christy whined again. "Who is that, anyway?"

"I guess I better let you go, *Greggie,*" Paris said snottily.

"Whatever," Greg said breezily, and he hung up.

Paris stared at the phone, wishing she could kick it across the room, or throw plates at the wall, or do *something* to deal with the impotent rage she felt just from talking with Greg.

Instead she opened the drawer on her nightstand and took out a chocolate candy bar, unwrapped it, and took a huge bite.

"No," she told herself. "I won't do this." She got up and strode to the bathroom, where she threw the candy into the toilet and flushed three times to make sure it went down. Then she went back to her bed and threw herself down on it, staring up at the ceiling.

I have sunk to the lowest of the low, she thought. *I am letting thoughts about a guy rule my life, something I vowed I would never do.*

And I don't know how to stop.

"Dang, I can't tell you how great this feels," Ty drawled, floating on his back in the Stanfields' pool. "That play is getting me mighty tense."

"I'm really glad you're here," Juliet said softly. She looked down at herself in her favorite bikini, bright aqua against her burnished skin. Ty looked so cute in his baggy, bright-colored trunks, the moon shining off the golden hairs on his taut, athletic chest.

She sighed happily and stared up at the moonlight, a smile on her lips. *Just being with Ty makes me so happy,* she thought. *I don't even need anything else!*

It was ten o'clock that night. Ty had called her when he'd gotten out of rehearsal, and she had invited him over for a swim. He had accepted eagerly, and clearly was happy to see her when he arrived.

But he was clearly preoccupied, too.

"I've never worked in a professional production before," Ty continued, swimming over to Juliet. "It's like a whole other thing."

"How did Austin manage to get out of rehearsal today?" Juliet asked. "I mean, he has the lead, doesn't he?"

"One of the leads," Ty agreed. "He told the director it was a major family crisis — I thought the guy was about to have a heart attack — but Austin was set on leaving, and he did. I thought it was beat, myself."

"Austin's used to getting his own way," Juliet admitted.

"Ain't that the truth?" Ty agreed. "But it was great for me, I got to play Brick this afternoon."

"Do you think it's good," Juliet asked, "that Austin and Fawn made up?"

"Sure," Ty said. "He loves her, I know that. He was miserable after their fight."

"But why did it happen, then?" Juliet asked.

"Got me," Ty said. "They're both scared, that's my guess. But I don't know when I've seen two people who love each other more, either."

Then why was Austin kissing Lexi? Juliet wanted to ask, but she would never betray Lexi's confidence, so she kept her mouth shut.

"I can't wait to see the play," she told him warmly.

"It's real soon now," Ty said. "I only have a bitty part, of course, but it might could be the start of something big, you never know!"

"Ty, remember when we met and you said you were embarrassed by your accent?" Juliet asked gently.

"Uh huh."

"Well, 'might could' is really, really southern . . ."

Ty laughed, righted himself in the water, and splashed Juliet hard. "Okay, Miss Stanfield, I stand corrected!"

Juliet laughed and splashed him back. "Well, you asked for it!"

He splashed her harder until she was screeching and giggling all at once. "Stop!" she yelled. "You can be as southern as you want, I promise!"

He stopped, grinned at her, and slowly wrapped his arms around her waist, pulling her close. "Have you ever had a moonshine kiss?"

"What is it?" Juliet whispered, gazing up into his shining brown eyes.

"See up there?" Ty cocked his head toward the sky. "The moon is full. That's when everyone in the backwoods can find their way to the still where the whiskey's made in the hollows. When you kiss by a full moon, it's called a moonshine kiss. It's a real southern boy's specialty."

Juliet smiled. "You made that up, didn't you?"

"I'll never tell." He softly brought his lips to hers, and her arms went around his neck. The kisses became more passionate, their bodies pressed together, until Juliet lost all track of where she was or who she was. All she wanted was the feeling of Ty holding her, kissing her, touching her, to never, ever stop and —

Abruptly she pulled away from him, breathing hard. "Ty, I . . . we . . ."

"What?" he whispered, reaching for her again.

"This is wonderful, but I . . . I need to slow down . . ."

"But why?"

"Because I just do, that's all," she said, her voice rising. "Do I have to have a reason?"

"No, you don't," he said, gently touching her wet hair.

"Maybe I'm just not ready for . . . that," she said awkwardly.

"Hey, it's okay, Juli," he told her. "I got a little carried away."

"Me, too," she admitted. "And I liked it."

He grinned at her. "Me, too." He reached for her hand

"But I'm not ready to . . . I mean, I haven't . . ." Juliet felt ridiculous trying to explain.

"I understand," Ty said. "You're only sixteen and — "

"A lot of girls I know are sleeping with their boyfriends," Juliet said. "But I don't think I'm ready for that."

"Like I said, it's okay," Ty assured her. "We don't have to rush anything." He let his fingers trail in the water. "You're special, Juli."

"I am?" she asked happily.

He nodded. "Sweet and smart and beautiful — "

"I'm not beautiful," Juliet said quickly.

"How can you say that?" Ty asked.

She was silent for a moment. "I suppose when I think of beautiful, I think of blond hair and blue eyes. And that's not me."

"Oh girl, don't you know that beauty comes in all colors and shapes? Don't you know how breathtakingly lovely you are?"

Tears of happiness came to Juliet's eyes. "No one ever said that to me before," she said softly.

"Well, I'm sayin' it," Ty drawled. "And I intend to keep on sayin' it until you believe it."

He opened his arms to her, and happily she moved toward him in the warm water. He put his arms around her and she laid her head on his chest. "You know, I was afraid when you didn't come to the engagement party that something was wrong with us," she admitted.

"I'm just busy," Ty said. "The play, and my job at the video store . . ."

"I know," Juliet said, nuzzling happily against his chest. "Now I know we have all the time in the world."

His body tensed, she could feel it. "What's wrong?" she asked him.

"Nothing."

"Not nothing," she said, lifting her head to gaze up at him. "What is it?"

"It's just . . . I've been thinking. About the fall . . ."

"When school starts?" Juliet said. "It'll be okay. Your classes can't take up more time than the play does now. We'll see each other."

"That's just it," Ty said. "In the fall . . . well, in the fall, I might not be in Stanfield at all."

Chapter 18

"This is going to be a blast," Fawn told Lexi, Paris, and Juliet, practically bouncing with happiness in her train seat. "I'm so glad I'm going to pick out my own wedding gown, and the three of you are fantastic to come with me!"

It was a week later, and they were on the train, speeding toward Bay Ridge, Brooklyn, and the largest collection of wedding gowns in the world, at Buchbaum's. Mrs. Stanfield wanted to come along, but Juliet had somehow talked her out of it — for which Fawn said she was eternally grateful. Fawn had talked her own mother out of making the trip, too. She figured her mother's idea of a bridal gown would be a simple, white, cotton hippie dress. It was not exactly what Fawn had in mind.

The only person she insisted should accompany her to pick out her dress was Lexi. Then

Juliet and Paris had volunteered to come along, mostly to support Lexi.

Lexi stared out the window and watched the world go by. Her feelings were so jumbled, her nerves so raw, that she barely knew what she felt anymore.

I still haven't spoken with Austin, she thought. *Maybe I never will. After that one time he came by the apartment, he never tried to talk with me again. Well, what is there to say, really?*

Fawn is so happy, and she insists it was just a big misunderstanding, that she and Austin were just both exhausted and stressed-out. So now they get to live happily ever after. And I get to wonder forever — why did he do it?

"You guys, we're the next stop," Juliet reminded them, reaching for the small patent leather backpack she'd brought and slinging it onto her back. She was wearing a short, pleated black skirt and pink-and-black paisley suspenders with a pale pink ribbed baby T-shirt. Black patent leather combat boots on her feet matched her backpack.

It's a good thing I got out of the house without Mom seeing me this morning, she thought with a grin. *She practically faints when I dress like this!*

Juliet looked over at the others, who had also spent time picking out the perfect outfit for their shopping trip. Paris, out of her usual baggy clothes, actually wore a short denim jumper over a plain white T-shirt. It was a new purchase. Lexi had on flowing, forest green striped pants with a drawstring waist, and a cropped, sleeveless green-and-burgundy shirt.

Fawn, per usual, looked the best of all in a fitted white suede skirt and a matching vest worn over a lacy camisole.

That looks like a Nicole Miller outfit to me, Juliet thought. Her mother had raised her on name designers and she knew them all. *Now how can Fawn afford a Nicole Miller?*

"This is us!" Fawn exclaimed as the train slowed to a stop. They all jumped off the train and headed to a nearby taxi stand.

"We have to be sure to really look at everything," Fawn said, as they got into the first available cab. She gave the driver the address of Buchbaum's. "I read in *Brides* magazine that this place is forty thousand square feet," Fawn told the girls. "There are over four thousand wedding gowns! And shoes and bridesmaid's dresses — "

"Hey, I have an idea!" Paris interrupted. "What if we pick out bridesmaid's dresses at Buch — whachamacallit."

"Buchbaum's," Fawn said. "But Mrs. Stanfield already has Madame Renaud's assistants sewing your dresses!"

"It was worth a try," Paris said with a sigh.

"Which reminds me, you all have to go in and see her next Monday," Fawn said. "For fittings."

"How are the bridesmaids from out of town doing it?" Juliet asked.

"Oh, they called their measurements in to Madame Renaud's," Fawn explained. "I guess they just don't get the special attention that you all get!"

"Lucky us," Paris muttered.

"Here it is!" Fawn cried as the driver stopped in front of the large, imposing stone building. Fawn handed the driver some money.

"Have a great wedding, dollface!" the driver called, as he sped away.

"Hello, welcome to Buchbaum's," an older woman with a thick New York accent greeted them just inside the door. She was heavyset, with very, very red hair set in a pompadour hairdo. She wore a black suit and black sneakers, and her rhinestone harlequin glasses hung from a chain around her neck. "Which one is the lovely bride?"

"I am," Fawn said. She felt dazed. All around her were rack after rack after rack of white wedding gowns. Bridal consultants were flitting back and forth, carrying armloads of dresses to and from dressing rooms. Dozens of women were looking through the racks, all talking at once.

"I'm Mrs. Garabaldi," the woman said, shaking Fawn's hand. "I'll be your bridal consultant. Whatever you want, whatever you need, we have it here at Buchbaum's."

"Thank you," Fawn said. "Oh, this is my sister, Lexi — she's my maid of honor — and Juliet and Paris, two of my bridesmaids."

"Charmed," Mrs. Garabaldi said. "So, come with me, we'll talk." She led them to some chairs. "Tell me everything you want, darling."

Fawn reached into her purse and pulled out the same photo she had shown to Mrs. Stanfield. "I was thinking . . . maybe something like this would be — "

"This would be sensational on you," Mrs. Garabaldi said quickly.

"Thanks!" Fawn said, happy for the show of support. "You have something like this, then?"

"Darling, this is Buchbaum's," Mrs. Garabaldi said. "If we don't have it, it doesn't exist."

"I was also thinking . . . maybe I could look at some other types of gowns, too," Fawn said. "Since I'm here — "

"And why not?" Mrs. Garabaldi cut her off as though she'd been doing it all her life. "You should look around and try on to your heart's content. Now, what kind of price range are we talking, darling?"

"Price is no object," Fawn said.

Mrs. Garabaldi grinned. "I only wish I could have said that about my own wedding gown. I had only two hundred dollars to spend, which bought junk, even back in the Dark Ages. Fortunately, my Aunt Bea could sew, you know what I mean?"

"That's nice — " Fawn said politely.

"Twenty-five years I was married to that man," Mrs. Garabaldi interrupted her. "And then one day he goes on a business trip and never comes home. Can you imagine?"

"Gee . . ." Fawn said, at a loss for words. The other girls, even Lexi — as depressed as she was — had to fight to keep from laughing.

" — But don't worry, that will never happen to you. So, let me show you to dressing room four, I'll bring some dresses, you'll have a ball. Long sleeves or short?"

"Uh, long, but not too warm," Fawn said. "The wedding is only a little more than a month away, and — "

Mrs. Garabaldi held her hands to her heart,

shocked. "You waited until a *month* before your wedding to get your wedding gown?"

"I . . . kind of did," Fawn said.

Mrs. Garabaldi shook her head sadly. "Neckline?"

"Sweetheart?" Fawn said tentatively. "Or off-the-shoulder?"

"And what size brassiere?" she asked briskly.

"Oh, I have a bra on," Fawn assured her.

"You need a wedding bra, darling," Mrs. Garabaldi explained. "Long-line and strapless."

"Oh," Fawn said, blushing. "Thirty-four C."

"Wonderful. And you're a perfect size eight — I can always tell. We'll talk veils and shoes afterward. Make yourself comfortable, darlings."

The girls all sat on the cushioned stools in the huge dressing room.

"Hey, is it only me, or do you guys find it très bizarre that they hired a woman whose husband deserted her as a wedding consultant?" Paris asked.

"And she tells people about it!" Fawn added with a laugh.

"Can you imagine, though," Juliet mused. "One day the love of your life just decides not to come home?"

Yeah, I can imagine, Paris said to herself. *My mom did it to my dad.* But she refused to let such somber thoughts color the moment.

"Oh, come on," Paris scoffed. "Just listening to that woman's voice for twenty-five years would send the guy running!"

"I'm serious!" Juliet said. "How totally devastating!"

"But Juli, they must have had terrible problems," Fawn said. "She just isn't telling us that part."

"To not ever see the guy you love, ever again . . ." Juliet's voice trailed off.

She wasn't thinking about Mr. and Mrs. Garabaldi. She was thinking about Ty and what he had told her.

He might drop out of college and move to Hollywood to try and get into the movies, she recalled. *He'd be all the way on the other side of the country, with all those gorgeous Hollywood blonds falling in love with his cute southern accent. I don't think I could stand it!*

"Hey, Juliet, did you hear me?" Fawn called to her.

"What?" Juliet asked, startled from her musings.

"I asked how you guys want to wear your hair for the wedding," Fawn said. "Whatever you three decide is what I'll tell the other bridesmaids, okay?"

"Why do we all have to wear our hair the same way?" Paris asked.

"So you'll look the same," Fawn explained.

"Fawn, I'm like this major blimp compared to everyone else," Paris said. "How could we possibly look the same?"

"Stop putting yourself down like that!" Lexi said sharply.

"And besides, you're much thinner," Juliet added.

"You're beautiful, Paris," Fawn said warmly. "You always have been."

Yeah, try telling Greg, Paris thought sourly. *Or should I say Greggie.*

"Are you wearing your hair up or down, Fawn?" Juliet asked.

"Up, I think," Fawn said. "With curls around my face and some hair hanging down, you know, in tendrils."

"So how about if we wear ours off our faces with flowered combs?" Juliet suggested. "In pink and white?"

"Very girly," Paris teased.

"It sounds lovely," Fawn agreed. "Lexi? Is that okay?"

"Sure," Lexi said flatly.

Fawn frowned at her. "What's wrong?"

"Nothing. I'm just tired," Lexi said quickly.

"Are you sure? You've been acting kind of strange all week."

Ever since Austin kissed me and then pretended it never happened, you mean, Lexi thought to herself.

"Maybe I picked up some kind of a bug," Lexi said.

"Or food poisoning," Fawn said, shaking her head. "I still can't believe that happened."

"It's kind of funny, when you stop and think about it," Paris said. "All the richest people in Stanfield in a barfathon!"

"I can't believe Austin and I had a fight about something so stupid," Fawn said. She smiled. "He's being so sweet now, he really is. You know what he told me last night? He thinks I should arrive at the club before the ceremony in a white carriage drawn by white horses, and he should arrive in a gray carriage drawn by gray horses!"

"Do the horses get to mate afterward?" Paris asked innocently.

"Honestly, Paris, you do not have a romantic bone in your body," Juliet chided her.

"It's so sweet of him, don't you think?" Fawn said. "I mean, he's so busy with the play, but he actually thought about the carriages and the horses . . ."

"Okay, darling, I've got gowns, gowns, and more gowns," Mrs. Garabaldi said, bustling back into the dressing room. She held up a dress that looked remarkably like the one Fawn had cut out of the magazine. "A Madeline Gardner," she said. "Straight out of a fairy tale, isn't it?"

"It's beautiful," Fawn agreed, her voice hushed.

"Now this one," Mrs. Garabaldi said, holding up another gown, "is a Miranda Sueg — she is the wedding designer of the moment, darling. We can hardly keep her gowns in stock." The dress was off-the-shoulder, with tiny bows traveling down the front of the sweeping skirt. Larger bows tied the sleeves above the elbow, and, finally, tiny bows were at each fitted wrist.

"Too many bows, I think," Fawn said politely.

"Oh, I agree, darling," Mrs. Garabaldi said. "So let's march on, shall we?" She hung up the Miranda Sueg and held up a simple, beautiful gown in ivory, perfectly stark and fitted, off-the-shoulder, with a small jacket to be worn over it for the ceremony.

"Then at the party you take off the jacket,"
Mrs. Garabaldi said, "instant gorgeous! With
the push-up-bra" — she handed the white,
strapless bra to Fawn — "you're walking sex
appeal, darling!"

"I don't think it's quite right," Fawn said.

"Of course not, you have taste," Mrs. Garabaldi approved. "So, how's this?"

Mrs. Garabaldi held out what was simply
the most beautiful wedding gown any of them
had ever seen, and they gasped.

"That's incredible!" Juliet cried.

"It is," Fawn agreed, her eyes huge.

The dress was not as ornate as the one in
the magazine. It had a high neck of delicate
lace, then sheer opaque silk over the bodice
and shoulders. A sweetheart neckline met the
silk, dipping low in the center. The arms and
bodice were a fine French lace sewn with tiny
seed pearls, and the same lace flowed in points
at the sweeping skirt.

And then there was the train. The same
perfect, delicate lace flowed from the back of
the gown in a stunning ten-foot-long train.

"Try it on," Mrs. Garabaldi urged.

Quickly Fawn took off her outfit and allowed
Mrs. Garabaldi to help her into the gown. She
did up the tiny pearl buttons in the back, then
stepped away from Fawn to survey the re-

sults. "Darling, this is you," she said. "I am an expert, and this is you."

"Oh, Fawn," Juliet gasped.

"I second that," Paris admitted.

Lexi had tears in her eyes. "It's gorgeous, Fawn."

Fawn looked at her reflection in the mirror, and her own eyes teared up, too. "This is my dress," she whispered. "I must be the luckiest girl in the world."

"You deserve it," Lexi said, hugging her sister. Even though her own heart felt battered and bruised, she really did love Fawn.

And Fawn was about to be the most beautiful bride in the world.

Chapter 19

As the curtain fell on the final scene of *Cat on a Hot Tin Roof,* Lexi, Juliet, and Paris, along with the rest of the audience, sat in hushed silence. Fawn sat next to Lexi, then Paris, then Juliet. Fawn and Lexi's parents were next to Fawn, and Juliet and Austin's parents sat next to Juliet. The group took up one entire row of seats set up inside the tent. Behind them sat Gerald and Ricky Littlefeather, Greg, Greg's parents, and various fraternity brothers of Austin and Ty's.

Mom and Dad are really dealing with this amazingly well, Juliet thought, looking over at her parents.

It was a Thursday evening of summer perfection. Juliet was in a wonderful mood. Everything was just going so well. The wedding was only two weeks away, and the final plans were really coming together. When she, Lexi, and

Paris had gone for the bridesmaid's dress fittings, Paris had been shocked to find that the dress actually looked good on her.

She was following the Fit for Life plan, which was basically eating healthy, low-fat meals and exercising, and it was slowly working. And she had found the perfect band for Fawn — a group called Bliss who had played at a recent ritzy bar mitzvah she and her father had attended in Syracuse. Bliss had had a cancellation of a gig for the night of Fawn's wedding, so they were available to play.

And there was more good news. Fawn and Mrs. Stanfield had finally come to an understanding, it seemed, and they were working together to plan the wedding — without fighting. The Mundys' health food restaurant was open again, and business was back almost to normal levels. Lexi was being completely supportive of her sister — even if she wasn't speaking to Austin. And Juliet and Ty spent all the time together that they possibly could.

So everyone is happy, Juliet thought, *which makes me happy. But I still don't know what's going to happen in the fall. And I can hardly bear to think about it . . .*

She tucked the scary thoughts about Ty's leaving into the back of her mind, and turned to smile at her mom.

Following the performance, the Stanfields were giving an opening-night party for the cast and friends of the cast at their home, and they didn't seem to be upset about Austin's interest in the theater at all. Tonight, anyway.

Suddenly, the audience began to applaud, and the cast came out to take their bows.

Sometimes my parents really surprise me, Juliet realized.

Mrs. Stanfield smiled back at her daughter. "I have such lovely children," she told Juliet.

"Marvelous production," Mr. Stanfield said heartily. "I'm really quite impressed."

"There's Ty!" Juliet cried, clapping her hands off as Ty took his bow. "He was so fantastic!"

The applause swelled as the principals joined those with smaller roles.

"Wasn't Austin wonderful?" Fawn cried to her sister, clapping as loudly as she could.

"He was really good," Lexi agreed, as she watched Austin smile that gorgeous smile of his at the audience.

When the entire cast took their group bow, Mr. and Mrs. Stanfield were the first ones to stand up. Fawn quickly jumped to her feet, too, and then the rest of the audience joined in, giving the cast a resounding standing ovation.

It must feel fantastic to have people applaud for you like that, Juliet thought. *No wonder Ty wants to be an actor. No wonder he wants to go to Hollywood and leave me behind . . .*

"Let's go backstage and see them!" Fawn suggested eagerly.

"Maybe we should give him some time to change," Sheila Mundy suggested, stepping out into the aisle.

"Oh, I can't wait, Mom," Fawn cried happily. "Gosh, wasn't he brilliant?"

"Ah, young love," Michael teased his daughter, giving her a hug. "Why don't you go by yourself, honey? We don't want to overwhelm the poor guy!"

Fawn, Mrs. Stanfield, and Juliet ended up going backstage to see Austin, and everyone else headed out for an early start on the party. Paris found herself next to Greg, who pulled a cigarette out as soon as they got outside the theater tent.

"You ought to give that up," Paris said.

"So I've heard," Greg said, lighting up.

"So . . . the play was good," Paris said, walking slowly beside him.

"It was okay."

"What, you aren't a theater lover?"

"Like I said, it was okay," Greg said tersely, taking a drag on his cigarette.

"Well, you're in a fabulous mood," Paris said sarcastically. "Lovely chatting with you."

She began to stride ahead of him, but Greg reached for her arm. "Hey, sorry about that." He caught up with her. "I'm in a lousy mood."

"And here you hid it so well," Paris marveled.

Greg smiled. "You know, you really tick me off sometimes, Paris, but there's just something about you . . ."

Paris tried not to feel thrilled by this compliment, and failed. Happiness surged through her.

"You want a lift to the party?" Greg asked.

"Sure," Paris said casually. She let Lexi know that she had a ride with Greg, then headed for Greg's black BMW. He was already sitting in the driver's seat, drumming his fingers on the steering wheel, a pensive look on his face.

"Okay, let's hit the party," Paris said happily. "This should be fun."

Greg stared off into the distance, still drumming his fingers.

Paris cocked her head at him. "Look, is something on your mind?"

He turned abruptly and looked at her. "No." He started up the car and headed toward the

Stanfield mansion. The radio wasn't on and Greg wasn't talking. The silence felt oppressive.

"So, wow, we're sure having some fun now, huh?" Paris finally said.

"Sorry," Greg said. "I'm . . . you're right. Something is on my mind. But let's not talk about it, okay?"

"How could we talk about it when I don't know what it is?" Paris pointed out.

"It's . . . don't you sometimes think Austin and Fawn should just call this whole thing off?" Greg blurted out.

"Oh, not that again," Paris groaned.

"Okay, forget I said anything — "

"Look, you just don't want to lose your partying bud," Paris said.

"Maybe," Greg said levelly.

"It's their lives," Paris said with a shrug. "Personally, I don't plan to get married until I've got an education and a bank account of my own — and I don't know if I even want to get married then. Or ever, maybe. But, hey, I'm not the Prince and Princess of Stanfield. I hope they live happily ever after."

"That only happens in fairy tales," Greg said, turning into the Stanfields' driveway. "And trust me, this is no fairy tale."

* * *

"And when that door got stuck in Act Two, I thought, 'Oh, Lord, please let me get this puppy open so I can make my entrance,'" Ty told Juliet, "'or this may be the very last play I ever get to be in!'"

"Juliet, can I talk with you a minute?"

Juliet turned away from Ty to look at Greg, who was standing behind her. The party was in full swing, the immense living room and dining room crowded with those involved in the play and their dozens of friends.

"Sure," Juliet said, though she was surprised at the serious look on Greg's face.

"Privately," Greg added.

"Oh, all right," Juliet said. "We can go to the study — I don't think anyone's in there."

She excused herself and silently walked with Greg to the study, then she turned to him, a question on her face. "What's up?"

Greg sighed and ran his fingers through his hair.

"Greg, this isn't like you!" Juliet teased. "You're never serious!"

"Yeah," Greg agreed. "And I wish I wasn't serious now."

Juliet sat on the leather sofa. A feeling of dread came over her. "What is it?"

Greg took the chair and leaned forward, his hands on his knees. "I've been going around and around about this, Juli, and I don't know if I'm doing the right thing . . ."

"About what?" Juliet asked. "What's wrong?"

"It's . . . it's about Austin."

Her face grew alarmed. "Is he sick or something? Is he flunking out of school?"

"No," Greg said. He sighed. "Man, this sucks. I keep thinking it's none of my business, I should just keep my mouth shut — "

"Well, now you have to tell me," Juliet said, "because whatever it is, you've got me scared to death."

Greg sighed again. "Look, you know I'm not exactly wild about the idea of Austin and Fawn getting married, right?"

"Is that what this is about?" Juliet asked. "Oh, Greg, you don't have anything to feel jealous about — "

"I'm not jealous, okay?" Greg exclaimed. "Look, it's true that I think Austin's too young, and I want to be able to hang out with him. And it's true that everything is going to change and I don't particularly dig it, but it's . . . it's more than that."

"What?"

He ran his fingers nervously through his hair again. "Austin might kill me for telling you this," Greg said in a low voice. He compressed his lips and finally shrugged, as if to say he was going to say what he had to say no matter what the consequences. "A few months ago, your parents dropped a bombshell on Austin. I can't believe they waited until he was twenty years old to tell him, but they did."

"Tell him what?" Juliet asked anxiously.

"It's like this," Greg began. "You've always known you're adopted — "

"It would have been a little difficult to keep it a secret," Juliet said wryly.

"Right," Greg agreed. "And I think that's probably the only reason your parents told you. Because Austin is adopted, too. And they never told him."

"That . . . that can't be true," Juliet stammered.

"It is true," Greg said in a flat voice. "Maybe I'm being a terrible friend to tell you, but — "

"I just don't believe it!" Juliet cried. "Why would my parents pretend he was their biological child? Why would they tell me the truth and not tell him?"

"I really don't know," Greg admitted. "Austin was really freaked out about it, too. I'm pretty sure I'm the only person he's told."

"He didn't even tell me . . ." Juliet said faintly.

"And he sure hasn't told Fawn," Greg added. "Now, don't you think that's a problem?"

"She wouldn't care — " Juliet began.

"Yeah, you're right," Greg agreed. "That's not the problem. What I mean is that a guy who can't tell the woman he's about to marry that he just found out he's adopted isn't ready to marry her, you know what I mean?"

Juliet put her hand to her forehead. She felt dizzy, faint, as if the room and everything she knew as reality was spinning crazily out of control. "I don't know what to think," she finally said.

"I don't blame you. And I don't know if you should tell Austin you know the truth, either. I might just lose my best friend over this. But I couldn't *not* say anything to *anyone*, you know?"

"I understand," Juliet managed to murmur.

"I thought about just going to Fawn, but I knew Austin would never forgive me for that," Greg said, shaking his head. "Listen, Austin loves you. And you know what it feels like, being adopted. Maybe you can talk with him."

"I just don't know what to do," Juliet said. Suddenly she felt like crying, but she bit her lips to hold back the tears.

"I'm sorry to have to lay this on you," Greg

said. "Maybe I shouldn't have done it . . ."

"No, I think you did the right thing," Juliet told him.

"It's just that if Austin is so freaked out over this that he couldn't tell Fawn, how can he possibly be ready to marry her?"

"Maybe he's planning to tell her — " Juliet began.

"He's not honest with her about anything, Juli — that he wants to be an actor, that he doesn't want to run the family trust . . . I mean, the only honest thing he tells Fawn is that he loves her. But what kind of love is that?"

Juliet didn't say a word, because she simply did not have an answer.

Chapter 20

"I got it, I got it!" Ricky Littlefeather called, as he leapt up in the water and deftly set the volleyball up for a spike. There were five kids on each side. One team was Juliet, Ricky, Paris, Lexi, and Gordon Shreeveport, who lived in the mansion next door to the Stanfields. The other team was made up of Greg, Ty, and three girls from Stanfield High who were friends of Juliet, Lexi, and Paris.

Fawn was with Sheila at Lockby's, the biggest department store at the mall, registering for a few last items in her china and silver patterns. And Austin had gone to purchase a new tuxedo for the wedding.

Mrs. Stanfield has actually backed off somewhat, Lexi thought as she watched Ty lunge for the ball on the other side of the net. *Or maybe it's just that she has everything completely ready.*

"Good set!" Lexi exclaimed, and Ricky grinned at her.

"I'm only a total klutz when I'm not doing sports."

Lexi laughed. Ricky really was a nice guy and they were getting to be friends. He had come over one afternoon a few days earlier to help his uncle at the Beansprout, and he and Lexi had gone out for ice cream. Now Juliet had finally organized her pool party, and Lexi, somewhat to her surprise, found she was really enjoying his company.

He's sweet and funny and smart, she thought. *He knows so much about American history and the Cherokee tribe — things I never even studied.*

But he's not Austin.

The thought came, unbidden, into her mind.

As much as she tried not to compare them, not to have any special feelings for Austin anymore, it seemed impossible. Oh, she could compartmentalize her feelings very well, and was happily helping Fawn with all the final details for the wedding.

But no matter how hard she tried, she couldn't seem to like another guy, not romantically, anyway.

"Lex, heads up!" Paris called, but it was too late, and the ball whacked her in the forehead.

"You okay?" Ricky asked, reaching out to touch her forehead gently.

"Yeah, I feel like an idiot, but I'm okay," Lexi said. "What's the score?"

"A bazzillion to nothing, our favor," Ty called from the other side of the net.

"Ha, we're slaughtering you," Paris called back happily.

Lexi smiled at her friend. Paris was actually appearing in coed company in a bathing suit. *Now, that's progress,* Lexi thought. *I just wish I could make that much progress in my own life.*

"Kids, the burgers are done," Mrs. Penny, one of the Stanfields' household assistants, called from the patio. "And the rest of the food is out here on the table. You can eat whenever you like!"

"Thanks, Mrs. Penny," Juliet called back.

I wonder what it's like to be so rich that you have people who do everything for you, Lexi mused. *It sure is not the Mundy family way of life! Well, I guess Fawn is about to find out!*

Still arguing good-naturedly about the score, the group got out of the pool to eat. As Lexi was drying off, she watched Juliet and Ty get their food and go sit together at the redwood picnic table. It seemed to Lexi that Juliet had been preoccupied for the last few days, but

Juliet didn't seem to want to talk about whatever was bothering her.

Greg looked over at Juliet, who tried to smile at him, and he gave her a strange look back.

That's not the first time I've seen something pass between the two of them, Lexi thought. *It's as if something is going on between them. Like they're sharing some . . . I don't know . . . intimate secret. But that's not possible. She's crazy about Ty, and Greg is . . . well I don't know what Greg is. I can't tell if he's interested in Paris or not.* Paris, Greg, and a bunch of other people sat down together on a huge blanket, laughing and joking around.

Lexi helped herself to all the salads, got herself a Coke and sat under the large oak tree. Ricky immediately came to sit with her. He practically tripped over his own feet and his paper plate nearly went flying. But he steadied himself, caught it neatly as if the whole thing had been a gigantic circus act, smiled sheepishly, and sank down next to Lexi.

"No burger?" he said, lifting his to his mouth.

"I don't eat meat," Lexi explained, forking up some egg salad.

"Oh, yeah, that's right, I forgot, the health

food thing." Ricky took a huge bite of his burger. "Does it bother you if I — "

"Not at all," Lexi assured him. "I watch people eat meat all the time. And I don't really do it because my parents own a health food restaurant, either. It's because of PETA."

"People for the Ethical Treatment of Animals," Ricky said, nodding. He took a slug from his can of Coke.

"You know about PETA?" Lexi asked, surprised.

"I've read about it," Ricky said. "I think it's a good thing."

"But you still eat meat," Lexi pointed out.

"Well, this is how I see it," Ricky said. "I don't eat anything from a pig, because I think pigs are very intelligent animals. It doesn't seem right to eat a living creature who has enough intelligence to have quality of life. But I don't mind eating cows or chickens, turkey, fish . . ."

"Well, none of it seems right to me," Lexi said. "I don't wear leather, either. It might seem weird, but — "

"Not at all," Ricky said, forking up some potato salad. "I think it's cool that you have strong convictions and you follow through on them. Most kids don't do that."

"Thanks," Lexi said with a small smile.

"I get pretty tired of people who spend all their time partying, you know?" Ricky said. "Like the biggest thing in their life is what their next buzz is gonna be. It's lame."

"I think so, too," Lexi said.

He smiled at her. "See? I knew we had a lot in common. Now maybe you'll actually go out with me!"

Heat came to Lexi's face. "I . . . I . . ." she stammered.

"What is it?" Ricky asked. "Another guy?"

"No," Lexi said, looking down at her paper plate.

"I don't want to be pushy," Ricky said. "Like, I can take no for an answer if it's really no — "

"There used to be another guy," Lexi tried to explain. "And I guess . . . I guess I'm not completely over him yet."

Ricky's face brightened. "That's it? Hey, that's great! I mean, I'm sorry that you're hurting, but I'm glad it's not that you just think I'm this dork from North Carolina — "

Lexi laughed. "No, nothing like that. But the truth is, I don't know how soon I'll be ready to . . . date or anything. And I guess you're going back home at the end of the summer."

"Oh, well, you never know," Ricky said mysteriously, shaking his beautiful black hair off his face. "I could always transfer to school here and live with my uncle."

"You wouldn't really do that, would you?" Lexi asked, shocked.

Ricky grinned. "I'm a man of many surprises," he said, lifting his burger again. "Many, many surprises."

". . . and I saw my china again, Lexi," Fawn gushed. "It's Lenox, white with a border of gold — real gold — and the silverware is gold, too, remember? Actually I guess it's called goldware!"

It was that evening, and as soon as Lexi got home Fawn came to her room to tell her all about her trip to Lockby's.

"I can't imagine any of my friends getting me any of this stuff," Fawn confided, sitting on the edge of Lexi's bed. "I mean, it costs a fortune! One place setting costs over a hundred dollars, can you imagine?"

"Not really," Lexi admitted, slipping into a clean T-shirt and cutoffs. She got some skin cream from her dresser and rubbed it into the dry skin on her arms.

"Mrs. Stanfield told me that her friends will make sure Austin and I end up with a complete service for twelve," Fawn went on. She laughed. "It's not like our friends are going to come over for pizza and we're going to break out the Lenox!"

"I guess you'll have to start having formal dinner parties," Lexi said. She put the top back on her skin cream. "So, did you and Austin decide where you're going to live?"

There had been an ongoing discussion about this. The Stanfields said that the mansion was so large, Fawn and Austin could certainly live there while they finished college, and then they would help them buy their own home. But Fawn wanted to get her own apartment with Austin right away.

"I think I've finally won that battle," Fawn said, her eyes shining. "You know those new apartments they just built out on Vaughn's Gap Road?"

Lexi nodded. "With the duck pond in front."

"Well, Austin and I went to look at one yesterday. It's so cute — a combination living/dining room, two bedrooms, and two baths. The kitchen is kind of small, but I don't know how to cook, anyway! And there's a pool and a tennis court — "

"Yes, but did Austin agree to living there instead of the family mansion?" Lexi asked.

Fawn smiled mischievously. "Let's just say I think I talked him into it."

"How did you do that?"

"I simply pointed out how at the mansion there would be a certain . . . lack of privacy," Fawn said.

"But the mansion is so huge that — "

"Not huge enough," Fawn said. "I might have taken out some of the sexy lingerie I just bought for our honeymoon and shown it to him while we were at that apartment. And I might have mentioned how I wouldn't be able to run around in anything like that at the mansion — "

Lexi laughed. "I have to hand it to you, that was kind of brilliant."

"I know," Fawn said. She reached for Lexi's hand. "Oh, Lex, I'm so happy. I didn't know I could be this happy."

"I'm happy for you, too," Lexi said, and found that except for one small place in her heart that continued to hurt, she meant it.

"Oh, I forgot to tell Mom about Mrs. Stanfield's — Leonia's — dress for the wedding!" Fawn realized, jumping up. "She changed her mind, and now her dress and Mom's dress won't complement each other!"

"Well, you can't expect Mom to change dresses just because Mrs. Stanfield did!"

"Well, I at least have to tell her!" Fawn leaned over and kissed Lexi's cheek, then she ran from the room.

Lexi slipped a Tori Amos tape into her tape deck, then she began to unpack her bag from the swim party. She took her wet bathing suit into the bathroom and dropped it into the sink so she could rinse out the chlorine. Laying on the edge of the tub was a bikini of Fawn's, pink-and-white polka-dot, that Lexi had almost worn instead of her own orange one-piece with the high-cut legs.

Guess I'd better return it, Lexi thought, *since Fawn was nice enough to lend it to me.* She picked up the bikini and padded down the hall to Fawn's room. The door was closed.

"Hey, Fawn?"

No answer.

I guess she's in the living room with Mom, Lexi thought. *Well, she won't mind if I just go in and leave her suit on her bed.*

Lexi opened the door, went in, and put the bathing suit on Fawn's bed. Over in one corner was a small pile of presents, some still in their torn wrapping, that Fawn had received at the tiny bridal shower Lexi had arranged for her earlier in the week.

I wanted to do a big shower, Lexi recalled, but Fawn wouldn't hear of it. *She said she was just too busy with everything else for yet another party. I suppose I can't blame her. So we had the world's smallest shower!*

Just as Lexi was about to leave and close the door, something caught her eye. A document on the letterhead of the Law Offices of Olden and Myers was sticking half out of Fawn's box of stationery on her nightstand. Lexi saw the words "The French Shoppe," but that's all she could make out.

Unless she took it out and really looked at it.

I shouldn't, she told herself.

But what if Fawn is in some kind of trouble?

With her heart thumping in her chest, Lexi slowly pulled the paper out of the box. Then she sat on Fawn's bed and read it, dumbfounded.

I, Fawn Mundy, admit to the following of my own free will. I am signing this confession voluntarily and am under no pressure from anyone. I have been caught shoplifting clothing from The French Shoppe. I admit to having shoplifted from The French Shoppe in the past. Each item I stole is listed below.

The French Shoppe has agreed not to press charges against me so long as I sign this confession and agree to pay The French Shoppe the retail price for all clothing that I have stolen, plus a twenty percent (20%) penalty, by this date next year.

In the event that I do not keep my word, or steal again, or do not pay for the clothes, The French Shoppe may use this letter as evidence against me in a court of law.

(signed)

Fawn Mundy

Below that was an itemized list of the clothing Fawn had stolen. Lexi recognized all the designer outfits she'd seen Fawn wear since she and Austin had become engaged.

"I can't believe it," Lexi whispered out loud, her hands shaking.

"Lexi!"

Lexi jumped up guiltily. Fawn was standing in the doorway, staring at her.

"Oh, Fawn — " Lexi began, holding out the terrible letter she'd just read.

"You had no right to sneak into my room!" Fawn cried, her face white.

"I was just returning your bathing suit," Lexi said. "And I saw this . . ."

Fawn strode across the room and grabbed the letter from Lexi. She shoved it into her top drawer. "Go away." She wouldn't turn around to look at her sister.

"Fawn, please — "

"I didn't want anyone to know — "

"Fawn, really — "

"Please, Lex," Fawn said, and Lexi could hear the shame in her voice, "please just forget you ever saw that."

Lexi went to her sister and gently touched her arm. "Fawn, I can't forget. I love you. You're in trouble and I want to help you."

Slowly Fawn turned around, her eyes filled with tears. "Oh, Lex, I'm so ashamed of myself! Mom and Dad would be so disappointed in me! Oh, God!"

Lexi led her sister, who was blinded by tears, to the bed. She handed her a Kleenex and let her cry.

"It was so awful, Lexi!" Fawn sobbed. "I was leaving The French Shoppe three days ago with this outfit, and the security guard stopped me at the door . . ."

Lexi reached for her sister's hand and held it tightly.

"They took me into the manager's office and said the sales clerk had seen me put a dress under my shirt, and they were going to c-call the police." Fawn could hardly choke out the words through her tears. "I took the dress out and showed it to them. It was the most humiliating moment of my life!

"And then . . . then I told them everything. That I had shoplifted four other outfits from them. They didn't know about any of those. But I felt so horrible, so guilty! How could I have done it, Lexi? How?"

"I . . . I guess you felt insecure about not having expensive clothes," Lexi said, searching for the right words.

"But to steal!" Fawn cried. "I hate myself for doing it, Lex! They were really wonderful to me. They said if I pay them back for everything they won't press charges. After the wedding I'm going to get a part-time job and pay them back every penny. I refuse to take a dime from Austin for this." She blew her nose hard, and wiped the tears off her cheeks.

"What did Austin say about it?" Lexi asked.

Fawn's eyes grew huge. "You don't think I actually *told* him about this, do you?"

"But he's going to be your husband," Lexi said. "You need to be able to tell him the good stuff and the bad stuff — "

"Oh, sure," Fawn said, blowing her nose again. "He'd really want to marry a thief. I could never, ever tell him in a million years. I would just die if he found out!" She clutched Lexi's hand. "You won't tell him, will you? Promise me!"

"But Fawn — "

"Promise!" she insisted, her voice panicked. "Please, Lexi, he would hate me!"

"No, he wouldn't — "

"Please, Lex. Don't you see? Austin has always been rich. He could never understand what it feels like to be insecure about . . . anything!"

Lexi sighed. "I won't tell him, Fawn. But I really think *you* should."

"Oh, God, I would die if he found out," Fawn groaned. "Because if Austin knew the truth, he would never, ever want to marry me. Never."

Chapter 21

THE HONOR OF YOUR PRESENCE
IS REQUESTED
AT THE MARRIAGE
OF
FAWN ELIZABETH MUNDY
TO
AUSTIN BAYLOR STANFIELD

The engraved words from the wedding invitation kept echoing in Lexi's head as she stood nervously at the back of the chapel. Just in front of her was Juliet, and in front of Juliet was Paris, each waiting for her perfectly choreographed and endlessly practiced moment to walk down the aisle with a groomsman.

Behind Lexi stood Fawn, with Mr. Mundy. All waiting to take the solemn steps that would lead to Austin and Fawn becoming husband and wife.

Married, Lexi thought. *Married forever.*

The beautiful organ music began, and little Betsy Stanfield, Austin's five-year-old cousin, started toward the altar, a basket of rose petals under her left arm. Happily, with every eye on her, she tossed rose petals to her left and to her right until she reached the altar.

Then, slowly, the couples of the bridal party made their way toward the altar. There were seven bridesmaids and seven groomsmen ahead of Lexi and her friends, so she watched each couple walk toward Reverend Collie, who smiled with encouragement.

Now it was Paris's turn. She took the arm of Peter Castle, one of Austin's friends from his fraternity, and walked lightly toward the minister in perfect step with the beautiful, emotional music.

Juliet, who would walk down the aisle with Jake Stanfield, her first cousin who had flown in from California, turned around to look at Lexi. "This is it," she whispered.

"Right," Lexi whispered back. She tried to smile at Juliet. *Is it my imagination, or does Juliet look as troubled as I do?* Lexi thought. *No, it couldn't be. Juliet doesn't know Fawn's terrible secret. I only wish I could have told her. But it wouldn't be fair. She's Austin's sister.*

In the days since Lexi had found out about

Fawn's shoplifting, she hadn't been able to eat or sleep. At night she would toss and turn, trying to figure out the best thing to do. Each day closer to the wedding, Lexi grew more anxious. The more she thought about Fawn and Austin, the more she worried.

He didn't tell her the truth about wanting to be an actor. She didn't tell him the truth about shoplifting designer clothes just to impress his family.

And he certainly never told her that he'd actually kissed her younger sister only weeks ago.

"Your turn, sweetie," Lexi's father whispered from behind her.

Lexi came back to the present with a start. She looked at Greg, who was Austin's best man, and held out her arm for him.

Greg had a grim look on his face. He shook his head as if he were resigned to fate, and reluctantly took Lexi's arm.

Greg really doesn't think they should be getting married, either, she realized.

Lexi took a deep breath and forced her feet forward down the narrow aisle, toward the minister's encouraging face.

What else can I do? Lexi thought helplessly. *I can't possibly stop the wedding. I don't have the right. And Fawn would never forgive me in*

*a million years. But I love her. How can I keep
my mouth shut when I love her?*

How can I?

Juliet watched Lexi as she slowly walked
down the aisle, her arm in Greg's, her face
ashen.

*I wish I could have confided in Lexi about
Austin's adoption,* she thought. *But I couldn't.
I haven't confronted my parents and I haven't
confronted Austin, either. Maybe I should have.
But I wanted to give Austin the chance to tell
everyone. And I kept thinking that any day now,
before the wedding, Austin would tell me himself, and then we could discuss it with Mom
and Dad, and then I could encourage him to
tell Fawn.*

*But he never said a word. And now it's too
late.*

She looked at Austin across the aisle, tall
and handsome, with such a hopeful look on his
face.

Oh, Austin, Juliet thought sadly, *why did you
think you had to hide it from me? And even
worse, why did you think you had to hide it from
Fawn? How can you marry her if you can't even
tell her the truth about yourself?*

*That's no basis for a marriage. No basis at
all.*

* * *

"Dearly beloved, we are gathered here to-day to witness the marriage vows of Fawn Elizabeth Mundy and Austin Baylor Stanfield," Reverend Collie intoned. "This is both a solemn and joyful occasion, when two people choose to become one under the laws of man, and more important, in the eyes of God."

Fawn smiled tremulously, her hands shaking a bit. She looked over at Austin, who stood beside her, and he met her gaze, looking just as nervous as she did. She brought her eyes back to the reverend as he continued to speak about the holy state of matrimony.

And then, finally, he was at the vows.

"Do you, Fawn Elizabeth Mundy, take this man, Austin Baylor Stanfield, to be your wedded husband in sickness and in health, for richer or for poorer, in good times and in bad, till death you do part?"

Oh, Fawn, Lexi thought, her heart catching in her chest. *I love you. And I'm so sorry if I hurt you in any way, but how can you go through with this without telling Austin the truth, and without him telling you the truth, and —*

"I do," Fawn managed in a shaky voice.

"And do you, Austin Baylor Stanfield, take this woman, Fawn Elizabeth Mundy, to be your wedded wife in sickness and in health, for richer or for poorer, in good times and in bad, till death you do part?"

Juliet gulped hard. *I should have talked to you, Austin. I'm a terrible sister,* she thought, *to let you agonize about everything alone, just because Mom and Dad had some messed up reason for never telling you that you're adopted. I'm so sorry. But please don't go through with this without being honest with Fawn, because how can you even start a marriage that isn't based on honesty, and —*

"I do," Austin replied solemnly.

Reverend Collie smiled and raised his head to look out over all the faces in the chapel. "If there is anyone present who does not feel that these two should now be joined in holy matrimony, let him or her speak now, or forever hold your peace."

Silence. And more silence.

And then a voice, one voice, which seemed to boom and echo throughout the hushed, sacred chapel —

"I do! I object!"

Reverend Collie looked shocked.

Everyone at the altar turned, aghast, to the person in the wedding party who had spoken, their faces full of anger and disapproval.

"I object!" the voice repeated. "Stop this wedding!"

Chapter 22

Paris could hardly believe it.

The words "I object!" had flown out of her mouth.

Everyone turned to her, gasping at once. All eyes were on her. Even the chapel seemed to be holding its breath.

"Look, I'm sorry, but — "

"Paris!" Fawn cried. "How could you?"

"If this is your idea of a joke, it isn't funny," Austin said, his face red with anger and embarrassment.

"It isn't a joke," Paris insisted, "and . . . well, I guess I'm not sorry, either."

"Young lady," Mr. Stanfield began, his tone dangerously sonorous, "how could you — "

"With all due respect, sir, I couldn't keep my mouth shut and live with myself," Paris said nervously. "And I'm glad I said it now at the rehearsal instead of tomorrow at the actual wedding!"

"I don't believe this!" Mrs. Stanfield cried, throwing her hands in the air.

"It is troubling," Reverend Collie said. "But if this young lady feels deeply enough to have spoken up, I think we ought to hear what she has to say."

Paris looked around the chapel at the large wedding party. "I . . . I don't want to do this in front of everyone," she said. "I'd like to talk with Austin and Fawn . . . and Juliet and Lexi. And Greg. Just the six of us."

"That is the most ridiculous thing I ever heard of!" Mrs. Stanfield exclaimed.

"But Leonia," Sheila Mundy said calmly, putting her hand on the other woman's arm, "isn't it better to let the kids talk this out in private?"

"There's nothing to talk out!" Mrs. Stanfield cried with exasperation.

Michael Mundy looked at Paris and scratched at his chin. "Is there? Something to talk out?"

"Yeah," Paris said firmly. "I didn't open my mouth for the big laugh value."

"I will never forgive you for this, Paris Goldman!" Fawn said, clearly close to tears. "Never!"

"Me, neither," Austin agreed, putting his arm around Fawn's shoulders. "Of all the lame stunts — "

"Paris is right," Juliet said, stepping forward.

"Juliet, really!" Mrs. Stanfield objected.

"She *is* right," Lexi agreed, stepping forward next to Juliet. "I should have said something, but I didn't have the nerve."

"And I should have said something, too, for that matter," Greg put in.

"I don't believe this is happening!" Fawn cried. "How could all of you do this to us?"

"You're supposed to be our friends!" Austin exclaimed.

"Children," Reverend Collie interrupted, "I know this is troubling to you. But . . ." he turned to Juliet. "Is it safe to assume that you love your brother?"

"Very much," Juliet replied fervently.

"And you love your sister?" Reverend Collie asked Lexi.

"I do," Lexi replied, gulping hard. "Even if I haven't always shown it."

"Please," Paris said to Fawn and Austin. "Just let us talk to you."

"Would you like me to be in the room, or would you prefer privacy?" Reverend Collie asked Fawn and Austin.

"We don't have to do this!" Austin sputtered.

"No, you don't have to," Reverend Collie agreed. "But I think you should."

Silence. And then, finally, "We would prefer privacy," Fawn said in a small voice. "At least, I would."

"Very well," Reverend Collie said. "Why don't you and Austin meet with me at my office at the church afterward. After all, it's only two blocks from here."

"But the rehearsal!" Mrs. Stanfield protested.

"I think we've rehearsed the majority of the ceremony for tomorrow," Reverend Collie said. "And if Austin and Fawn decide to proceed with the wedding, I will certainly offer them my blessing."

Mrs. Behmmann, the wedding consultant at the country club, who'd stopped in to look at the rehearsal, strode up the aisle, swiping at her forehead with a lace hanky.

"This is very, very unusual . . ." she said nervously.

"And just what are we supposed to do now?" Mrs. Stanfield asked, her voice high and stressed. She took her husband's arm.

"Mom, Dad, go home," Austin said firmly.

"But we're supposed to be having the rehearsal dinner!" Mr. Stanfield objected. "This is simply not acceptable!"

Austin turned to Mrs. Behmmann. "Could we hold the rehearsal dinner for an hour?"

"Well, yes, I suppose we could, if it's necessary," she said, clearly distressed.

"It seems to be necessary," Austin said grimly. "Our so-called friends have seen to that."

"There's a small conference room down the hall you can use to . . . talk," Mrs. Behmmann offered.

"Thank you," Fawn said, trying to maintain some dignity.

Mrs. Behmmann dabbed at her forehead again. "Everything is planned for this wedding. It's the largest wedding we've ever done here at the club. I can't just . . . I mean what should I . . ."

"It's all right," Austin assured her. "Nothing horrible is going to happen." He turned to Fawn. "Are you okay?"

"No, I'm not okay!" Tears filled her eyes.

"Let's just go get this over with," Austin said in a steely voice. He reached for Fawn's hand and headed out of the chapel.

"Hey, man, I — " Greg began, his hand on Austin's shoulder.

"I'm not interested in anything you have to

say," Austin said, his voice cold and cutting. "Just stay away from me."

Juliet turned around, her eyes searching for Ty, who, although he wasn't in the wedding party, had come along to the rehearsal. Juliet had invited him to the informal dinner at the club that was to follow the dress rehearsal.

He nodded at her and mouthed "see you later," and Juliet smiled back gratefully.

When the six of them reached the conference room, Austin took charge immediately. "Okay, Paris. You got us into this. You have exactly two minutes to say whatever you have to say."

Paris shook her hair off her face nervously. "Look, I'm sorry if you hate me for this, but I only did it because I thought it was the right thing to do. And I couldn't live with myself if I kept my mouth shut."

She looked over at Greg, Juliet, and Lexi. "Here's the thing. Greg, Lexi, and Juliet have all confided in me," she said to Austin and Fawn. "Stuff about the two of you, stuff you guys haven't even told each other. But everyone's been too afraid to say anything to you . . ."

"We — we don't have to stand here and listen to this," Fawn sputtered, folding her arms defensively.

"Are the four of you judge and jury now?" Austin asked furiously.

"Don't you get it?" Paris cried with exasperation. "You guys are totally lying to each other! It's crazy!"

No one spoke. Time seemed to stand still.

"Paris is right," Greg finally said. "It's time for you guys to come clean with each other."

"You think I don't know why you're doing this?" Austin sneered at Greg. "You just don't want to lose me as a partying buddy. I found someone to love, and you feel left out. That's the truth, isn't it, buddy?"

"Partly," Greg admitted, staring Austin down. "But it's not everything. How come you never told Fawn that you really want to be an actor?"

Fawn turned to Austin. "You want to be an actor?" she asked with surprise. "Like, as a *job*?"

Austin reddened. "I don't know. Maybe."

"But you never told me that!" Fawn said. "I thought this was some . . . some *hobby*."

"It's not like it's some kind of firm decision," Austin protested. "It's just a dream . . ."

"But I want to know your dreams!" Fawn exclaimed.

"You mean you wouldn't care if I didn't want

to go to law school and then run the family trust?" Austin asked.

"I wouldn't care if you didn't even *have* the trust!" Fawn told him fervently. "That's not why I fell in love with you!"

Austin shook his head in happy wonder. "Really, Fawn?"

"Really," she told him.

He wrapped his arms around her, pulling her close. "I was so sure that you'd be upset, and I still don't know if I'm really going to give acting a full-time shot or not, but . . . it's great to know that you'd be there for me."

"No matter what," Fawn promised.

"And Austin," Juliet began slowly, "this is hard for me to ask you, but . . ." She looked over at Greg, then back at her brother. "How come you haven't told Fawn that you're adopted, just like me?"

"You're *what??*" Fawn gasped.

The blood drained from Austin's face. He stared hard at Greg. "How could you do this to me?"

"I'm sorry, Austin, but — "

"Sorry doesn't cut it!" Austin yelled.

"You're *adopted?*" Fawn echoed incredulously. "And you never told me?"

"He didn't even know until a little while

ago," Juliet said. "And Austin hasn't even told me. The only person he told was Greg — "

"And Greg decided he had the right to tell my sister," Austin seethed. "Some best friend."

"So what if he told Juliet?" Paris asked. "You might as well know that Juliet told me, too. But it was only because she was so worried about you!"

Juliet's eyes searched her brother's. "Austin, I don't know why Mom and Dad didn't tell you the truth all these years. I can't think of any good reason for it. But why didn't you tell me?"

"And more important, why didn't you tell Fawn?" Paris asked.

Austin stared at his sister hard for a moment, then he looked away. "I would have told you both. Eventually."

Fawn touched Austin's arm. "Did you think it would matter to me?"

"I don't know," Austin confessed. "But can't you understand — I just found out myself! I . . . I needed time to digest it, you know? I mean, it just came at me out of nowhere!"

"But we could have digested it together!" Fawn exclaimed. "Maybe I could have helped you figure things out."

Austin gulped hard and took a deep breath. "It was . . . like, this total bombshell. I just . . . at first I was just floored, you know? Like, 'wow, I'm not even a Stanfield!' "

He looked over at Juliet, who looked as if he had kicked her in the stomach. "But then I thought about you, Juli," he said quickly. "How you are one hundred percent my sister, and one hundred percent Stanfield. How I couldn't love you more than I do, no matter who gave birth to you . . ."

Juliet nodded at her brother, too overcome to speak.

". . . and I realized it was some stupid trip of Mom and Dad's. It was like they had made this dumb mistake not telling me the truth, and every year they didn't tell me just made the mistake one year tougher to undo . . ."

"We'll have to talk with them, Austin," Juliet said. "Together."

Austin smiled at his sister, then he turned to Fawn. "I don't blame you if you're ticked at me — "

"Oh, Austin, I'm not!" Fawn cried. "I don't care that you're adopted, and I think your parents were really wrong to keep it from you. But I feel terrible that you didn't think you could be honest with me — "

"I don't know why you feel terrible," Lexi said boldly. "After all, you haven't been honest with him, either!"

"Lexi, don't!" Fawn gasped. "You promised!"

"Well, I didn't promise," Paris said. "I'm sorry, Fawn, but Lexi told me, and now I'm not going to keep my mouth shut. You can hate me forever if you want, but — "

"You don't have to say anything," Fawn interrupted. "I'll tell him myself." Fawn turned to Austin. She took a deep breath. "Austin, this is . . . the hardest thing I've ever done. But you need to know that . . . I was caught shoplifting from The French Shoppe."

"You stole clothing?" Austin asked incredulously.

Fawn nodded, her face etched with pain and humiliation. "Expensive designer stuff. A lot. The outfits I wore every time I had to go somewhere with your parents . . ."

"But . . . but why?" Austin wondered.

"Because I wanted to impress you and your parents," Fawn admitted.

"But I don't care about things like that!" Austin protested.

"Maybe you don't," Fawn said, her chin jutting forward. "But your mother does. Don't try to tell me she doesn't!"

"Maybe she does," Austin said. "But . . . you're not marrying my mother!"

"Don't you see?" Fawn cried. "I'm marrying into your family! I just wanted your parents to like me!" Tears filled her eyes. "Believe me, I know how stupid it was. I betrayed everything I believe in . . ."

Tears overcame her, and Austin took her into his arms. "I'm so sorry you felt like you had to do that, Fawn," he said, his voice muffled against her hair.

"No, I'm the one who's sorry," Fawn managed to gulp out. "I'm so sorry. I've promised them I'd get a job and pay them back every penny . . ."

"We can pay them together — " Austin began.

"No!" Fawn insisted. "I did it and I'm going to pay for it myself!"

"All right," Austin said, still holding her close. "We'll do it your way." He rocked her slowly in his arms. "Fawn, I'm so sorry, so sorry I lied to you — "

"Me, too," she said, shuddering through her tears. "I was such an idiot! But I was so afraid — "

"Me, too — "

"And I didn't want to lose you — "

As Fawn cried in his arms, Austin looked at

Lexi. They both knew that there was still one lie, one unspoken betrayal that Austin and Fawn had not shared. Austin's eyes searched Lexi's.

What's the right thing to do? she wondered. *Should I tell Fawn that he kissed me, or that I thought I was in love with him and that he was falling in love with me, too?*

But as she watched her sister in Austin's arms, she realized something. What she had felt for Austin hadn't really been love. It had been some childhood fantasy of Austin that she had weaved her dreams around for years. But the real Austin had never belonged to her, and he never would. The place in her heart that had hurt for so very long had finally stopped hurting. Fawn loved Austin and Austin loved Fawn. They belonged together.

And Lexi was free at last.

"I'm so glad everything is out in the open," Lexi said, staring hard at Austin. Her eyes told him that their kiss would remain a secret.

"Do you hate us?" Paris asked.

"I still feel ambushed," Austin said. "But . . . you did us a favor." He looked over at Greg. "I'm sorry about — "

"Forget it," Greg said. "Everything is cool."

"You know, maybe we should . . . should

go for some premarital counseling," Fawn said, blowing her nose again.

"Gee, that gives you twenty-four hours to get healthy before the big 'I do's'!" Paris cracked.

Austin's eyes searched Fawn's. "Do you . . . still want to get married?"

"Do you?"

"I love you, Fawn," Austin said. "And if you're willing to take on a guy who messes up as much as I do, I want to marry you tomorrow more than anything in the world."

"Me, too," Fawn said. "But I want us to go to counseling together, okay?"

"No Stanfield has ever gone to — "

"Austin!" Juliet cried. "Don't act like such an idiot!"

"You're right," Austin agreed. "I need to talk to someone about . . . all this adoption stuff. And I'll do everything I can to make our marriage work. I don't want to lose you, Fawn. God, I'd die if I lost you . . ."

"It will never happen," Fawn vowed. "We're in this together, Austin Stanfield, for better or for worse. And I'm done lying to you."

"Yeah, me, too," Austin agreed. "Even though this honesty stuff is not easy . . ."

"We'll find someone to help us learn," Fawn said. "We'll learn together."

"Very nineties!" Paris approved, applauding. "I'm proud of you!"

"Just wait until you get married," Fawn warned Paris, but there was love in her voice. "We will show you no mercy!"

"Don't hold your breath," Paris said. "Frankly, marriage before the age of, like, *forty* is not my idea of a swell time, you know what I mean?"

But neither Fawn nor Austin answered her, because they were lost in a kiss so full of love that it seemed to fill the room with its sweetness.

Chapter 23

"Let me just fix your veil," Lexi told her sister. She carefully adjusted the delicate lace off the back of the seed pearl crown that sat on Fawn's head.

It was just the two of them in Fawn's room. Fawn had decided she wanted to get dressed for her wedding at home, in her own room, with only Lexi to help her put on her wedding gown.

Earlier that day, Fawn had her hair and nails done. Lexi and Sheila both had their nails done, too, but each decided to do her own hair. Then Juliet had come over to do Fawn's makeup, which was understated perfection in delicate shades of the palest pink.

Now Fawn and Lexi stood next to each other, gazing at their reflections in the mirror on Fawn's dresser. "Do I look okay?" Fawn asked her sister.

"Oh, Fawn," Lexi said tremulously, "you look perfect."

And for once I can say that without any jealousy, Lexi realized happily.

"You look rather wonderful yourself," Fawn said with a smile.

Lexi gazed at her reflection in her bridesmaid's dress. Contrary to what Paris had thought, the design Mrs. Stanfield had selected looked good on all the bridesmaids. Fawn had selected the color and the material — a pale pink watered silk with pale pink silk pumps dyed to match.

Fawn turned and looked around her room. "I can't believe this won't be my room anymore," she murmured.

"It's still your room," Lexi said. "It's not like Mom and Dad are renting it out!"

"But it won't be home," Fawn said sadly. She tried to smile. "It's not that I'm not happy, because I am. It's just that . . . well, I guess it's scary, letting go of one part of your life to begin another . . ."

"I guess it is," Lexi agreed. "Hey, I have an idea — I'll be right back." Lexi lifted the bottom of her dress so she could dash to her room, where she found the tiny, blue stuffed bunny Fawn had given her on her eighth birthday, which she had kept on her nightstand all these years. She brought the bunny back to Fawn and handed it to her.

"Mr. Bunny!" Fawn exclaimed.

"Gosh, how many years ago did I give him to you?"

"Eight," Lexi said. "You were twelve. And I was all upset because Mom and Dad said we couldn't have a pet because you were allergic. So you got me Mr. Bunny instead."

"I guess he was a poor substitute for the real thing," Fawn said, smoothing down Mr. Bunny's raggedy ears.

"No, he was wonderful," Lexi said. "And now I want you to take him with you. To remind you of home."

"Oh, Lex — "

"What's that saying?" Lexi asked. "A bride is supposed to have something old, something new, something borrowed, and something blue. Well, Mr. Bunny is old, borrowed, and blue — three out of four isn't bad!"

Fawn smiled at her sister, tears filling her eyes. "I love you, Lex."

"I love you, too," Lexi said sincerely. "But Juliet will kill me if I let you cry off her perfectly applied makeup, so no tears!" She grabbed a tissue from the dresser and carefully blotted Fawn's eyes.

"Lex, about yesterday — " Fawn began.

"We don't have to talk about it anymore, unless you want to," Lexi said quickly.

"I . . . I guess I do," Fawn said. "I'm not stupid. I don't think that Austin and I won't have any problems. And I don't think that we're going to live happily ever after just because we were finally honest with each other . . ."

Lexi nodded thoughtfully.

"I guess what I want to say is, well, this acting-like-an-adult stuff is really hard!" Fawn exclaimed. "But . . . I'm going to give it everything I've got. And I believe Austin will, too."

Lexi grinned at her sister. "I only hope I can say that when I get married."

"Oh, you'll be disgustingly mature," Fawn said with a laugh. "You already are!"

There was a knock on Fawn's door.

"It's Mom and Dad," Sheila called in.

"Come on in," Fawn called. She turned to face her parents, neither of whom had ever seen her in her wedding gown.

"Oh Fawn," Sheila breathed, clapping her hand to her mouth. "Oh, honey, you are so beautiful!"

"Thanks, Mom," Fawn said, her eyes tearing up again.

Michael's eyes filled, too. "Fawn, you're absolutely lovely, inside and out. And I'm proud to be your dad." He strode to his daughter and took her in his arms.

"The two of you look so wonderful," Fawn told them earnestly. "I mean it."

Sheila Mundy had on a long, graceful gown of mauve and rose chiffon, and Michael had on a perfectly fitted tuxedo with a rose paisley vest. Fawn knew her parents had dressed like this to please her, and her heart filled with love all over again.

"You guys, we can't all stand here crying, you know," Lexi said, fighting back her own tears. "We have a wedding to go to!"

"The carriage just arrived in front," Sheila said, dabbing at her own eyes.

"I guess this is it, then," Fawn said. She looked around her room one last time.

"This is still your home, honey," Sheila said gently, as if reading her daughter's mind. "And it always will be."

"Let's go out through the inn," Michael suggested.

Sheila and Lexi carefully lifted Fawn's train, and the four of them made their way to the front of the inn. When she walked through the lobby, Fawn was surprised to see all the guests there, waiting to get a peek at her. When they saw her they oohed and ahhed, and broke into spontaneous applause.

The Mundys walked out into the bright sunlight. There, at the end of the brick path that led to the road, was a white carriage with gold filigree, drawn by two beautiful, white horses. The coachman was dressed in white tails and a white top hat, and he stood waiting for Fawn, his hat in his hands.

The path that led to the carriage had been strewn with rose petals by Sheila and Michael while Fawn was getting dressed.

"This is like a dream come true!" Fawn cried, her eyes shining.

"Your chariot awaits, milady," Michael told his daughter, bowing from the waist.

Lexi and Sheila lifted Fawn's train again, and the foursome walked to the carriage and were helped in by the coachman.

The drive to the Stanfield Country Club was a short one, and Fawn found that another crowd had gathered in front of the club in hopes of seeing the bride. The videographer was there, as planned, to shoot Fawn and her family as they emerged from the coach.

Down the street Fawn could see a gray coach approaching, drawn by two sleek, gray stallions. "That's Austin!" she cried. "I have to go right in — I don't want him to see me before the wedding — it's bad luck!"

Fawn hurried into the country club and the

videographer turned his camera to Austin's approaching carriage. She found all her bridesmaids crowded into the tiny bridal room.

"Lex, I can't even breathe in here!" Fawn whispered to her sister.

"What do you want me to do?" Lexi asked.

"Maybe everyone could go out but you, Juliet, and Paris," Fawn suggested. "And Mom, of course."

Lexi smiled at her sister. "Consider it done." She quickly — and nicely — managed to shoo the other bridesmaids out of the room until it was just the five of them.

"Much better," Fawn said, sitting on the rose velvet loveseat. "Thanks."

"Let me just fix the curls in the back," Sheila said, carefully touching her daughter's hair under her veil.

"And I need to touch up your makeup," Juliet said, eyeing Fawn critically.

"What, no 'Hello, Fawn, gee, you look kind of nice'?" Fawn asked.

"Hey, I take pride in my work," Juliet said, getting out her makeup bag. Then she smiled at Fawn. "And I think the most beautiful bride in the world deserves the most perfect makeup."

"You are looking disgustingly fantastic," Paris agreed good-naturedly.

"You look rather disgustingly cute yourself," Fawn teased Paris, as Juliet brushed pale pink blush over her cheeks.

"I do, don't I?" Paris agreed happily, looking at her reflection in the mirror. "I better get lots of photos tonight. I may never, ever look this good again, and I'm going to need photographic proof!"

Fawn just smiled and looked happy as her bridesmaids and her mother buzzed around her, fixing this, adjusting that.

A stranger looking in might think Fawn isn't nervous, Lexi thought fondly, *but I know better.*

Fawn still had Mr. Bunny clutched tightly in her hands.

The organ music swelled into the wedding march, and Fawn slowly walked down the aisle, her father at her side. The fine, imported lace veil over her face didn't hide her beauty; rather, it enhanced the planes and shadows of her radiant face.

Austin gazed at her with total love and awe as she made her way to her place beside him.

Someday I'm going to fall in love with the guy who is perfect for me, Lexi thought, *and when I stand beside him at the altar he will look at me just like that.*

"Dearly beloved, we are gathered together

on this joyous occasion to witness the marriage vows of Fawn Elizabeth Mundy and Austin Baylor Stanfield," Reverend Collie began.

Lexi's eyes gazed over at her best friends. There was Juliet, looking beautiful in her pale pink gown. And there was Paris, blond and voluptuous — a completely different kind of beauty, but equally lovely — looking happy and radiant in hers.

I'm so lucky to have them as best friends, Lexi thought. *It's kind of like a marriage in a certain way — because I know Paris and Juliet will always be there for me, in good times and in bad, come what may . . .*

"Do you, Fawn Elizabeth Mundy, take this man, Austin Baylor Stanfield," Reverend Collie began, "to be your wedded husband in sickness and in health, for richer or for poorer, in good times and in bad, till death you do part?"

"I do," Fawn said.

Reverend Collie smiled at her, then turned to Austin. "And do you, Austin Baylor Stanfield, take this woman, Fawn Elizabeth Mundy, to be your wedded wife in sickness and in health, for richer or for poorer, in good times and in bad, till death you do part?"

"I do," Austin replied.

"Now it is time for the ring ceremony," Reverend Collie explained. "The ring is a symbol of the joining of this couple for eternity. Who has the rings?"

Greg stepped forward. "I do," he said, and handed the rings to Reverend Collie.

"Austin, if you would place the ring on Fawn's finger," Reverend Collie instructed, "and repeat after me. With this ring . . ."

Then Fawn placed a gold band on Austin's finger, and she, too, repeated the ring vows after Reverend Collie.

"And now we come to an important point in our ceremony," Reverend Collie said. "The time to receive blessings from your friends, family, all who love you. May their love help carry you through times of trouble, and add joy to your heart during times of happiness and celebration." His eyes swept over the huge crowd of people. "If anyone here now has reason to believe that these two should not be joined in holy matrimony, let him or her speak now, or forever hold your peace."

A hushed silence filled the chapel. And it seemed as if everyone from the wedding rehearsal turned as one to stare at Paris.

Paris smiled and gave Austin and Fawn the tiniest thumbs-up, so tiny that only the wedding party could see.

And Reverend Collie. He breathed a sigh of relief and beamed at Austin and Fawn.

"With the power vested in me by the State of New York, I now pronounce you husband and wife. You may kiss your bride!"

Austin lifted Fawn's veil, then he took her into his arms and kissed her with such love and tenderness that it took everyone's breath away.

"Ladies and gentlemen, may I present Austin and Fawn Mundy-Stanfield!" Reverend Collie exclaimed happily.

Fawn and Austin turned and walked together back down the aisle, hundreds of faces beaming at them.

"Mundy-Stanfield?" Juliet asked Lexi when they, too, reached the back of the chapel.

"Hey," Lexi said with a laugh, "Fawn may have married a Stanfield, but you can't get the Mundy out of the girl that easily!"

Chapter 24

"Dance?" Greg asked Paris.

"Sure," Paris agreed. Bliss, the band, was playing a slow love song. Paris stepped into Greg's arms.

After more than an hour of posing for the wedding photographer while the wedding guests had hors d'oeuvres in the Opal Room, the wedding party had finally been released to join in the fun. Fawn and Austin had danced their first dance to "Forever Love" by Whitney Houston, then Fawn had danced a sentimental dance with her dad to "Sunrise, Sunset."

The dinner had been fantastic, the food incredible, and now the party was in full swing.

"Some wedding, huh?" Greg said, moving gracefully to the music.

"Unbelievable," Paris agreed. "Kind of excessive, but in a nice way."

Greg laughed. "You might just be the funniest girl I ever met."

"Yeah, but everyone knows you don't get around much," Paris said with a straight face.

He looked down at her. "Are you sure you're only sixteen?"

"Last time I checked."

"Too bad," Greg murmured.

"What's wrong with sixteen?" Paris asked.

"Nothing, if I were seventeen," Greg said. "But I'm twenty."

"Wow, ancient," Paris quipped. "But don't worry. I have been known to have friends as ancient as you in the past."

"Friends?" Greg asked.

"Friends," Paris said firmly. "You're a party guy, Greg, right?"

"If you mean am I looking for a serious relationship right now, the answer is no," he said honestly.

"How about any kind of a relationship?" Paris asked.

Greg shrugged. "The truth is — I just want to have fun. With different girls."

"Cool," Paris said with a shrug. "Like I said, a party dude. And aside from it being a really dumb waste of time, there's nothing wrong with that. But I'm not a party kind of babe."

Greg looked at Paris with new respect. "Maybe not," he said, "but you are some incredibly cool kind of woman."

"Yeah," Paris agreed with a grin. "I guess that's true."

"So . . . where does that leave us?" Greg asked her.

"Friends," Paris said. "If I ever change my mind, you'll be the first to know."

Greg shook his head. "Since when did you get to be so self-confident, Miss Goldman?"

"It's a recent development," Paris admitted. "Kind of like a work-in-progress."

Greg threw his head back and laughed as he pulled Paris closer into his arms.

"Someday I'm going to have a wedding this perfect," Juliet told Ty. After dancing wildly through three fast songs in a row, they had come out onto the balcony overlooking the rolling hills of the golf course to get some fresh air.

"You'll sure be a beautiful bride, Juliet," Ty said quietly.

But will I be your bride? Juliet wondered silently to herself. She didn't dare say anything like that out loud. She hadn't even had the nerve to ask Ty if he'd made a decision about staying in Stanfield.

But she knew the moment had come.

"Ty — "

"I know what you're going to ask, Juli," Ty said quietly.

Something in his tone of voice scared her, and she could feel her heartbeat galloping in her chest.

"I'm going to Hollywood," Ty said. "I'm leaving in two weeks."

Juliet gulped hard. "I . . . I see," she said, trying not to let her voice shake.

Ty turned to her. "It's the hardest decision I've ever had to make, Juliet," he told her. "Because it means leaving behind the girl I love."

Juliet turned to him. "You — ?"

"I love you," Ty said.

"Oh, Ty, I love you, too!" Juliet cried, throwing her arms around his neck. "But if you love me how can you — "

"Up and leave?" Ty finished for her. "I've been awake so many nights, asking myself that same question, tellin' myself I'd have to be the biggest kind of fool to walk away from you . . ."

He stared out at the moonlit sky, as if searching for words. "But if I never gave myself this chance to try, I'm afraid we'd never work out, Juli. I'm afraid I'd end up resenting you for keeping me here, and I'd end up killing all the love we have for each other . . ."

"But . . . but I can't stand to have you go!" Juliet cried.

"It's not forever," Ty promised, taking her into his arms. "Shoot, I have no idea what I'm gonna run into out in Hollywood. I hear that town has chewed up people a lot smarter and more talented than me. But if I'm still there when you graduate, you could go to college in Los Angeles — "

"UCLA!" Juliet said eagerly.

"Or maybe I'll end up right back here at college," Ty continued. "But either way we'll be together again. And we'll write, and call, and see each other as often as we can . . ."

"It's not the same," Juliet said, choking on the tears that began again.

"I know," Ty agreed sadly. "But I'm betting that we love each other enough to make it work." He tipped her chin up to him, and he kissed her lips.

"Oh, Ty, I love you so much!"

He kissed her again, pulling her so close she could feel his heart beating as wildly as hers. Then he gently pulled away. "Hey, I almost forgot. I got a present for you."

"Really?" Juliet asked, trying to stem her sobs. "What is it?"

Please let it be a ring, Juliet prayed. *Or a necklace. Something personal that I can wear when he's gone . . .*

Ty pulled a small, rectangular package out of the pocket of his tuxedo. It was wrapped in plain brown paper.

Juliet's heart sank. It definitely wasn't jewelry. She opened the package quickly. It was a book, entitled *The People of Viet Nam.* She gave him a questioning look.

"I remember you told me you don't know anything about your birth culture," Ty said. "And you said you wanted to learn about it. So I thought . . ."

"Thanks," Juliet said, trying hard not to feel disappointed. "I guess it would be good to know where I come from."

"And this is for you, too," Ty said, taking a small, square package out of his other pocket.

Juliet tore open the wrapping paper, which covered a blue velvet jeweler's box. She opened the box, and inside was a slender gold bracelet from which hung a small gold heart.

"Oh, Ty!" Juliet cried, overwhelmed with happiness. She slipped it on her wrist.

"Now you'll know that my heart is always with you," Ty said.

"And mine will always be with you," Juliet whispered. "Always." She wrapped her arms around his neck and raised her face for a kiss that she wished would never end.

Lexi watched Fawn and Austin as they danced, gazing deeply into each other's eyes.

It must be wonderful to be loved like that, Lexi thought with longing.

"Hi."

Lexi turned. Ricky Littlefeather was standing next to her, holding two plates of dessert. In his black tuxedo, with his shiny black hair falling over his forehead, he looked extremely cute.

"I thought you might want dessert," Ricky said. "No animal by-products, and I promise not to spill anything on you for at least fifteen minutes."

Lexi laughed and took the plate of petits fours. "Thanks. Are you having fun?"

"Well, the truth of the matter is I've been trying to get up the nerve to come talk to you for the past hour," Ricky said, shaking his hair off his face.

"Why would it take nerve to talk to me?" Lexi asked with surprise.

Ricky shrugged. "Got me. There's just something about you."

"No one ever told me I was intimidating before," Lexi said, biting into a tiny petit four.

"You're not," Ricky said. "You're totally nice and sweet and easy to be with. You care about more than what outfit you're going to wear tomorrow, and you're a really good friend to your friends. In fact you're so cool that if I hadn't made such a jerk out of myself the first time we met, you'd probably be ready to run away with me by now."

Lexi laughed. "Oh, is that the plan?"

"Could be," Ricky said seriously. He put his dessert plate down on the nearest table and cocked his head at Lexi. "Let me ask you a question . . . about that guy you broke up with who broke your heart."

"Yes?" Lexi asked.

"Are you still hung up on him?"

Lexi thought a moment. "No," she said honestly. "I'm not."

Ricky's face lit up. "Yeah?"

"Yeah," Lexi admitted. "I really think I'm finally over him."

"Whoever he was, he didn't deserve you," Ricky said fervently. "So, let me ask you another question. Once I asked you out, and you said no, because of that guy — the one you're no longer hung up on."

"Uh-huh . . ." Lexi agreed.

"So what would happen if I asked you out again, now that he's history?" Ricky asked. "This is only a theoretical question, you understand, so just in case you still say no I won't feel like the biggest jerk on the planet."

"If you asked me out again," Lexi said slowly, "I would probably say yes."

"Probably . . . probably is good," Ricky said, nodding. "How about tomorrow night? And if you plan to say yes, the question is more than theoretical," he added.

"The answer is yes," Lexi said.

"Yes!" Ricky echoed, pumping his fist in the air with triumph.

"I don't know if I'm ready for a . . . a relationship or anything," Lexi warned him.

"Hey, all we're talking about here is a first date," Ricky said. "I promise not to discuss 'relationship' until at least the second one."

"After which you'll be going back to North Carolina," Lexi reminded him.

Ricky folded his arms. "Does Stanfield High have a good baseball team?"

"They won the district championship last year," Lexi said.

"How about tennis?" Ricky asked.

"They're terrific," Lexi said. "Juliet plays girls' varsity."

"Cool, those are my best sports," Ricky said.

"You mean you're actually going to — "

"I told you I'm a man of many surprises," Ricky said mildly. "You should have listened. Care to dance?"

Lexi stepped into Ricky's arms, still reeling from what he had just told her. "You're really going to move here and go to Stanfield High?" Lexi asked in amazement.

"Looks that way," Ricky said, turning Lexi smoothly to the music.

Oh God, he's going to step on my feet, Lexi feared.

But her feet never got stepped on. When Ricky was moving to music, he was utterly graceful.

"Please tell me you're not moving here for me," Lexi said.

"I'm not moving here for you," Ricky echoed.

"Thank goodness — "

"Not completely, anyway," Ricky continued. "Stanfield High is supposed to be a great school, which should help me get into a great college."

"Oh, well, yeah, Stanfield High is really

strong academically," Lexi agreed.

"I believe in strong academics," Ricky said with mock solemnity. Then his eyes danced at Lexi, and a smile twitched at his lips. "I also happen to believe in love at first sight. But we can talk about that on our third date."

And with that he swept her into his arms and danced her breathlessly around the dance floor.

Lexi saw Paris across the room, laughing with Greg, and she saw Juliet come in from outside, hand in hand with Tyler. Then she gazed at Fawn and Austin, who were swaying together, talking to Sheila and Michael, their arms around each other's waists.

Soon Fawn and Austin would escape this party. They would run outside where, Lexi knew, the gray coach driven by gray horses awaited to take them to the Marriott, where they would spend their wedding night. And tomorrow they would leave for their honeymoon, two weeks in Hawaii.

But tonight, just at this moment, they were content to be here, surrounded by so many people who loved them so much.

I really believe they're going to make it, Lexi thought. *They're finally being honest with each other. And they both found out that they're loved for who they really are, not the perfect person they thought they had to pretend to be.*

Her eyes misted with tears. *So much love,* Lexi thought, *so many hearts so full of hope.*

She smiled at Ricky, who smiled back and held her close.

And my heart is hopeful, too, Lexi realized. *Something wonderful could happen to me. And when it does, I have the greatest family and the greatest friends in the world to share it with.*

She looked at Ricky's handsome face again.

It isn't for sure. I don't know him yet at all. But it is possible.

Something wonderful might just be happening right now . . .